PENGUIN ENGLISH LIBRARY

The Valley of Fear

Sir Arthur Conan Doyle (1859–1930) was born in Edinburgh and studied medicine at the university, after an education in Jesuit schools in Lancashire and Austria. He had an active career as a doctor and ophthalmologist, including volunteering in Bloemfontein during the Boer War, but also in the public sphere as Deputy-Lieutenant of Surrey, writer of widely read historical works and political pamphlets, vociferous opponent of miscarriages of justice and twice parliamentary candidate (although he was never elected). Yet it was for his brilliant creation of the first scientific detective, Sherlock Holmes, that he achieved great fame – so great that after he killed Holmes off to concentrate on his historical work, he was forced to bring the character back to life. In later life, Conan Doyle was converted to Spiritualism, writing works such as *The Coming of the Fairies*, and was a friend of the magician Houdini. He died of a heart attack in 1930, at the age of seventy-one.

The Valley of Fear

SIR ARTHUR CONAN DOYLE

...

PENGUIN ENGLISH
LIBRARY

PENGUIN BOOKS

Published by the Penguin Group
Penguin Books Ltd, 80 Strand, London WC2R ORL, England
Penguin Group (USA) Inc., 375 Hudson Street, New York, New York 10014, USA
Penguin Group (Canada), 90 Eglinton Avenue East, Suite 700, Toronto, Ontario, Canada M4P 2Y3
(a division of Pearson Penguin Canada Inc.)
Penguin Ireland, 25 St Stephen's Green, Dublin 2, Ireland (a division of Penguin Books Ltd)
Penguin Group (Australia), 707 Collins Street, Melbourne, Victoria 3008, Australia
(a division of Pearson Australia Group Pty Ltd)
Penguin Books India Pvt Ltd, 11 Community Centre, Panchsheel Park, New Delhi – 110 017, India
Penguin Group (NZ), 67 Apollo Drive, Rosedale, Auckland 0632, New Zealand
(a division of Pearson New Zealand Ltd)
Penguin Books (South Africa) (Pty) Ltd, Block D, Rosebank Office Park,
181 Jan Smuts Avenue, Parktown North, Guateng, South Africa 2193

Penguin Books Ltd, Registered Offices: 80 Strand, London WC2R ORL, England

www.penguin.com

First published by Smith, Elder 1915
Published in Penguin Books 1981
First published in the Penguin English Library 2014
003

Cover illustration: Coralie Bickford-Smith

The Essay by David Cannadine © 2014

Set in 11/13 pt Dante MT Std
Typeset by Jouve (UK), Milton Keynes
Printed in Great Britain by Clays Ltd, St Ives plc

A CIP catalogue record for this book is available from the British Library

ISBN: 978-0-141-39556-2

www.greenpenguin.co.uk

MIX
Paper from
responsible sources
FSC
www.fsc.org   FSC™ C018179

Penguin Books is committed to a sustainable
future for our business, our readers and our planet.
This book is made from Forest Stewardship
Council™ certified paper.

Contents

Contents

PART ONE

The Tragedy of Birlstone

Chapter One

The Warning

'I am inclined to think –' said I.

'I should do so,' Sherlock Holmes remarked, impatiently.

I believe that I am one of the most long-suffering of mortals, but I admit that I was annoyed at the sardonic interruption.

'Really, Holmes,' said I, severely, 'you are a little trying at times.'

He was too much absorbed with his own thoughts to give any immediate answer to my remonstrance. He leaned upon his hand, with his untasted breakfast before him, and he stared at the slip of paper which he had just drawn from its envelope. Then he took the envelope itself, held it up to the light, and very carefully studied both the exterior and the flap.

'It is Porlock's writing,' said he, thoughtfully. 'I can hardly doubt that it is Porlock's writing, though I have only seen it twice before. The Greek "e" with the peculiar top flourish is distinctive. But if it is from Porlock, then it must be something of the very first importance.'

He was speaking to himself rather than to me, but my vexation disappeared in the interest which the words awakened.

'Who, then, is Porlock?' I asked.

'Porlock, Watson, is a *nom de plume*, a mere identification mark, but behind it lies a shifty and evasive personality. In a former letter he frankly informed me that the name was not his own, and defied me ever to trace him among the teeming millions of this great city. Porlock is important, not for himself, but for the great man with whom he is in touch. Picture to yourself the pilot-fish with the shark, the jackal with the lion – anything that is insignificant in companionship with what is formidable. Not only formidable, Watson, but sinister – in the highest degree sinister.

That is where he comes within my purview. You have heard me speak of Professor Moriarty?'

'The famous scientific criminal, as famous among crooks as –'

'My blushes, Watson,' Holmes murmured, in a deprecating voice.

'I was about to say "as he is unknown to the public".'

'A touch – a distinct touch!' cried Holmes. 'You are developing a certain unexpected vein of pawky humour, Watson, against which I must learn to guard myself. But in calling Moriarty a criminal you are uttering libel in the eyes of the law, and there lies the glory and the wonder of it. The greatest schemer of all time, the organizer of every devilry, the controlling brain of the underworld – a brain which might have made or marred the destiny of nations. That's the man. But so aloof is he from general suspicion – so immune from criticism – so admirable in his management and self-effacement, that for those very words that you have uttered he could hale you to a court and emerge with your year's pension as a solatium for his wounded character. Is he not the celebrated author of *The Dynamics of an Asteroid* – a book which ascends to such rarefied heights of pure mathematics that it is said that there was no man in the scientific press capable of criticizing it? Is this a man to traduce? Foul-mouthed doctor and slandered professor – such would be your respective roles. That's genius, Watson. But if I am spared by lesser men our day will surely come.'

'May I be there to see!' I exclaimed, devoutly. 'But you were speaking of this man Porlock.'

'Ah, yes – the so-called Porlock is a link in the chain some little way from its great attachment. Porlock is not quite a sound link, between ourselves. He is the only flaw in that chain so far as I have been able to test it.'

'But no chain is stronger than its weakest link.'

'Exactly, my dear Watson. Hence the extreme importance of Porlock. Led on by some rudimentary aspirations towards right, and encouraged by the judicious stimulation of an occasional ten-pound note sent to him by devious methods, he has once or twice given me advance information which has been of value – that highest value which anticipates and prevents rather than avenges crime. I cannot doubt that if we had the cipher we should find that this communication is of the nature that I indicate.'

Again Holmes flattened out the paper upon his unused plate. I rose and, leaning over him, stared down at the curious inscription, which ran as follows:

534 C2 13 127 36 31 4 17 21 41
DOUGLAS 109 293 5 37 BIRLSTONE
26 BIRLSTONE 9 127 171

'What do you make of it, Holmes?'

'It is obviously an attempt to convey secret information.'

'But what is the use of a cipher message without the cipher?'

'In this instance, none at all.'

'Why do you say "in this instance"?'

'Because there are many ciphers which I would read as easily as I do the apocrypha of the agony column. Such crude devices amuse the intelligence without fatiguing it. But this is different. It is clearly a reference to the words in a page of some book. Until I am told which page and which book I am powerless.'

'But why "Douglas" and "Birlstone"?'

'Clearly because those are words which were not contained in the page in question.'

'Then why has he not indicated the book?'

'Your native shrewdness, my dear Watson, that innate cunning which is the delight of your friends, would surely prevent you from enclosing cipher and message in the same envelope. Should it miscarry you are undone. As it is, both have to go wrong before any harm comes from it. Our second post is now overdue, and I shall be surprised if it does not bring us either a further letter of explanation or, as is more probable, the very volume to which these figures refer.'

Holmes's calculation was fulfilled within a very few minutes by the appearance of Billy, the page, with the very letter which we were expecting.

'The same writing,' remarked Holmes, as he opened the envelope, 'and actually signed,' he added, in an exultant voice, as he unfolded the epistle. 'Come, we are getting on, Watson.'

His brow clouded, however, as he glanced over the contents.

'Dear me, this is very disappointing! I fear, Watson, that all our expectations come to nothing. I trust that the man Porlock will come to no harm.

' "Dear Mr Holmes," he says, "I will go no further in this matter. It is too dangerous. He suspects me. I can see that he suspects me. He came to me quite unexpectedly after I had actually addressed this envelope with the intention of sending you the key to the cipher. I was able to cover it up. If he had seen it, it would have gone hard with me. But I read suspicion in his eyes. Please burn the cipher message, which can now be of no use to you. – Fred Porlock." '

Holmes sat for some little time twisting this letter between his fingers, and frowning, as he stared into the fire.

'After all,' he said at last, 'there may be nothing in it. It may be only his guilty conscience. Knowing himself to be a traitor, he may have read the accusation in the other's eyes.'

'The other being, I presume, Professor Moriarty?'

'No less. When any of that party talk about "he", you know whom they mean. There is one predominant "he" for all of them.'

'But what can he do?'

'Hum! That's a large question. When you have one of the first brains of Europe up against you and all the powers of darkness at his back, there are infinite possibilities. Anyhow, friend Porlock is evidently scared out of his senses. Kindly compare the writing in the note with that upon its envelope, which was done, he tells us, before this ill-omened visit. The one is clear and firm; the other hardly legible.'

'Why did he write at all? Why did he not simply drop it?'

'Because he feared I would make some inquiry after him in that case, and possibly bring trouble on him.'

'No doubt,' said I. 'Of course' – I had picked up the original cipher message and was bending my brows over it – 'it's pretty maddening to think that an important secret may lie here on this slip of paper, and that it is beyond human power to penetrate it.'

Sherlock Holmes had pushed away his untasted breakfast and lit the unsavoury pipe which was the companion of his deepest meditations.

'I wonder!' said he, leaning back and staring at the ceiling. 'Perhaps there are points which have escaped your Machiavellian intellect. Let us consider the problem in the light of pure reason. This man's reference is to a book. That is our point of departure.'

'A somewhat vague one.'

'Let us see, then, if we can narrow it down. As I focus my mind upon it, it seems rather less impenetrable. What indications have we as to this book?'

'None.'

'Well, well, it is surely not quite so bad as that. The cipher message begins with a large 534, does it not? We may take it as a working hypothesis that 534 is the particular page to which the cipher refers. So our book has already become a *large* book, which is surely something gained. What other indications have we as to the nature of this large book? The next sign is C2. What do you make of that, Watson?'

'Chapter the second, no doubt.'

'Hardly that, Watson. You will, I am sure, agree with me that if the page be given, the number of the chapter is immaterial. Also that if page 534 only finds us in the second chapter, the length of the first one must have been really intolerable.'

'Column!' I cried.

'Brilliant, Watson. You are scintillating this morning. If it is not column, then I am very much deceived. So now, you see, we begin to visualize a large book, printed in double columns, which are each of a considerable length, since one of the words is numbered in the document as the two hundred and ninety-third. Have we reached the limits of what reason can supply?'

'I fear that we have.'

'Surely you do yourself an injustice. One more coruscation, my dear Watson. Yet another brain-wave. Had the volume been an unusual one he would have sent it to me. Instead of that he had intended, before his plans were nipped, to send me the clue in this envelope. He says so in his note. This would seem to indicate that the book is one which he thought that I would have no difficulty in finding for myself. He had it, and he imagined that I would have it too. In short, Watson, it is a very common book.'

'What you say certainly sounds plausible.'

'So we have contracted our field of search to a large book, printed in double columns and in common use.'

'The Bible!' I cried, triumphantly.

'Good, Watson, good! But not, if I may say so, quite good enough. Even if I accepted the compliment for myself, I could hardly name any volume which would be less likely to lie at the elbow of one of Moriarty's associates. Besides, the editions of Holy Writ are so numerous that he could hardly suppose that two copies would have the same pagination. This is clearly a book which is standardized. He knows for certain that his page 534 will exactly agree with my page 534.'

'But very few books would correspond with that.'

'Exactly. Therein lies our salvation. Our search is narrowed down to standardized books which any one may be supposed to possess.'

'Bradshaw!'

'There are difficulties, Watson. The vocabulary of *Bradshaw* is nervous and terse, but limited. The selection of words would hardly lend itself to the sending of general messages. We will eliminate *Bradshaw*. The dictionary is, I fear, inadmissible for the same reason. What, then, is left?'

'An almanack.'

'Excellent, Watson! I am very much mistaken if you have not touched the spot. An almanack! Let us consider the claims of *Whitaker's Almanack*. It is in common use. It has the requisite number of pages. It is in double columns. Though reserved in its earlier vocabulary, it becomes, if I remember right, quite garrulous towards the end.' He picked up the volume from his desk. 'Here is page 534, column two, a substantial block of print dealing, I perceive, with the trade and resources of British India. Jot down the words, Watson. Number thirteen is "Mahratta". Not, I fear, a very auspicious beginning. Number one hundred and twenty-seven is "Government", which at least makes sense, though somewhat irrelevant to ourselves and Professor Moriarty. Now let us try again. What does the Mahratta Government do? Alas! the next word is "pigs'-bristles". We are undone, my good Watson! It is finished.'

He had spoken in jesting vein, but the twitching of his bushy eyebrows bespoke his disappointment and irritation. I sat helpless and unhappy, staring into the fire. A long silence was broken by a sudden exclamation from Holmes, who dashed at a cupboard, from which he emerged with a second yellow-covered volume in his hand.

'We pay the price, Watson, for being too up-to-date,' he cried. 'We are before our time, and suffer the usual penalties. Being the seventh of January, we have very properly laid in the new almanack. It is more than likely that Porlock took his message from the old one. No doubt he would have told us so had his letter of explanation been written. Now let us see what page 534 has in store for us. Number thirteen is "There", which is much more promising. Number one hundred and twenty-seven is "is" – "There is" ' – Holmes's eyes were gleaming with excitement, and his thin, nervous fingers twitched as he counted the words – ' "danger". Ha! ha! Capital! Put that down, Watson. "There is danger – may – come – very – soon – one". Then we have the name "Douglas" – "rich – country – now – at – Birlstone – House – Birlstone – confidence – is – pressing". There, Watson! what do you think of pure reason and its fruits? If the greengrocer had such a thing as a laurelwreath I should send Billy round for it.'

I was staring at the strange message which I had scrawled, as he deciphered it, upon a sheet of foolscap on my knee.

'What a queer, scrambling way of expressing his meaning!' said I.

'On the contrary, he has done quite remarkably well,' said Holmes. 'When you search a single column for words with which to express your meaning, you can hardly expect to get everything you want. You are bound to leave something to the intelligence of your correspondent. The purport is perfectly clear. Some devilry is intended against one Douglas, whoever he may be, residing as stated, a rich country gentleman. He is sure – "confidence" was as near as he could get to "confident" – that it is pressing. There is our result, and a very workmanlike little bit of analysis it was.'

Holmes had the impersonal joy of the true artist in his better work, even as he mourned darkly when it fell below the high level to which he aspired. He was still chuckling over his success when Billy swung open the door and Inspector MacDonald of Scotland Yard was ushered into the room.

Those were the early days at the end of the 'eighties, when Alec MacDonald was far from having attained the national fame which he has now achieved. He was a young but trusted member of the detective force, who had distinguished himself in several cases which had been entrusted to him. His tall, bony figure gave promise of exceptional physical strength, while his great cranium and deep-set, lustrous eyes spoke no less clearly of the keen intelligence which twinkled out from behind his bushy eyebrows. He was a silent, precise man, with a dour nature and a hard Aberdonian accent. Twice already in his career had Holmes helped him to attain success, his own sole reward being the intellectual joy of the problem. For this reason the affection and respect of the Scotchman for his amateur colleague were profound, and he showed them by the frankness with which he consulted Holmes in every difficulty. Mediocrity knows nothing higher than itself, but talent instantly recognizes genius, and MacDonald had talent enough for his profession to enable him to perceive that there was no humiliation in seeking the assistance of one who already stood alone in Europe, both in his gifts and in his experience. Holmes was not prone to friendship, but he was tolerant of the big Scotchman, and smiled at the sight of him.

'You are an early bird, Mr Mac,' said he. 'I wish you luck with your worm. I fear this means that there is some mischief afoot.'

'If you said "hope" instead of "fear" it would be nearer the truth, I'm thinking, Mr Holmes,' the inspector answered, with a knowing grin. 'Well, maybe a wee nip would keep out the raw morning chill. No, I won't smoke, I thank you. I'll have to be pushing on my way, for the early hours of a case are the precious ones, as no man knows better than your own self. But – but –'

The inspector had stopped suddenly, and was staring with a look of absolute amazement at a paper upon the table. It was the sheet upon which I had scrawled the enigmatic message.

'Douglas!' he stammered. 'Birlstone! What's this, Mr Holmes? Man, it's witchcraft! Where in the name of all that is wonderful did you get those names?'

'It is a cipher that Dr Watson and I have had occasion to solve. But why – what's amiss with the names?'

The inspector looked from one to the other of us in dazed astonishment.

'Just this,' said he, 'that Mr Douglas, of Birlstone Manor House, was horribly murdered this morning.'

Chapter Two

Mr Sherlock Holmes Discourses

It was one of those dramatic moments for which my friend existed. It would be an over-statement to say that he was shocked or even excited by the amazing announcement. Without having a tinge of cruelty in his singular composition, he was undoubtedly callous from long over-stimulation. Yet, if his emotions were dulled, his intellectual perceptions were exceedingly active. There was no trace then of the horror which I had myself felt at this curt declaration, but his face showed rather the quiet and interested composure of the chemist who sees the crystals falling into position from his over-saturated solution.

'Remarkable!' said he; 'remarkable!'

'You don't seem surprised.'

'Interested, Mr Mac, but hardly surprised. Why should I be surprised? I receive an anonymous communication from a quarter which I know to be important, warning me that danger threatens a certain person. Within an hour I learn that this danger has actually materialized, and that the person is dead. I am interested, but, as you observe, I am not surprised.'

In a few short sentences he explained to the inspector the facts about the letter and the cipher. MacDonald sat with his chin on his hands, and his great sandy eyebrows bunched into a yellow tangle.

'I was going down to Birlstone this morning,' said he. 'I had come to ask you if you cared to come with me – you and your friend here. But from what you say we might perhaps be doing better work in London.'

'I rather think not,' said Holmes.

'Hang it all, Mr Holmes!' cried the inspector. 'The papers will be full of the Birlstone Mystery in a day or two, but where's the mystery if there is a man in London who prophesied the crime before ever it occurred? We have only to lay our hands on that man and the rest will follow.'

'No doubt, Mr Mac. But how did you propose to lay your hands on the so-called Porlock?'

MacDonald turned over the letter which Holmes had handed him.

'Posted in Camberwell – that doesn't help us much. Name, you say, is assumed. Not much to go on, certainly. Didn't you say that you have sent him money?'

'Twice.'

'And how?'

'In notes to Camberwell post-office.'

'Did you never trouble to see who called for them?'

'No.'

The inspector looked surprised and a little shocked.

'Why not?'

'Because I always keep faith. I had promised when he first wrote that I would not try to trace him.'

'You think there is some one behind him?'

'I *know* there is.'

'This Professor that I have heard you mention?'

'Exactly.'

Inspector MacDonald smiled, and his eyelid quivered as he glanced towards me.

'I won't conceal from you, Mr Holmes, that we think in the C.I.D. that you have a wee bit of a bee in your bonnet over this Professor. I made some inquiries myself about the matter. He seems to be a very respectable, learned, and talented sort of man.'

'I'm glad you've got as far as to recognize the talent.'

'Man, you can't but recognize it. After I heard your view, I made it my business to see him. I had a chat with him on eclipses – how the talk got that way I canna think – but he had out a reflector lantern and a globe and made it all clear in a minute. He lent me a book, but I don't mind saying that it was a bit above my head, though I had a good Aberdeen upbringing. He'd have made a grand meenister, with his thin face and grey hair and solemn-like way of talking. When he put his hand on my shoulder as we were parting, it was like a father's blessing before you go out into the cold, cruel world.'

Holmes chuckled and rubbed his hands.

'Great!' he cried; 'great! Tell me, friend MacDonald; this pleasing and touching interview was, I suppose, in the Professor's study?'

'That's so.'

'A fine room, is it not?'

'Very fine – very handsome indeed, Mr Holmes.'

'You sat in front of his writing-desk?'

'Just so.'

'Sun in your eyes and his face in the shadow?'

'Well, it was evening, but I mind that the lamp was turned on my face.'

'It would be. Did you happen to observe a picture over the Professor's head?'

'I don't miss much, Mr Holmes. Maybe I learned that from you. Yes, I saw the picture – a young woman with her head on her hands, keeking at you sideways.'

'That painting was by Jean Baptiste Greuze.'

The inspector endeavoured to look interested.

'Jean Baptise Greuze,' Holmes continued, joining his fingertips and leaning well back in his chair, 'was a French artist who flourished between the years 1750 and 1800. I allude, of course, to his working career. Modern criticism has more than endorsed the high opinion formed of him by his contemporaries.'

The inspector's eyes grew abstracted.

'Hadn't we better –' he said.

14

'We are doing so,' Holmes interrupted. 'All that I am saying has a very direct and vital bearing upon what you have called the Birlstone Mystery. In fact, it may in a sense be called the very centre of it.'

MacDonald smiled feebly, and looked appealingly to me.

'Your thoughts move a bit too quick for me, Mr Holmes. You leave out a link or two, and I can't get over the gap. What in the whole wide world can be the connection between this dead painting man and the affair at Birlstone?'

'All knowledge comes useful to the detective,' remarked Holmes. 'Even the trivial fact that in the year 1865 a picture by Greuze, entitled "La Jeune Fille à l'agneau", fetched not less than four thousand pounds – at the Portalis sale – may start a train of reflection in your mind.'

It was clear that it did. The inspector looked honestly interested.

'I may remind you,' Holmes continued, 'that the Professor's salary can be ascertained in several trustworthy books of reference. It is seven hundred a year.'

'Then how could he buy –'

'Quite so. How could he?'

'Aye, that's remarkable,' said the inspector, thoughtfully. 'Talk away, Mr Holmes. I'm just loving it. It's fine.'

Holmes smiled. He was always warmed by genuine admiration – the characteristic of the real artist.

'What about Birlstone?' he asked.

'We've time yet,' said the inspector, glancing at his watch. 'I've a cab at the door, and it won't take us twenty minutes to Victoria. But about this picture – I thought you told me once, Mr Holmes, that you had never met Professor Moriarty.'

'No, I never have.'

'Then how do you know about his rooms?'

'Ah, that's another matter. I have been three times in his rooms, twice waiting for him under different pretexts and leaving before he came. Once – well, I can hardly tell about the once to an official detective. It was on the last occasion that I took the liberty of running over his papers, with the most unexpected results.'

'You found something compromising?'

'Absolutely nothing. That was what amazed me. However, you have now seen the point of the picture. It shows him to be a very wealthy man. How did he acquire wealth? He is unmarried. His younger brother is a station-master in the West of England. His chair is worth seven hundred a year. And he owns a Greuze.'

'Well?'

'Surely the inference is plain.'

'You mean that he has a great income, and that he must earn it in an illegal fashion?'

'Exactly. Of course, I have other reasons for thinking so – dozens of exiguous threads which lead vaguely up towards the centre of the web where the poisonous motionless creature is lurking. I only mention the Greuze because it brings the matter within the range of your own observation.'

'Well, Mr Holmes, I admit that what you say is interesting. It's more than interesting – it's just wonderful. But let us have it a little clearer if you can. Is it forgery, coining, burglary? Where does the money come from?'

'Have you ever read of Jonathan Wild?'

'Well, the name has a familiar sound. Someone in a novel, was he not? I don't take much stock of detectives in novels – chaps that do things and never let you see how they do them. That's just inspiration, not business.'

'Jonathan Wild wasn't a detective, and he wasn't in a novel. He was a master criminal, and he lived last century – 1750 or thereabouts.'

'Then he's no use to me. I'm a practical man.'

'Mr Mac, the most practical thing that ever you did in your life would be to shut yourself up for three months and read twelve hours a day at the annals of crime. Everything comes in circles, even Professor Moriarty. Jonathan Wild was the hidden force of the London criminals, to whom he sold his brains and his organization on a fifteen per cent commission. The old wheel turns and the same spoke comes up. It's all been done before and will be again. I'll tell you one or two things about Moriarty which may interest you.'

'You'll interest me right enough.'

'I happen to know who is the first link in his chain – a chain with this Napoleon-gone-wrong at one end and a hundred broken fighting men, pickpockets, blackmailers, and card-sharpers at the other, with every sort of crime in between. His chief of staff is Colonel Sebastian Moran, as aloof and guarded and inaccessible to the law as himself. What do you think he pays him?'

'I'd like to hear.'

'Six thousand a year. That's paying for brains, you see – the American business principle. I learned that detail quite by chance. It's more than the Prime Minister gets. That gives you an idea of Moriarty's gains and of the scale on which he works. Another point. I made it my business to hunt down some of Moriarty's cheques lately – just common innocent cheques that he pays his household bills with. They were drawn on six different banks. Does that make any impression on your mind?'

'Queer, certainly. But what do you gather from it?'

'That he wanted no gossip about his wealth. No single man should know what he had. I have no doubt that he has twenty banking accounts – the bulk of his fortune abroad in the Deutsche Bank or the Crédit Lyonnais as likely as not. Some time when you have a year or two to spare I commend to you the study of Professor Moriarty.'

Inspector MacDonald had grown steadily more impressed as the conversation proceeded. He had lost himself in his interest. Now his practical Scotch intelligence brought him back with a snap to the matter in hand.

'He can keep, anyhow,' said he. 'You've got us sidetracked with your interesting anecdotes, Mr Holmes. What really counts is your remark that there is some connection between the Professor and the crime. That you get from the warning received through the man Porlock. Can we for our present practical needs get any farther than that?'

'We may form some conception as to the motives of the crime. It is, as I gather from your original remarks, an inexplicable, or at least an unexplained, murder. Now, presuming that the source of the crime is as we suspect it to be, there might be two different motives. In the first place, I may tell you that Moriarty rules with a rod of iron over his people. His discipline is tremendous. There is only one punishment in his code. It is death. Now, we might suppose that this murdered man – this Douglas, whose approaching fate was known by one of the arch-criminal's subordinates – had in some way betrayed the chief. His punishment followed and would be known to all, if only to put the fear of death into them.'

'Well, that is one suggestion, Mr Holmes.'

'The other is that it has been engineered by Moriarty in the ordinary course of business. Was there any robbery?'

'I have not heard.'

'If so it would, of course, be against the first hypothesis and in favour of the second. Moriarty may have been engaged to engineer it on a promise of part spoils, or he may have been paid so much down to manage it. Either is possible. But, whichever it may be, or if it is some third combination, it is down at Birlstone that we must seek the solution. I know our man too well to suppose that he has left anything up here which may lead us to him.'

'Then to Birlstone we must go!' cried MacDonald, jumping from his chair. 'My word! it's later than I thought. I can give you gentlemen five minutes for preparation, and that is all.'

'And ample for us both,' said Holmes, as he sprang up and hastened to change from his dressing-gown to his coat. 'While we are on our way, Mr Mac, I will ask you to be good enough to tell me all about it.'

'All about it' proved to be disappointingly little, and yet there was enough to assure us that the case before us might well be worthy of the expert's closest attention. He brightened and rubbed his thin hands together as he listened to the meagre but remarkable details. A long series of sterile weeks lay behind us, and here, at last, there was a fitting object for those remarkable powers which, like all special gifts, become irksome to their owner when they are not in use. That razor brain blunted and rusted with inaction. Sherlock Holmes's eyes glistened, his pale cheeks took a warmer hue, and his whole eager face shone with an inward light when the call for work reached him. Leaning forward in the cab, he listened intently to MacDonald's short sketch of the problem which awaited us in Sussex. The inspector was himself dependent, as he explained to us, upon a scribbled account forwarded to him by the milk train in the early hours of the morning. White Mason, the local officer, was a personal friend, and hence MacDonald had been notified very much more promptly than is usual at Scotland Yard when provincials need their assistance. It is a very cold scent upon which the Metropolitan expert is generally asked to run.

'Dear Inspector MacDonald,' said the letter which he read to us, 'official requisition for your services is in separate envelope. This is for your private eye. Wire me what train in the morning you can get for Birlstone, and I will meet it – or have it met if I am too occupied. This case is a snorter. Don't waste a moment in getting started. If you can bring Mr Holmes, please do so, for he will find something after his own heart. You would think the whole thing had been fixed up for theatrical effect, if there wasn't a dead man in the middle of it. My word, it *is* a snorter!'

'Your friend seems to be no fool,' remarked Holmes.

'No sir; White Mason is a very live man, if I am any judge.'

'Well, have you anything more?'

'Only that he will give us every detail when we meet.'

'Then how did you get at Mr Douglas and the fact that he had been horribly murdered?'

'That was in the enclosed official report. It didn't say "horrible". That's not a recognized official term. It gave the name John Douglas. It mentioned that his injuries had been in the head, from the discharge of a shot-gun. It also mentioned the hour of the alarm, which was close on to midnight last night. It added that the case was undoubtedly one of murder, but that no arrest had been made, and that the case was one which presented some very perplexing and extraordinary features. That's absolutely all we have at present, Mr Holmes.'

'Then, with your permission, we will leave it at that, Mr Mac. The temptation to form premature theories upon insufficient data is the bane of our profession. I can only see two things for certain at present: a great brain in London and a dead man in Sussex. It's the chain between that we are going to trace.'

Chapter Three

The Tragedy of Birlstone

And now for a moment I will ask leave to remove my own insignificant personality and to describe events which occurred before we arrived upon the scene by the light of knowledge which came to us afterwards. Only in this way can I make the reader appreciate the people concerned and the strange setting in which their fate was cast.

The village of Birlstone is a small and very ancient cluster of half-timbered cottages on the northern border of the county of Sussex. For centuries it had remained unchanged, but within the last few years its picturesque appearance and situation have attracted a number of well-to-do residents, whose villas peep out from the woods around. These woods are locally supposed to be the extreme fringe of the great Weald forest, which thins away until it reaches the northern chalk downs. A number of small shops have come into being to meet the wants of the increased population, so that there seems some prospect that Birlstone may soon grow from an ancient village into a modern town. It is the centre for a considerable area of country, since Tunbridge Wells, the nearest place of importance, is ten or twelve miles to the eastward, over the borders of Kent.

About half a mile from the town, standing in an old park famous for its huge beech trees, is the ancient Manor House of Birlstone. Part of this venerable building dates back to the time of the first Crusade, when Hugo de Capus built a fortalice in the centre of the estate, which had been granted to him by the Red King. This was destroyed by fire in 1543, and some of its smoke-blackened corner-stones were used when, in Jacobean times, a brick country house rose upon the ruins of the feudal castle. The

Manor House, with its many gables and its small, diamond-paned windows, was still much as the builder had left it in the early seventeenth century. Of the double moats which had guarded its more warlike predecessor the outer had been allowed to dry up, and served the humble function of a kitchen garden. The inner one was still there, and lay, forty feet in breadth, though now only a few feet in depth, round the whole house. A small stream fed it and continued beyond it, so that the sheet of water, though turbid, was never ditch-like or unhealthy. The groundfloor windows were within a foot of the surface of the water. The only approach to the house was over a drawbridge, the chains and windlass of which had long been rusted and broken. The latest tenants of the Manor House had, however, with characteristic energy, set this right, and the drawbridge was not only capable of being raised, but actually was raised every evening and lowered every morning. By thus renewing the custom of the old feudal days the Manor House was converted into an island during the night – a fact which had a very direct bearing upon the mystery which was soon to engage the attention of all England.

The house had been untenanted for some years, and was threatening to moulder into a picturesque decay when the Douglases took possession of it. This family consisted of only two individuals, John Douglas and his wife. Douglas was a remarkable man both in character and in person; in age he may have been about fifty, with a strong-jawed, rugged face, a grizzling moustache, peculiarly keen grey eyes, and a wiry, vigorous figure which had lost nothing of the strength and activity of youth. He was cheery and genial to all, but somewhat offhand in his manners, giving the impression that he had seen life in social strata on some far lower horizon than the county society of Sussex. Yet, though looked at with some curiosity and reserve by his more cultivated neighbours, he soon acquired a great popularity among the villagers, subscribing handsomely to all local objects, and attending their smoking concerts, and other functions, where, having a remarkably rich tenor voice, he was always ready to oblige with an excellent song. He appeared to have plenty of money, which was said to have been gained in the Californian goldfields, and it was clear from his own talk and that of his wife that he had spent a part of his life in America. The good impression which had been produced by his generosity and by his democratic manners was increased by a reputation gained for utter indifference to danger. Though a wretched rider, he turned out at every meet, and took the most amazing falls in his determination to hold his own with the best. When the vicarage caught fire he distinguished himself also by the fearlessness with which he re-entered the building to save property, after the local fire brigade had given it up as impossible. Thus it came about that John Douglas, of the Manor House, had within five years won himself quite a reputation in Birlstone.

His wife, too, was popular with those who had made her acquaintance, though, after the English fashion, the callers upon a stranger who settled in the county without introductions were few and far between. This mattered less to her as she was retiring by disposition and very much absorbed, to all appearance, in her husband and her domestic duties. It was known that she was an English lady who had met Mr Douglas in London, he being at that time a widower. She was a beautiful woman, tall, dark, and slender, some twenty years younger than her husband, a disparity which seemed in no wise to mar the contentment of their family life. It was remarked sometimes, however, by those who knew them best that the confidence between the two did not appear to be complete, since the wife was either very reticent about her husband's past life or else, as seemed more likely, was very imperfectly informed about it. It had also been noted and commented upon by a few observant people that there were signs sometimes of some nerve-strain upon the part of Mrs Douglas, and that she would display acute uneasiness if her absent husband should ever be particularly late in his return. In a quiet countryside, where all gossip is welcome, this weakness of the lady of the Manor House did not pass without remark, and it bulked larger upon people's memory when the events arose which gave it a very special significance.

There was yet another individual whose residence under that roof was, it is true, only an intermittent one, but whose presence at the time of the strange happenings which will now be narrated brought his name prominently before the public. This was Cecil James Barker, of Hales Lodge, Hampstead. Cecil Barker's tall, loose-jointed figure was a familiar one in the main street of Birlstone village, for he was a frequent and welcome visitor at the Manor House. He was the more noticed as being the only friend of the past unknown life of Mr Douglas who was ever seen in his new English surroundings. Barker was himself an undoubted Englishman, but by his remarks it was clear that he had first known Douglas in America, and had there lived on intimate terms with him. He appeared to be a man of considerable wealth, and was reputed to be a bachelor. In age he was rather younger than Douglas, forty-five at the most, a tall, straight, broad-chested fellow, with a clean-shaven, prize-fighter face, thick, strong, black eyebrows, and a pair of masterful black eyes which might, even without the aid of his very capable hands, clear a way for him through a hostile crowd. He neither rode nor shot, but spent his days in wandering round the old village with his pipe in his mouth, or in driving with his host, or in his absence with his hostess, over the beautiful countryside. 'An easy-going, free-handed gentleman,' said Ames, the butler. 'But, my word, I had rather not be the man that crossed him.' He was cordial and intimate with Douglas, and he was no less friendly with his wife, a friendship which more than once seemed to cause some irritation to the husband, so that even the servants were able to perceive his annoyance. Such was the third person who was one of the family when the catastrophe occurred. As to the other denizens of the old building, it will suffice out of a large household to mention the prim, respectable, and capable Ames and Mrs Allen, a buxom and cheerful person, who relieved the lady of some of her household cares. The other six servants in the house bear no relation to the events of the night of January 6th.

It was at eleven forty-five that the first alarm reached the small local police-station in the charge of Sergeant Wilson, of the Sussex Constabulary. Mr Cecil Barker, much excited, had rushed up to the door and pealed furiously upon the bell. A terrible tragedy had occurred at the Manor House, and Mr John Douglas had been murdered. That was the breathless burden of his message. He had hurried back to the house, followed within a few minutes by the police-sergeant, who arrived at the scene of the crime a little past twelve o'clock, after taking prompt steps to warn the county authorities that something serious was afoot.

On reaching the Manor House the sergeant had found the drawbridge down, the windows lighted up, and the whole household in a state of wild confusion and alarm. The white-faced servants were huddling together in the hall, with the frightened butler wringing his hands in the doorway. Only Cecil Barker seemed to be master of himself and his emotions. He had opened the door which was nearest to the entrance, and had beckoned to the sergeant to follow him. At that moment there arrived Dr Wood, a brisk and capable general practitioner from the village. The three men entered the fatal room together, while the horror-stricken butler followed at their heels, closing the door behind him to shut out the terrible scene from the maid-servants.

The dead man lay upon his back, sprawling with outstretched limbs in the centre of the room. He was clad only in a pink dressing-gown, which covered his night clothes. There were carpet slippers upon his bare feet. The doctor knelt beside him, and held down the hand-lamp which had stood on the table. One glance at the victim was enough to show the healer that his presence could be dispensed with. The man had been horribly injured. Lying across his chest was a curious weapon, a shot-gun with the barrel sawn off a foot in front of the triggers. It was clear that this had been fired at close range, and that he had received the whole charge in the face, blowing his head almost to pieces. The triggers had been wired together, so as to make the simultaneous discharge more destructive.

The country policeman was unnerved and troubled by the tremendous responsibility which had come so suddenly upon him.

'We will touch nothing until my superiors arrive,' he said, in a hushed voice, staring in horror at the dreadful head.

'Nothing has been touched up to now,' said Cecil Barker. 'I'll answer for that. You see it all exactly as I found it.'

'When was that?' The sergeant had drawn out his notebook.

'It was just half-past eleven. I had not begun to undress, and I was sitting by the fire in my bedroom, when I heard the report. It was not very loud – it seemed to be muffled. I rushed down. I don't suppose it was thirty seconds before I was in the room.'

'Was the door open?'

'Yes, it was open. Poor Douglas was lying as you see him. His bedroom candle was burning on the table. It was I who lit the lamp some minutes afterwards.'

'Did you see no one?'

'No. I heard Mrs Douglas coming down the stair behind me, and I rushed out to prevent her from seeing this dreadful sight. Mrs Allen, the housekeeper, came and took her away. Ames had arrived, and we ran back into the room once more.'

'But surely I have heard that the drawbridge is kept up all night.'

'Yes, it was up until I lowered it.'

'Then how could any murderer have got away? It is out of the question. Mr Douglas must have shot himself.'

'That was our first idea. But see.' Barker drew aside the curtain, and showed that the long, diamond-paned window was open to its full extent. 'And look at this!' He held the lamp down and illuminated a smudge of blood like the mark of a boot-sole upon the wooden sill. 'Some one has stood there in getting out.'

'You mean that some one waded across the moat?'

'Exactly.'

'Then, if you were in the room within half a minute of the crime, he must have been in the water at that very moment.'

'I have not a doubt of it. I wish to Heaven that I had rushed to the window. But the curtain screened it, as you can see, and so it never occurred to me. Then I heard the step of Mrs Douglas, and I could not let her enter the room. It would have been too horrible.'

'Horrible enough!' said the doctor, looking at the shattered head and the terrible marks which surrounded it. 'I've never seen such injuries since the Birlstone railway smash.'

'But, I say,' remarked the police-sergeant, whose slow, bucolic common sense was still pondering over the open window. 'It's all very well your saying that a man escaped by wading this moat, but what I ask you is – how did he ever get into the house at all if the bridge was up?'

'Ah, that's the question,' said Barker.

'At what o'clock was it raised?'

'It was nearly six o'clock,' said Ames, the butler.

'I've heard,' said the sergeant, 'that it was usually raised at sunset. That would be nearer half-past four than six at this time of year.'

'Mrs Douglas had visitors to tea,' said Ames. 'I couldn't raise it until they went. Then I wound it up myself.'

'Then it comes to this,' said the sergeant. 'If anyone came from outside – *if* they did – they must have got in across the bridge before six and been in hiding ever since, until Mr Douglas came into the room after eleven.'

'That is so. Mr Douglas went round the house every night the last thing before he turned in to see that the lights were right.

That brought him in here. The man was waiting, and shot him. Then he got away through the window and left his gun behind him. That's how I read it – for nothing else will fit the facts.'

The sergeant picked up a card which lay beside the dead man upon the floor. The initials V. V., and under them the number 341, were rudely scrawled in ink upon it.

'What's this?' he asked, holding it up.

Barker looked at it with curiosity.

'I never noticed it before,' he said. 'The murderer must have left it behind him.'

' "V. V. 341." I can make no sense of that.'

The sergeant kept turning it over in his big fingers.

'What's V. V.? Somebody's initials, maybe. What have you got there, Dr Wood?'

It was a good-sized hammer which had been lying upon the rug in front of the fireplace – a substantial, workmanlike hammer. Cecil Barker pointed to a box of brass-headed nails upon the mantelpiece.

'Mr Douglas was altering the pictures yesterday,' he said. 'I saw him myself standing upon that chair and fixing the big picture above it. That accounts for the hammer.'

'We'd best put it back on the rug where we found it,' said the sergeant, scratching his puzzled head in his perplexity. 'It will want the best brains in the force to get to the bottom of this thing. It will be a London job before it is finished.' He raised the hand-lamp and walked slowly round the room. 'Halloa!' he cried, excitedly, drawing the window curtain to one side. 'What o'clock were those curtains drawn?'

'When the lamps were lit,' said the butler. 'It would be shortly after four.'

'Some one has been hiding here, sure enough.' He held down the light, and the marks of muddy boots were very visible in the corner. 'I'm bound to say this bears out your theory, Mr Barker. It looks as if the man got into the house after four, when the curtains were drawn, and before six, when the bridge was raised. He slipped into this room because it was the first that he saw. There was no other place where he could hide, so he popped in behind this curtain. That all seems clear enough. It is likely that his main idea was to burgle the house, but Mr Douglas chanced to come upon him, so he murdered him and escaped.'

'That's how I read it,' said Barker. 'But, I say, aren't we wasting precious time? Couldn't we start out and scour the country before the fellow gets away?'

The sergeant considered for a moment.

'There are no trains before six in the morning, so he can't get away by rail. If he goes by road with his legs all dripping, it's odds that some one will notice him. Anyhow, I can't leave here myself until I am relieved. But I think none of you should go until we see more clearly how we all stand.'

The doctor had taken the lamp and was narrowly scrutinizing the body.

'What's this mark?' he asked. 'Could this have any connection with the crime?'

The dead man's right arm was thrust out from his dressing-gown and exposed as high as the elbow. About halfway up the forearm was a curious brown design, a triangle inside a circle, standing out in vivid relief upon the lard-coloured skin.

'It's not tattooed,' said the doctor, peering through his glasses. 'I never saw anything like it. The man has been branded at some time, as they brand cattle. What is the meaning of this?'

'I don't profess to know the meaning of it,' said Cecil Barker; 'but I've seen the mark on Douglas any time this last ten years.'

'And so have I,' said the butler. 'Many a time when the master has rolled up his sleeves I have noticed that very mark. I've often wondered what it could be.'

'Then it has nothing to do with the crime, anyhow,' said the sergeant. 'But it's a rum thing all the same. Everything about this case is rum. Well, what is it now?'

The butler had given an exclamation of astonishment, and was pointing at the dead man's outstretched hand.

'They've taken his wedding-ring!' he gasped.

'What!'

'Yes, indeed! Master always wore his plain gold wedding-ring on the little finger of his left hand. That ring with the rough nugget on it was above it, and the twisted snake-ring on the third finger. There's the nugget, and there's the snake, but the wedding-ring is gone.'

'He's right,' said Barker.

'Do you tell me,' said the sergeant, 'that the wedding-ring was *below* the other?'

'Always!'

'Then the murderer, or whoever it was, first took off this ring you call the nugget-ring, then the wedding-ring, and afterwards put the nugget-ring back again.'

'That is so.'

The worthy country policeman shook his head.

'Seems to me the sooner we get London on to this case the better,' said he. 'White Mason is a smart man. No local job has ever been too much for White Mason. It won't be long now before he is here to help us. But I expect we'll have to look to London before we are through. Anyhow, I'm not ashamed to say that it is a deal too thick for the likes of me.'

Chapter Four

Darkness

At three in the morning the chief Sussex detective, obeying the urgent call from Sergeant Wilson, of Birlstone, arrived from head-quarters in a light dog-cart behind a breathless trotter. By the five-forty train in the morning he had sent his message to Scotland Yard, and he was at the Birlstone station at twelve o'clock to welcome us. Mr White Mason was a quiet, comfortable-looking person, in a loose tweed suit, with a clean-shaven, ruddy face, a stoutish body, and powerful bandy legs adorned with gaiters, looking like a small farmer, a retired game-keeper, or anything upon earth except a very favourable specimen of the provincial criminal officer.

'A real downright snorter, Mr MacDonald,' he kept repeating. 'We'll have the pressmen down like flies when they understand it. I'm hoping we will get our work done before they get poking their noses into it and messing up all the trails. There has been nothing like this that I can remember. There are some bits that will come home to you, Mr Holmes, or I am mistaken. And you also, Dr Watson, for the medicos will have a word to say before we finish. Your room is at the Westville Arms. There's no other place, but I hear that it is clean and good. The man will carry your bags. This way, gentlemen, if *you* please.'

He was a very bustling and genial person, this Sussex detective. In ten minutes we had all found our quarters. In ten more we were seated in the parlour of the inn and being treated to a rapid sketch of those events which have been outlined in the previous chapter. MacDonald made an occasional note, while Holmes sat absorbed with the expression of surprised and reverent admiration with which the botanist surveys the rare and precious bloom.

'Remarkable!' he said, when the story was unfolded. 'Most remarkable! I can hardly recall any case where the features have been more peculiar.'

'I thought you would say so, Mr Holmes,' said White Mason, in great delight. 'We're well up with the times in Sussex. I've told you now how matters were, up to the time when I took over from Sergeant Wilson between three and four this morning. My word, I made the old mare go! But I need not have been in such a hurry as it turned out, for there was nothing immediate that I could do. Sergeant Wilson had all the facts. I checked them and considered them, and maybe added a few on my own.'

'What were they?' asked Holmes, eagerly.

'Well, I first had the hammer examined. There was Dr Wood there to help me. We found no signs of violence upon it. I was hoping that, if Mr Douglas defended himself with the hammer, he might have left his mark upon the murderer before he dropped it on the mat. But there was no stain.'

'That, of course, proves nothing at all,' remarked Inspector MacDonald. 'There has been many a hammer murder and no trace on the hammer.'

'Quite so. It doesn't prove it wasn't used. But there might have been stains, and that would have helped us. As a matter of fact, there were none. Then I examined the gun. They were buck-shot cartridges, and, as Sergeant Wilson pointed out, the triggers were wired together so that if you pulled on the hinder one both barrels were discharged. Whoever fixed that up had made up his mind that he was going to take no chances of missing his man. The sawn gun was not more than two feet long; one could carry it easily under one's coat. There was no complete maker's name, but the printed letters "P E N" were on the fluting between the barrels, and the rest of the name had been cut off by the saw.'

'A big "P" with a flourish above it – "E" and "N" smaller?' asked Holmes.

'Exactly.'

'Pennsylvania Small Arm Company – well-known American firm,' said Holmes.

White Mason gazed at my friend as the little village practitioner looks at the Harley Street specialist who by a word can solve the difficulties that perplex him.

'That is very helpful, Mr Holmes. No doubt you are right. Wonderful – wonderful! Do you carry the names of all the gunmakers in the world in your memory?'

Holmes dismissed the subject with a wave.

'No doubt it is an American shot-gun,' White Mason continued. 'I seem to have read that a sawed-off shot-gun is a weapon used in some parts of America. Apart from the name upon the barrel, the idea had occurred to me. There is some evidence, then, that this man who entered the house and killed its master was an American.'

MacDonald shook his head. 'Man, you are surely travelling over-fast,' said he. 'I have heard no evidence yet that any stranger was ever in the house at all.'

'The open window, the blood on the sill, the queer card, marks of boots in the corner, the gun.'

'Nothing there that could not have been arranged. Mr Douglas was an American, or had lived long in America. So had Mr Barker. You don't need to import an American from outside in order to account for American doings.'

'Ames, the butler –'

'What about him? Is he reliable?'

'Ten years with Sir Charles Chandos – as solid as a rock. He has been with Douglas ever since he took the Manor House five years ago. He has never seen a gun of this sort in the house.'

'The gun was made to conceal. That's why the barrels were sawn. It would fit into any box. How could he swear there was no such gun in the house?'

'Well, anyhow, he had never seen one.'

MacDonald shook his obstinate Scotch head. 'I'm not

convinced yet that there was ever any one in the house,' said he. 'I'm asking you to conseedar' – his accent became more Aberdonian as he lost himself in his argument – 'I'm asking you to conseedar what it involves if you suppose that this gun was ever brought into the house and that all these strange things were done by a person from outside. Oh, man, it's just inconceivable! It's clean against common sense. I put it to you, Mr Holmes, judging it by what we have heard.'

'Well, state your case, Mr Mac,' said Holmes, in his most judicial style.

'The man is not a burglar, supposing that he ever existed. The ring business and the card point to premeditated murder for some private reason. Very good. Here is a man who slips into a house with the deliberate intention of committing murder. He knows, if he knows anything, that he will have a deeficulty in making his escape, as the house is surrounded with water. What weapon would he choose? You would say the most silent in the world. Then he could hope, when the deed was done, to slip quickly from the window, to wade the moat, and to get away at his leisure. That's understandable. But is it understandable that he should go out of his way to bring with him the most noisy weapon he could select, knowing well that it will fetch every human being in the house to the spot as quick as they can run, and that it is all odds that he will be seen before he can get across the moat? Is that credible, Mr Holmes?'

'Well, you put your case strongly,' my friend replied, thoughtfully. 'It certainly needs a good deal of justification. May I ask, Mr White Mason, whether you examined the farther side of the moat at once, to see if there were any signs of the man having climbed out from the water?'

'There were no signs, Mr Holmes. But it is a stone ledge, and one could hardly expect them.'

'No tracks or marks?'

'None.'

'Ha! Would there be any objection, Mr White Mason, to our going down to the house at once? There may possibly be some small point which might be suggestive.'

'I was going to propose it, Mr Holmes, but I thought it well to put you in touch with all the facts before we go. I suppose, if anything should strike you –' White Mason looked doubtfully at the amateur.

'I have worked with Mr Holmes before,' said Inspector Mac-Donald. 'He plays the game.'

'My own idea of the game, at any rate,' said Holmes, with a smile. 'I go into a case to help the ends of justice and the work of the police. If ever I have separated myself from the official force, it is because they have first separated themselves from me. I have no wish ever to score at their expense. At the same time, Mr White Mason, I claim the right to work in my own way and give my results at my own time – complete, rather than in stages.'

'I am sure we are honoured by your presence and to show you all we know,' said White Mason, cordially. 'Come along, Dr Watson, and when the time comes we'll all hope for a place in your book.'

We walked down the quaint village street with a row of pollarded elms on either side of it. Just beyond were two ancient stone pillars, weather-stained and lichen-blotched, bearing upon their summits a shapeless something which had once been the ramping lion of Capus of Birlstone. A short walk along the winding drive, with such sward and oaks around it as one only sees in rural England; then a sudden turn, and the long, low, Jacobean house of dingy, liver-coloured brick lay before us, with an old-fashioned garden of cut yews on either side of it. As we approached it there were the wooden drawbridge and the beautiful broad moat, as still and luminous as quicksilver in the cold winter sunshine. Three centuries had flowed past the old Manor House, centuries of births and homecomings, of country dances and of the meetings of fox-hunters. Strange that now in its old age this dark business should have cast its shadow upon the venerable walls. And yet those strange peaked roofs and quaint overhung gables were a fitting covering to grim and terrible intrigue. As I looked at the deep-set windows and the long sweep of the dull-coloured, water-lapped front I felt that no more fitting scene could be set for such a tragedy.

'That's the window,' said White Mason: 'that one on the immediate right of the drawbridge. It's open just as it was found last night.'

'It looks rather narrow for a man to pass.'

'Well, it wasn't a fat man, anyhow. We don't need your deductions, Mr Holmes, to tell us that. But you or I could squeeze through all right.'

Holmes walked to the edge of the moat and looked across. Then he examined the stone ledge and the grass border beyond it.

'I've had a good look, Mr Holmes,' said White Mason. 'There is nothing there; no sign that any one has landed. But why should he leave any sign?'

'Exactly. Why should he? Is the water always turbid?'

'Generally about this colour. The stream brings down the clay.'

'How deep is it?'

'About two feet at each side and three in the middle.'

'So we can put aside all idea of the man having been drowned in crossing?'

'No; a child could not be drowned in it.'

We walked across the drawbridge, and were admitted by a quaint, gnarled, dried-up person who was the butler – Ames. The poor old fellow was white and quivering from the shock. The village sergeant, a tall, formal, melancholy man, still held his vigil in the room of fate. The doctor had departed.

'Anything fresh, Sergeant Wilson?' asked White Mason.

'No, sir.'

'Then you can go home. You've had enough. We can send for you if we want you. The butler had better wait outside. Tell him to warn Mr Cecil Barker, Mrs Douglas, and the housekeeper that we may want a word with them presently. Now, gentlemen, perhaps you will allow me to give you the views I have formed first, and then you will be able to arrive at your own.'

He impressed me, this country specialist. He had a solid grip of fact and a cool, clear, common-sense brain, which should take him some way in his profession. Holmes listened to him intently, with no sign of that impatience which the official exponent too often produced.

'Is it suicide or is it murder – that's our first question, gentlemen, is it not? If it were suicide, then we have to believe that this man began by taking off his wedding-ring and concealing it; that he then came down here in his dressing-gown, trampled mud into a corner behind the curtain in order to give the idea someone had waited for him, opened the window, put the blood on the –'

'We can surely dismiss that,' said MacDonald.

'So I think. Suicide is out of the question. Then a murder has been done. What we have to determine is whether it was done by someone outside or inside the house.'

'Well, let's hear the argument.'

'There are considerable difficulties both ways, and yet one or the other it must be. We will suppose first that some person or persons inside the house did the crime. They got this man down here at a time when everything was still, and yet no one was asleep. They then did the deed with the queerest and noisiest weapon in the world, so as to tell every one what had happened – a weapon that was never seen in the house before. That does not seem a very likely start, does it?'

'No, it does not.'

'Well, then, everyone is agreed that after the alarm was given only a minute at the most had passed before the whole household – not Mr Cecil Barker alone, though he claims to have been the first, but Ames and all of them – were on the spot. Do you tell me that in that time the guilty person managed to make footmarks in the corner, open the window, mark the sill with blood, take the wedding-ring off the dead man's finger, and all the rest of it? It's impossible!'

'You put it very clearly,' said Holmes. 'I am inclined to agree with you.'

'Well, then, we are driven back to the theory that it was done by someone from outside. We are still faced with some big difficulties, but, anyhow, they have ceased to be impossibilities. The man got into the house between four-thirty and six – that is to say, between dusk and the time when the bridge was raised. There had been some visitors, and the door was open, so there was nothing to prevent him. He may have been a common burglar, or he may have had some private grudge against Mr Douglas. Since Mr Douglas has spent most of his life in America, and this shot-gun seems to be an American weapon, it would seem that the private grudge is the more likely theory. He slipped into this room because it was the first he came to, and he hid behind the curtain. There he remained until past eleven at night. At that time Mr Douglas entered the room. It was a short interview, if there were any interview at all, for Mrs Douglas declares that her husband had not left her more than a few minutes when she heard the shot.'

'The candle shows that,' said Holmes.

'Exactly. The candle, which was a new one, is not burned more than half an inch. He must have placed it on the table before he was attacked, otherwise, of course, it would have fallen when he fell. This shows that he was not attacked the instant that he entered the room. When Mr Barker arrived the lamp was lit and the candle put out.'

'That's all clear enough.'

'Well, now, we can reconstruct things on those lines. Mr Douglas enters the room. He puts down the candle. A man appears from behind the curtain. He is armed with this gun. He demands the wedding-ring – Heaven only knows why, but so it must have been. Mr Douglas gave it up. Then either in cold blood or in the course of a struggle – Douglas may have gripped the hammer that was found upon the mat – he shot Douglas in this horrible way. He dropped his gun and also, it would seem, this queer card, "V. V. 341", whatever that may mean, and he made his escape through the window and across the moat at the very moment when Cecil Barker was discovering the crime. How's that, Mr Holmes?'

'Very interesting, but just a little unconvincing.'

'Man, it would be absolute nonsense if it wasn't that anything else is even worse,' cried MacDonald. 'Somebody killed the man, and whoever it was I could clearly prove to you that he should have done it some other way. What does he mean by allowing his retreat to be cut off like that? What does he mean by using a shot-gun when silence was his one chance of escape? Come, Mr Holmes, it's up to you to give us a lead, since you say Mr White Mason's theory is unconvincing.'

Holmes had sat intently observant during this long discussion, missing no word that was said, with his keen eyes darting to right and to left, and his forehead wrinkled with speculation.

'I should like a few more facts before I get so far as a theory, Mr Mac,' said he, kneeling down beside the body. 'Dear me! these injuries are really appalling. Can we have the butler in for a moment? . . . Ames, I understand that you have often seen this very unusual mark, a branded triangle inside a circle, upon Mr Douglas's forearm?'

'Frequently, sir.'

'You never heard any speculation as to what it meant?'

'No, sir.'

'It must have caused great pain when it was inflicted. It is undoubtedly a burn. Now, I observe, Ames, that there is a small piece of plaster at the angle of Mr Douglas's jaw. Did you observe that in life?'

'Yes, sir; he cut himself in shaving yesterday morning.'

'Did you ever know him cut himself in shaving before?'

'Not for a very long time, sir.'

'Suggestive!' said Holmes. 'It may, of course, be a mere coincidence, or it may point to some nervousness which would indicate that he had reason to apprehend danger. Had you noticed anything unusual in his conduct yesterday, Ames?'

'It struck me that he was a little restless and excited, sir.'

'Ha! The attack may not have been entirely unexpected. We do seem to make a little progress, do we not? Perhaps you would rather do the questioning, Mr Mac?'

'No, Mr Holmes; it's in better hands.'

'Well, then, we will pass to this card – "V. V. 341". It is rough cardboard. Have you any of the sort in the house?'

'I don't think so.'

Holmes walked across to the desk and dabbed a little ink from each bottle on to the blotting-paper. 'It has not been printed in this room,' he said; 'this is black ink, and the other purplish. It has been done by a thick pen, and these are fine. No, it has been done elsewhere, I should say. Can you make anything of the inscription, Ames?'

'No, sir, nothing.'

'What do you think, Mr Mac?'

'It gives me the impression of a secret society of some sort. The same with this badge upon the forearm.'

'That's my idea, too,' said White Mason.

'Well, we can adopt it as a working hypothesis, and then see how far our difficulties disappear. An agent from such a society makes his way into the house, waits for Mr Douglas, blows his head nearly off with this weapon, and escapes by wading the moat, after leaving a card beside the dead man which will, when mentioned in the papers, tell other members of the society that vengeance has been done. That all bangs together. But why this gun, of all weapons?'

'Exactly.'

'And why the missing ring?'

'Quite so.'

'And why no arrest? It's past two now. I take it for granted that since dawn every constable within forty miles has been looking out for a wet stranger?'

'That is so, Mr Holmes.'

'Well, unless he has a burrow close by, or a change of clothes ready, they can hardly miss him. And yet they *have* missed him up to now.' Holmes had gone to the window and was examining with his lens the bloodmark upon the sill. 'It is clearly the tread of a shoe. It is remarkably broad – a splay foot, one would say. Curious, because, so far as one can trace any footmark in this mud-stained corner, one would say it was a more shapely sole. However, they are certainly very indistinct. What's this under this side table?'

'Mr Douglas's dumb-bells,' said Ames.

'Dumb-bell – there's only one. Where's the other?'

'I don't know, Mr Holmes. There may have been only one. I have not noticed them for months.'

'One dumb-bell –' Holmes said, seriously, but his remarks were interrupted by a sharp knock at the door. A tall, sunburned, capable-looking, clean-shaven man looked in at us. I had no difficulty in guessing that it was the Cecil Barker of whom I had heard. His masterful eyes travelled quickly with a questioning glance from face to face.

'Sorry to interrupt your consultation,' said he, 'but you should hear the latest.'

'An arrest?'

'No such luck. But they've found his bicycle. The fellow left his bicycle behind him. Come and have a look. It is within a hundred yards of the hall door.'

We found three or four grooms and idlers standing in the drive inspecting a bicycle which had been drawn out from a clump of evergreens in which it had been concealed. It was a well-used Rudge-Whitworth, splashed as from a considerable journey. There was a saddle-bag with spanner and oil-can, but no clue as to the owner.

'It would be a grand help to the police,' said the inspector, 'if these things were numbered and registered. But we must be thankful for what we've got. If we can't find where he went to, at least we are likely to get where he came from. But what in the name of all that is wonderful made the fellow leave it behind? And how in the world has he got away without it? We don't seem to get a gleam of light in the case, Mr Holmes.'

'Don't we?' my friend answered, thoughtfully. 'I wonder!'

Chapter Five

The People of the Drama

'Have you seen all you want of the study?' asked White Mason as we re-entered the house.

'For the time,' said the inspector; and Holmes nodded.

'Then perhaps you would now like to hear the evidence of some of the people in the house? We could use the dining-room, Ames. Please come yourself first and tell us what you know.'

The butler's account was a simple and a clear one, and he gave a convincing impression of sincerity. He had been engaged five years ago when Mr Douglas first came to Birlstone. He understood that Mr Douglas was a rich gentleman who had made his money in America. He had been a kind and considerate employer – not quite what Ames was used to, perhaps, but one can't have everything. He never saw any signs of apprehension in Mr Douglas – on the contrary, he was the most fearless man he had ever known. He ordered the drawbridge to be pulled up every night because it was the ancient custom of the old house, and he liked to keep the old ways up. Mr Douglas seldom went to London or left the village, but on the day before the crime he had been shopping at Tunbridge Wells. He, Ames, had observed some restlessness and excitement on the part of Mr Douglas upon that day, for he had seemed impatient and irritable, which was unusual with him. He had not gone to bed that night, but was in the pantry at the back of the house, putting away the silver, when he heard the bell ring violently. He heard no shot, but it was hardly possible he should, as the pantry and kitchens were at the very back of the house and there were several closed doors and a long passage between. The housekeeper had come out of her room, attracted by the violent ringing of the bell. They had gone to the front of the house together. As they reached the bottom of the stair he had seen Mrs Douglas coming down it. No, she was not hurrying – it did not seem to him that she was particularly agitated. Just as she reached the bottom of the stair Mr Barker had rushed out of the study. He had stopped Mrs Douglas and begged her to go back.

'For God's sake, go back to your room!' he cried. 'Poor Jack is dead. You can do nothing. For God's sake, go back!'

After some persuasion upon the stairs Mrs Douglas had gone back. She did not scream. She made no outcry whatever. Mrs Allen, the housekeeper, had taken her upstairs and stayed with her in the bedroom. Ames and Mr Barker had then returned to the study, where they had found everything exactly as the police had seen it. The candle was not lit at that time, but the lamp was burning. They had looked out of the window, but the night was very dark and nothing could be seen or heard. They had then rushed out into the hall, where Ames had turned the windlass which had lowered the drawbridge. Mr Barker had then hurried off to get the police.

Such, in its essentials, was the evidence of the butler.

The account of Mrs Allen, the housekeeper, was, so far as it went, a corroboration of that of her fellow-servant. The housekeeper's room was rather nearer to the front of the house than the pantry in which Ames had been working. She was preparing to go to bed when the loud ringing of the bell had attracted her attention. She was a little hard of hearing. Perhaps that was why she had not heard the sound of the shot, but in any case the study was a long way off. She remembered hearing some sound which she imagined to be the slamming of a door. That was a good deal earlier – half an hour at least before the ringing of the bell. When Mr Ames ran to the front she went with him. She saw Mr Barker, very pale and excited, come out of the study. He intercepted Mrs Douglas, who was coming down the stairs. He entreated her to go back, and she answered him, but what she said could not be heard.

'Take her up. Stay with her!' he had said to Mrs Allen.

She had therefore taken her to the bedroom and endeavoured to soothe her. She was greatly excited, trembling all over, but made no other attempt to go downstairs. She just sat in her dressing-gown by her bedroom fire with her head sunk in her hands. Mrs Allen stayed with her most of the night. As to the other servants, they had all gone to bed, and the alarm did not reach them until just before the police arrived. They slept at the extreme back of the house, and could not possibly have heard anything.

So for the housekeeper – who could add nothing on cross-examination save lamentations and expressions of amazement.

Mr Cecil Barker succeeded Mrs Allen as a witness. As to the occurrences of the night before, he had very little to add to what he had already told the police. Personally, he was convinced that the murderer had escaped by the window. The blood-stain was conclusive, in his opinion, upon that point. Besides, as the bridge was up there was no other possible way of escaping. He could not explain what had become of the assassin, or why he had not taken his bicycle, if it were indeed his. He could not possibly have been drowned in the moat, which was at no place more than three feet deep.

In his own mind he had a very definite theory about the murder. Douglas was a reticent man, and there were some chapters in his life of which he never spoke. He had emigrated to America from Ireland when he was a very young man. He had prospered well, and Barker had first met him in California, where they had become partners in a successful mining claim at a place called Benito Canyon. They had done very well, but Douglas had suddenly sold out and started for England. He was a widower at that time. Barker had afterwards realized his money and come to live in London. Thus they had renewed their friendship. Douglas had given him the impression that some danger was hanging over his head, and he had always looked upon his sudden departure from California, and also his renting a house in so quiet a place in England, as being connected with this peril. He imagined that some secret society, some implacable organization, was on Douglas's track which would never rest until it killed him. Some remarks of his had given him this idea, though he had never told him what the society was, nor how he had come to offend it. He could only suppose that the legend upon the placard had some reference to this secret society.

'How long were you with Douglas in California?' asked Inspector MacDonald.

'Five years altogether.'

'He was a bachelor, you say?'

'A widower.'

'Have you ever heard where his first wife came from?'

'No; I remember his saying that she was of Swedish extraction, and I have seen her portrait. She was a very beautiful woman. She died of typhoid the year before I met him.'

'You don't associate his past with any particular part of America?'

'I have heard him talk of Chicago. He knew that city well and had worked there. I have heard him talk of the coal and iron districts. He had travelled a good deal in his time.'

'Was he a politician? Had this secret society to do with politics?'

'No; he cared nothing about politics.'

'You have no reason to think it was criminal?'

'On the contrary, I never met a straighter man in my life.'

'Was there anything curious about his life in California?'

'He liked best to stay and to work at our claim in the mountains. He would never go where other men were if he could help it. That's why I first thought that someone was after him. Then when he left so suddenly for Europe I made sure that it was so. I believe that he had a warning of some sort. Within a week of his leaving half a dozen men were inquiring for him.'

'What sort of men?'

'Well, they were a mighty hard-looking crowd. They came up to the claim and wanted to know where he was. I told them that he was gone to Europe and that I did not know where to find him. They meant him no good – it was easy to see that.'

'Were these men Americans – Californians?'

'Well, I don't know about Californians. They were Americans all right. But they were not miners. I don't know what they were, and was very glad to see their backs.'

'That was six years ago?'

'Nearer seven.'

'And then you were together five years in California, so that this business dates back not less than eleven years at the least?'

'That is so.'

'It must be a very serious feud that would be kept up with such earnestness for as long as that. It would be no light thing that would give rise to it.'

'I think it shadowed his whole life. It was never quite out of his mind.'

'But if a man had a danger hanging over him, and knew what it was, don't you think he would turn to the police for protection?'

'Maybe it was some danger that he could not be protected against. There's one thing you should know. He always went about armed. His revolver was never out of his pocket. But, by bad luck, he was in his dressing-gown and had left it in the bedroom last night. Once the bridge was up I guess he thought he was safe.'

'I should like these dates a little clearer,' said MacDonald. 'It is quite six years since Douglas left California. You followed him next year, did you not?'

'That is so.'

47

'And he has been married for five years. You must have returned about the time of his marriage.'

'About a month before. I was his best man.'

'Did you know Mrs Douglas before her marriage?'

'No, I did not. I had been away from England for ten years.'

'But you have seen a good deal of her since?'

Barker looked sternly at the detective.

'I have seen a good deal of *him* since,' he answered. 'If I have seen her, it is because you cannot visit a man without knowing his wife. If you imagine there is any connection –'

'I imagine nothing, Mr Barker. I am bound to make every inquiry which can bear upon the case. But I mean no offence.'

'Some inquiries are offensive,' Barker answered, angrily.

'It's only the facts that we want. It is in your interest and everyone's interests that they should be cleared up. Did Mr Douglas entirely approve your friendship with his wife?'

Barker grew paler, and his great strong hands were clasped convulsively together.

'You have no right to ask such questions!' he cried. 'What has this to do with the matter you are investigating?'

'I must repeat the question.'

'Well, I refuse to answer.'

'You can refuse to answer, but you must be aware that your refusal is in itself an answer, for you would not refuse if you had not something to conceal.'

Barker stood for a moment, with his face set grimly and his strong black eyebrows drawn low in intense thought. Then he looked up with a smile.

'Well, I guess you gentlemen are only doing your clear duty, after all, and that I have no right to stand in the way of it. I'd only ask you not to worry Mrs Douglas over this matter, for she has enough upon her just now. I may tell you that poor Douglas had just one fault in the world, and that was his jealousy. He was fond of me – no man could be fonder of a friend. And he was devoted to his wife. He loved me to come here and was for ever sending for me. And yet if his wife and I talked together or there seemed any sympathy between us, a kind of wave of jealousy would pass over him and he would be off the handle and saying the wildest things in a moment. More than once I've sworn off coming for that reason, and then he would write me such penitent, imploring letters that I just had to. But you can take it from me, gentlemen, if it was my last word, that no man ever had a more loving, faithful wife – and I can say, also, no friend could be more loyal than I.'

It was spoken with fervour and feeling, and yet Inspector Mac-Donald could not dismiss the subject.

'You are aware,' said he, 'that the dead man's wedding-ring has been taken from his finger?'

'So it appears,' said Barker.

'What do you mean by "appears"? You know it as a fact.'

The man seemed confused and undecided.

'When I said "appears", I meant that it was conceivable that he had himself taken off the ring.'

'The mere fact that the ring should be absent, whoever may have removed it, would suggest to anyone's mind, would it not, that the marriage and the tragedy were connected?'

Barker shrugged his broad shoulders.

'I can't profess to say what it suggests,' he answered. 'But if you mean to hint that it could reflect in any way upon this lady's honour' – his eyes blazed for an instant, and then with an evident effort he got a grip upon his own emotions – 'well, you are on the wrong track, that's all.'

'I don't know that I've anything else to ask you at present,' said MacDonald, coldly.

'There was one small point,' remarked Sherlock Holmes. 'When you entered the room there was only a candle lighted upon the table, was there not?'

'Yes, that was so.'

'By its light you saw that some terrible incident had occurred?'

'Exactly.'

'You rang at once for help?'

'Yes.'

'And it arrived very speedily?'

'Within a minute or so.'

'And yet when they arrived they found that the candle was out and that the lamp had been lighted. That seems very remarkable.'

Again Barker showed some signs of indecision.

'I don't see that it was remarkable, Mr Holmes,' he answered, after a pause. 'The candle threw a very bad light. My first thought was to get a better one. The lamp was on the table, so I lit it.'

'And blew out the candle?'

'Exactly.'

Holmes asked no further question, and Barker, with a deliberate look from one to the other of us, which had, as it seemed to me, something of defiance in it, turned and left the room.

Inspector MacDonald had sent up a note to the effect that he would wait upon Mrs Douglas in her room, but she had replied that she would meet us in the dining-room. She entered now, a tall and beautiful woman of thirty, reserved and self-possessed to a remarkable degree, very different from the tragic and distracted figure that I had pictured. It is true that her face was pale and drawn, like that of one who has endured a great shock, but her manner was composed, and the finely moulded hand which she rested upon the edge of the table was as steady as my own. Her sad, appealing eyes travelled from one to the other of us with a curiously inquisitive expression. That questioning gaze transformed itself suddenly into abrupt speech.

'Have you found out anything yet?' she asked.

Was it my imagination that there was an undertone of fear rather than of hope in the question?

'We have taken every possible step, Mrs Douglas,' said the inspector. 'You may rest assured that nothing will be neglected.'

'Spare no money,' she said, in a dead, even tone. 'It is my desire that every possible effort should be made.'

'Perhaps you can tell us something which may throw some light upon the matter.'

'I fear not, but all I know is at your service.'

'We have heard from Mr Cecil Barker that you did not actually see – that you were never in the room where the tragedy occurred?'

'No; he turned me back upon the stairs. He begged me to return to my room.'

'Quite so. You had heard the shot and you had at once come down.'

'I put on my dressing-gown and then came down.'

'How long was it after hearing the shot that you were stopped on the stair by Mr Barker?'

'It may have been a couple of minutes. It is so hard to reckon time at such a moment. He implored me not to go on. He assured me that I could do nothing. Then Mrs Allen, the housekeeper, led me upstairs again. It was all like some dreadful dream.'

'Can you give us any idea how long your husband had been downstairs before you heard the shot?'

'No, I cannot say. He went from his dressing-room and I did not hear him go. He did the round of the house every night, for he was nervous of fire. It is the only thing that I have ever known him nervous of.'

'That is just the point which I want to come to, Mrs Douglas. You have only known your husband in England, have you not?'

'Yes. We have been married five years.'

'Have you heard him speak of anything which occurred in America and which might bring some danger upon him?'

Mrs Douglas thought earnestly before she answered.

'Yes,' she said at last. 'I have always felt that there was a danger hanging over him. He refused to discuss it with me. It was not from want of confidence in me – there was the most complete love and confidence between us – but it was out of his desire to keep all alarm away from me. He thought I should brood over it if I knew all, and so he was silent.'

'How did you know it, then?'

Mrs Douglas's face lit with a quick smile.

'Can a husband ever carry about a secret all his life and a woman who loves him have no suspicion of it? I knew it in many ways. I knew it by his refusal to talk about some episodes in his American life. I knew it by certain precautions he took. I knew it by certain words he let fall. I knew it by the way he looked at unexpected strangers. I was perfectly certain that he had some powerful enemies, that he believed they were on his track and that he was always on his guard against them. I was so sure of it that for years I have been terrified if ever he came home later than was expected.'

'Might I ask,' said Holmes, 'what the words were which attracted your attention?'

' "The Valley of Fear",' the lady answered. 'That was an expression he has used when I questioned him. "I have been in the Valley of Fear. I am not out of it yet." "Are we never to get out of the Valley of Fear?" I have asked him, when I have seen him more serious than usual. "Sometimes I think that we never shall," he has answered.'

'Surely you asked him what he meant by the Valley of Fear?'

'I did; but his face would become very grave and he would shake his head. "It is bad enough that one of us should have been in its shadow," he said. "Please God it shall never fall upon you." It was some real valley in which he had lived and in which something terrible had occurred to him – of that I am certain – but I can tell you no more.'

'And he never mentioned any names?'

'Yes; he was delirious with fever once when he had his hunting accident three years ago. Then I remember that there was a name that came continually to his lips. He spoke it with anger and a sort of horror. McGinty was the name – Bodymaster McGinty. I asked him, when he recovered, who Bodymaster McGinty was, and whose body he was master of. "Never of mine, thank God!" he answered, with a laugh, and that was all I could get from him. But there is a connection between Bodymaster McGinty and the Valley of Fear.'

'There is one other point,' said Inspector MacDonald. 'You met Mr Douglas in a boarding-house in London, did you not, and became engaged to him there? Was there any romance, anything secret or mysterious, about the wedding?'

'There was romance. There is always romance. There was nothing mysterious.'

'He had no rival?'

'No; I was quite free.'

'You have heard, no doubt, that his wedding-ring has been taken. Does that suggest anything to you? Suppose that some enemy of his old life had tracked him down and committed this crime, what possible reason could he have for taking his wedding-ring?'

For an instant I could have sworn that the faintest shadow of a smile flickered over the woman's lips.

'I really cannot tell,' she answered. 'It is certainly a most extraordinary thing.'

'Well, we will not detain you any longer, and we are sorry to have put you to this trouble at such a time,' said the inspector. 'There are some other points, no doubt, but we can refer to you as they arise.'

She rose, and I was again conscious of that quick, questioning glance with which she had just surveyed us: 'What impression has my evidence made upon you?' The question might as well have been spoken. Then, with a bow, she swept from the room.

'She's a beautiful woman – a very beautiful woman,' said Mac-Donald, thoughtfully, after the door had closed behind her. 'This man Barker has certainly been down here a good deal. He is a man who might be attractive to a woman. He admits that the dead man was jealous, and maybe he knew best himself what cause he had for jealousy. Then there's that wedding-ring. You can't get past that. The man who tears a wedding-ring off a dead man's – What do you say to it, Mr Holmes?'

My friend had sat with his head upon his hands, sunk in the deepest thought. Now he rose and rang the bell.

'Ames,' he said, when the butler entered, 'where is Mr Cecil Barker now?'

'I'll see, sir.'

He came back in a moment to say that Mr Barker was in the garden.

'Can you remember, Ames, what Mr Barker had upon his feet last night when you joined him in the study?'

'Yes, Mr Holmes. He had a pair of bedroom slippers. I brought him his boots when he went for the police.'

'Where are the slippers now?'

'They are still under the chair in the hall.'

'Very good, Ames. It is, of course, important for us to know which tracks may be Mr Barker's and which from outside.'

'Yes, sir. I may say that I noticed that the slippers were stained with blood – so, indeed, were my own.'

'That is natural enough, considering the condition of the room. Very good, Ames. We will ring if we want you.'

A few minutes later we were in the study. Holmes had brought with him the carpet slippers from the hall. As Ames had observed, the soles of both were dark with blood.

'Strange!' murmured Holmes, as he stood in the light of the window and examined them minutely. 'Very strange indeed!'

Stooping with one of his quick, feline pounces he placed the slipper upon the bloodmark on the sill. It exactly corresponded. He smiled in silence at his colleagues.

The inspector was transfigured with excitement. His native accent rattled like a stick upon railings.

'Man!' he cried, 'there's not a doubt of it! Barker has just marked the window himself. It's a good deal broader than any boot-mark. I mind that you said it was a splay foot, and here's the explanation. But what's the game, Mr Holmes – what's the game?'

'Aye, what's the game?' my friend repeated, thoughtfully.

White Mason chuckled and rubbed his fat hands together in his professional satisfaction.

'I said it was a snorter!' he cried. 'And a real snorter it is!'

Chapter Six

A Dawning Light

The three detectives had many matters of detail into which to inquire, so I returned alone to our modest quarters at the village inn; but before doing so I took a stroll in the curious old-world garden which flanked the house. Rows of very ancient yew trees, cut into strange designs, girded it round. Inside was a beautiful stretch of lawn with an old sundial in the middle, the whole effect so soothing and restful that it was welcome to my somewhat jangled nerves. In that deeply peaceful atmosphere one could forget or remember only as some fantastic nightmare that darkened study with the sprawling, blood-stained figure upon the floor. And yet as I strolled round it and tried to steep my soul in its gentle balm, a strange incident occurred which brought me back to the tragedy and left a sinister impression on my mind.

I have said that a decoration of yew trees circled the garden. At the end which was farthest from the house they thickened into a continuous hedge. On the other side of this hedge, concealed from the eyes of any one approaching from the direction of the house, there was a stone seat. As I approached the spot I was aware of voices, some remark in the deep tones of a man, answered by a little ripple of feminine laughter. An instant later I had come round the end of the hedge, and my eyes lit upon Mrs Douglas and the man Barker before they were aware of my presence. Her appearance gave me a shock. In the dining-room she had been demure and discreet. Now all pretence of grief had passed away from her. Her eyes shone with the joy of living, and her face still quivered with amusement at some remark of her companion. He sat forward, his hands clasped and his forearms on his knees, with an answering smile upon his bold, handsome face. In an instant – but it was just one instant too late – they resumed their solemn masks as my figure came into view. A hurried word or two passed between them, and then Barker rose and came towards me.

'Excuse me, sir,' said he, 'but am I addressing Dr Watson?'

I bowed with a coldness which showed, I dare say, very plainly the impression which had been produced upon my mind.

'We thought that it was probably you, as your friendship with Mr Sherlock Holmes is so well known. Would you mind coming over and speaking to Mrs Douglas for one instant?'

I followed him with a dour face. Very clearly I could see in my mind's eye that shattered figure upon the floor. Here within a few hours of the tragedy were his wife and his nearest friend laughing together behind a bush in the garden which had been his. I greeted the lady with reserve. I had grieved with her grief in the dining-room. Now I met her appealing gaze with an unresponsive eye.

'I fear you think me callous and hard-hearted?' said she.

I shrugged my shoulders.

'It is no business of mine,' said I.

'Perhaps some day you will do me justice. If you only realized –'

'There is no need why Dr Watson should realize,' said Barker, quickly. 'As he has himself said, it is no possible business of his.'

'Exactly,' said I, 'and so I will beg leave to resume my walk.'

'One moment, Dr Watson,' cried the woman, in a pleading voice. 'There is one question which you can answer with more authority than anyone else in the world, and it may make a very great difference to me. You know Mr Holmes and his relations with the police better than anyone else can do. Supposing that a matter were brought confidentially to his knowledge, is it absolutely necessary that he should pass it on to the detectives?'

'Yes, that's it,' said Barker, eagerly. 'Is he on his own or is he entirely in with them?'

'I really don't know that I should be justified in discussing such a point.'

'I beg – I implore that you will, Dr Watson. I assure you that you will be helping us – helping me greatly if you will guide us on that point.'

There was such a ring of sincerity in the woman's voice that for the instant I forgot all about her levity and was moved only to do her will.

'Mr Holmes is an independent investigator,' I said. 'He is his own master, and would act as his own judgement directed. At the same time he would naturally feel loyalty towards the officials who were working on the same case, and he would not conceal from them anything which would help them in bringing a criminal to justice. Beyond this I can say nothing, and I would refer you to Mr Holmes himself if you want fuller information.'

So saying I raised my hat and went upon my way, leaving them still seated behind that concealing hedge. I looked back as I rounded the far end of it, and saw that they were still talking very earnestly together, and, as they were gazing after me, it was clear that it was our interview that was the subject of their debate.

'I wish none of their confidences,' said Holmes, when I reported to him what had occurred. He had spent the whole afternoon at the Manor House in consultation with his two colleagues, and returned about five with a ravenous appetite for a high tea which I had ordered for him. 'No confidences, Watson, for they are mighty awkward if it comes to an arrest for conspiracy and murder.'

'You think it will come to that?'

He was in his most cheerful and *débonnaire* humour.

'My dear Watson, when I have exterminated that fourth egg I will be ready to put you in touch with the whole situation. I don't say that we have fathomed it – far from it – but when we have traced the missing dumb-bell –'

'The dumb-bell!'

'Dear me, Watson, is it possible that you have not penetrated the fact that the case hangs upon the missing dumb-bell? Well, well, you need not be downcast, for, between ourselves, I don't think that either Inspector Mac or the excellent local practitioner has grasped the overwhelming importance of this incident. One dumb-bell, Watson! Consider an athlete with one dumb-bell. Picture to yourself the unilateral development – the imminent danger of a spinal curvature. Shocking, Watson; shocking!'

He sat with his mouth full of toast and his eyes sparkling with mischief, watching my intellectual entanglement. The mere sight of his excellent appetite was an assurance of success, for I had very clear recollections of days and nights without a thought of food, when his baffled mind had chafed before some problem whilst his thin, eager features became more attenuated with the asceticism of complete mental concentration. Finally he lit his pipe and, sitting in the ingle-nook of the old village inn, he talked slowly and at random about his case, rather as one thinks aloud than as one who makes a considered statement.

'A lie, Watson – a great big, thumping, obtrusive, uncompromising lie – that's what meets us on the threshold. There is our starting point. The whole story told by Barker is a lie. But Barker's story is corroborated by Mrs Douglas. Therefore she is lying also. They are both lying and in a conspiracy. So now we have the clear problem – why are they lying, and what is the truth which they are trying so hard to conceal? Let us try, Watson, you and I, if we can get behind the lie and reconstruct the truth.

'How do I know that they are lying? Because it is a clumsy fabrication which simply *could* not be true. Consider! According to the story given to us the assassin had less than a minute after the murder had been committed to take that ring, which was under another ring, from the dead man's finger, to replace the other ring – a thing which he would surely never have done – and to put that singular card beside his victim. I say that this was obviously impossible. You may argue – but I have too much respect for your judgement, Watson, to think that you will do so – that the ring may have been taken before the man was killed. The fact that the candle had only been lit a short time shows that there had been no lengthy interview. Was Douglas, from what we hear of his fearless character, a man who would be likely to give up his wedding-ring at such short notice, or could we conceive of his giving it up at all? No, no, Watson, the assassin was alone with the dead man for some time with the lamp lit. Of that I have no doubt at all. But the gunshot was apparently the cause of death. Therefore the gunshot must have been fired some time earlier than we are told. But there could be no mistake about such a matter as that. We are in the presence, therefore, of a deliberate conspiracy upon the part of the two people who heard the gunshot – of the man Barker and of the woman Douglas. When on the top of this I am able to show that the bloodmark upon the windowsill was deliberately placed there by Barker in order to give a false clue to the police, you will admit that the case grows dark against him.

'Now we have to ask ourselves at what hour the murder actually did occur. Up to half-past ten the servants were moving about the house, so it was certainly not before that time. At a quarter to eleven they had all gone to their rooms with the exception of Ames, who was in the pantry. I have been trying some experiments after you left us this afternoon, and I find that no noise which MacDonald can make in the study can penetrate to me in the pantry when the doors are all shut. It is otherwise, however, from the housekeeper's room. It is not so far down the corridor, and from it I could vaguely hear a voice when it was very loudly raised. The sound from a shot-gun is to some extent muffled when the discharge is at very close range, as it undoubtedly was in this instance. It would not be very loud, and yet in the silence of the night it should have easily penetrated to Mrs Allen's room.

She is, as she has told us, somewhat deaf, but none the less she mentioned in her evidence that she did hear something like a door slamming half an hour before the alarm was given. Half an hour before the alarm was given would be a quarter to eleven. I have no doubt that what she heard was the report of the gun, and that this was the real instant of the murder. If this is so, we have now to determine what Mr Barker and Mrs Douglas, presuming that they are not the actual murderers, could have been doing from a quarter to eleven, when the sound of the gunshot brought them down, until a quarter past eleven, when they rang the bell and summoned the servants. What were they doing, and why did they not instantly give the alarm? That is the question which faces us, and when it has been answered we will surely have gone some way to solve our problem.'

'I am convinced myself,' said I, 'that there is an understanding between those two people. She must be a heartless creature to sit laughing at some jest within a few hours of her husband's murder.'

'Exactly. She does not shine as a wife even in her own account of what occurred. I am not a whole-souled admirer of woman-kind, as you are aware, Watson, but my experience of life has taught me that there are few wives having any regard for their husbands who would let any man's spoken word stand between them and that husband's dead body. Should I ever marry, Watson, I should hope to inspire my wife with some feeling which would prevent her from being walked off by a housekeeper when my corpse was lying within a few yards of her. It was badly stage-managed, for even the rawest of investigations must be struck by the absence of the usual feminine ululation. If there had been nothing else, this incident alone would have suggested a pre-arranged conspiracy to my mind.'

'You think, then, definitely, that Barker and Mrs Douglas are guilty of the murder?'

'There is an appalling directness about your questions,

Watson,' said Holmes, shaking his pipe at me. 'They come at me like bullets. If you put it that Mrs Douglas and Barker know the truth about the murder and are conspiring to conceal it, then I can give you a whole-souled answer. I am sure they do. But your more deadly proposition is not so clear. Let us for a moment consider the difficulties which stand in the way.

'We will suppose that this couple are united by the bonds of a guilty love and that they have determined to get rid of the man who stands between them. It is a large supposition, for discreet inquiry among servants and others has failed to corroborate it in any way. On the contrary, there is a good deal of evidence that the Douglases were very attached to each other.'

'That I am sure cannot be true,' said I, thinking of the beautiful, smiling face in the garden.

'Well, at least they gave that impression. However, we will suppose that they are an extraordinarily astute couple, who deceive everyone upon this point and who conspire to murder the husband. He happens to be a man over whose head some danger hangs –'

'We have only their word for that.'

Holmes looked thoughtful.

'I see, Watson. You are sketching out a theory by which everything they say from the beginning is false. According to your idea, there was never any hidden menace or secret society or Valley of Fear or Boss Mac-Somebody or anything else. Well, that is a good, sweeping generalization. Let us see what that brings us to. They invent this theory to account for the crime. They then play up to the idea by leaving this bicycle in the park as a proof of the existence of some outsider. The stain on the windowsill conveys the same idea. So does the card upon the body, which might have been prepared in the house. That all fits into your hypothesis, Watson. But now we come on the nasty angular, uncompromising bits which won't slip into their places. Why a cut-off shot-gun of all weapons – and an American one at that?

How could they be so sure that the sound of it would not bring someone on to them? It's a mere chance, as it is, that Mrs Allen did not start out to inquire for the slamming door. Why did your guilty couple do all this, Watson?'

'I confess that I can't explain it.'

'Then, again, if a woman and her lover conspire to murder a husband, are they going to advertise their guilt by ostentatiously removing his wedding-ring after his death? Does that strike you as very probable, Watson?'

'No, it does not.'

'And once again, if the thought of leaving a bicycle concealed outside had occurred to you, would it really have seemed worth doing when the dullest detective would naturally say this is an obvious blind, as the bicycle is the first thing which the fugitive needed in order to make his escape?'

'I can conceive of no explanation.'

'And yet there should be no combination of events for which the wit of man cannot conceive an explanation. Simply as a mental exercise, without any assertion that it is true, let me indicate a possible line of thought. It is, I admit, mere imagination, but how often is imagination the mother of truth?

'We will suppose that there *was* a guilty secret, a really shameful secret, in the life of this man Douglas. This leads to his murder by someone who is, we will suppose, an avenger – someone from outside. This avenger, for some reason which I confess I am still at a loss to explain, took the dead man's wedding-ring. The vendetta might conceivably date back to the man's first marriage and the ring be taken for some such reason. Before this avenger got away Barker and the wife had reached the room. The assassin convinced them that any attempt to arrest him would lead to the publication of some hideous scandal. They were converted to this idea and preferred to let him go. For this purpose they probably lowered the bridge, which can be done quite noiselessly, and then raised it again. He made his escape, and for some reason thought that he could do so more safely on foot than on the bicycle. He therefore left his machine where it would not be discovered until he had got safely away. So far we are within the bounds of possibility, are we not?'

'Well, it is possible, no doubt,' said I, with some reserve.

'We have to remember, Watson, that whatever occurred is certainly something very extraordinary. Well now, to continue our supposititious case, the couple – not necessarily a guilty couple – realize after the murderer is gone that they have placed themselves in a position in which it may be difficult for them to prove that they did not themselves either do the deed or connive at it. They rapidly and rather clumsily meet the situation. The mark was put by Barker's blood-stained slipper upon the windowsill to suggest how the fugitive got away. They obviously were the two who must have heard the sound of the gun, so they gave the alarm exactly as they would have done, but a good half-hour after the event.'

'And how do you propose to prove all this?'

'Well, if there were an outsider he may be traced and taken. That would be the most effective of all proofs. But if not – well, the resources of science are far from being exhausted. I think that an evening alone in that study would help me much.'

'An evening alone!'

'I propose to go up there presently. I have arranged it with the estimable Ames, who is by no means whole-hearted about Barker. I shall sit in that room and see if its atmosphere brings me inspiration. I'm a believer in the *genius loci*. You smile, friend Watson. Well, we shall see. By the way, you have that big umbrella of yours, have you not?'

'It is here.'

'Well, I'll borrow that, if I may.'

'Certainly, but what a wretched weapon! If there is danger –'

'Nothing serious, my dear Watson, or I should certainly ask for your assistance. But I'll take the umbrella. At present I am only awaiting the return of our colleagues from Tunbridge Wells, where they are at present engaged in trying for a likely owner to the bicycle.'

It was nightfall before Inspector MacDonald and White Mason came back from their expedition, and they arrived exultant, reporting a great advance in our investigation.

'Man, I'll admeet that I had my doubts if there was ever an outsider,' said MacDonald, 'but that's all past now. We've had the bicycle identified, and we have a description of our man, so that's a long step on our journey.'

'It sounds to me like the beginning of the end,' said Holmes; 'I'm sure I congratulate you both with all my heart.'

'Well, I started from the fact that Mr Douglas had seemed disturbed since the day before, when he had been at Tunbridge Wells. It was at Tunbridge Wells, then, that he had become conscious of some danger. It was clear, therefore, that if a man had come over with a bicycle it was from Tunbridge Wells that he might be expected to have come. We took the bicycle over with us and showed it at the hotels. It was identified at once by the manager of the Eagle Commercial as belonging to a man named Hargrave who had taken a room there two days before. This bicycle and a small valise were his whole belongings. He had registered his name as coming from London, but had given no address. The valise was London-made and the contents were British, but the man himself was undoubtedly an American.'

'Well, well,' said Holmes, gleefully, 'you have indeed done some solid work whilst I have been sitting spinning theories with my friend. It's a lesson in being practical, Mr Mac.'

'Aye, it's just that, Mr Holmes,' said the inspector with satisfaction.

'But this may all fit in with your theories,' I remarked.

'That may or may not be. But let us hear the end, Mr Mac. Was there nothing to identify this man?'

'So little that it was evident he had carefully guarded himself against identification. There were no papers or letters and no marking upon the clothes. A cycle-map of the county lay upon his bedroom table. He had left the hotel after breakfast yesterday morning upon his bicycle, and no more was heard of him until our inquiries.'

'That's what puzzles me, Mr Holmes,' said White Mason. 'If the fellow did not want the hue and cry raised over him, one would imagine that he would have returned and remained at the hotel as an inoffensive tourist. As it is, he must know that he will be reported to the police by the hotel manager, and that his disappearance will be connected with the murder.'

'So one would imagine. Still he has been justified of his wisdom up to date at any rate, since he has not been taken. But his description – what of that?'

MacDonald referred to his notebook.

'Here we have it so far as they could give it. They don't seem to have taken any very particular stock of him, but still the porter, the clerk, and the chambermaid are all agreed that this about covers the points. He was a man about five foot nine in height, fifty or so years of age, his hair slightly grizzled, a greyish moustache, a curved nose and a face which all of them described as fierce and forbidding.'

'Well, bar the expression, that might almost be a description of Douglas himself,' said Holmes. 'He is just over fifty, with grizzled hair and moustache and about the same height. Did you get anything else?'

'He was dressed in a heavy grey suit with a reefer jacket, and he wore a short yellow overcoat and a soft cap.'

'What about the shot-gun?'

'It is less than two feet long. It could very well have fitted into his valise. He could have carried it inside his overcoat without difficulty.'

'And how do you consider that all this bears upon the general case?'

'Well, Mr Holmes,' said MacDonald, 'when we have got our man – and you may be sure that I had his description on the wires within five minutes of hearing it – we shall be able to judge. But even as it stands, we have surely gone a long way. We know that an American calling himself Hargrave came to Tunbridge Wells two days ago with bicycle and valise. In the latter was a sawn-off shot-gun, so he came with the deliberate purpose of crime. Yesterday morning he set off for this place upon his bicycle with his gun concealed in his overcoat. No one saw him arrive, so far as we can learn, but he need not pass through the village to reach the park gates, and there are many cyclists upon the road. Presumably he at once concealed his cycle among the laurels, where it was found, and possibly lurked there himself, with his eye on the house waiting for Mr Douglas to come out. The shot-gun is a strange weapon to use inside a house, but he had intended to use it outside, and then it has very obvious advantages, as it would be impossible to miss with it, and the sound of shots is so common in an English sporting neighbourhood that no particular notice would be taken.'

'That is all very clear!' said Holmes.

'Well, Mr Douglas did not appear. What was he to do next? He left his bicycle and approached the house in the twilight. He found the bridge down and no one about. He took his chance, intending, no doubt, to make some excuse if he met anyone. He met no one. He slipped into the first room that he saw and concealed himself behind the curtain. From thence he could see the drawbridge go up and he knew that his only escape was through the moat. He waited until a quarter past eleven, when Mr Douglas, upon his usual nightly round, came into the room. He shot him and escaped, as arranged. He was aware that the bicycle would be described by the hotel people and be a clue against him, so he left it there and made his way by some other means to London or to some safe hiding-place which he had already arranged. How is that, Mr Holmes?'

'Well, Mr Mac, it is very good and very clear so far as it goes. That is your end of the story. My end is that the crime was committed half an hour earlier than reported; that Mrs Douglas and Mr Barker are both in a conspiracy to conceal something; that they aided the murderer's escape – or at least, that they reached the room before he escaped – and that they fabricated evidence of his escape through the window, whereas in all probability they had themselves let him go by lowering the bridge. That's *my* reading of the first half.'

The two detectives shook their heads.

'Well, Mr Holmes, if this is true we only tumble out of one mystery into another,' said the London inspector.

'And in some ways a worse one,' added White Mason. 'The lady has never been in America in her life. What possible connection could she have with an American assassin which would cause her to shelter him?'

'I freely admit the difficulties,' said Holmes. 'I propose to make a little investigation of my own tonight, and it is just possible that it may contribute something to the common cause.'

'Can we help you, Mr Holmes?'

'No, no! Darkness and Dr Watson's umbrella. My wants are simple. And Ames – the faithful Ames – no doubt he will stretch a point for me. All my lines of thought lead me back invariably to the one basic question – why should an athletic man develop his frame upon so unnatural an instrument as a single dumb-bell?'

It was late that night when Holmes returned from his solitary excursion. We slept in a double-bedded room, which was the best that the little country inn could do for us. I was already asleep when I was partly awakened by his entrance.

'Well, Holmes,' I murmured, 'have you found out anything?'

He stood beside me in silence, his candle in his hand. Then the tall lean figure inclined towards me.

'I say, Watson,' he whispered, 'would you be afraid to sleep in the same room as a lunatic, a man with softening of the brain, an idiot whose mind has lost its grip?'

'Not in the least,' I answered in astonishment.

'Ah, that's lucky,' he said, and not another word would he utter that night.

Chapter Seven

The Solution

Next morning, after breakfast, we found Inspector MacDonald and Mr White Mason seated in close consultation in the small parlour of the local police-sergeant. Upon the table in front of them were piled a number of letters and telegrams, which they were carefully sorting and docketing. Three had been placed upon one side.

'Still on the track of the elusive bicyclist?' Holmes asked, cheerfully. 'What is the latest news of the ruffian?'

MacDonald pointed ruefully to his heap of correspondence.

'He is at present reported from Leicester, Nottingham, Southampton, Derby, East Ham, Richmond, and fourteen other places. In three of them – East Ham, Leicester, and Liverpool – there is a clear case against him and he has actually been arrested. The country seems to be full of fugitives with yellow coats.'

'Dear me!' said Holmes, sympathetically. 'Now, Mr Mac, and you, Mr White Mason, I wish to give you a very earnest piece of advice. When I went into this case with you I bargained, as you will no doubt remember, that I should not present you with half-proved theories, but that I should retain and work out my own ideas until I had satisfied myself that they were correct. For this reason I am not at the present moment telling you all that is in my mind. On the other hand, I said that I would play the game fairly by you, and I do not think it is a fair game to allow you for one unnecessary moment to waste your energies upon a profitless task. Therefore I am here to advise you this morning, and my advice to you is summed up in three words: Abandon the case.'

MacDonald and White Mason stared in amazement at their celebrated colleague.

'You consider it hopeless?' cried the inspector.

'I consider *your* case to be hopeless. I do not consider that it is hopeless to arrive at the truth.'

'But this cyclist. He is not an invention. We have his description, his valise, his bicycle. The fellow must be somewhere. Why should we not get him?'

'Yes, yes; no doubt he is somewhere, and no doubt we shall get him, but I would not have you waste your energies in East Ham or Liverpool. I am sure that we can find some shorter cut to a result.'

'You are holding something back. It's hardly fair of you, Mr Holmes.' The inspector was annoyed.

'You know my methods of work, Mr Mac. But I will hold it back for the shortest time possible. I only wish to verify my details in one way, which can very readily be done, and then I make my bow and return to London, leaving my results entirely at your service. I owe you too much to act otherwise, for in all my experience I cannot recall any more singular and interesting study.'

'This is clean beyond me, Mr Holmes. We saw you when we returned from Tunbridge Wells last night, and you were in general agreement with our results. What has happened since then to give you a completely new idea of the case?'

'Well, since you ask me, I spent as I told you that I would, some hours last night at the Manor House.'

'Well, what happened?'

'Ah! I can only give you a very general answer to that for the moment. By the way, I have been reading a short, but clear and interesting, account of the old building, purchasable at the modest sum of one penny from the local tobacconist.' Here Holmes drew a small tract, embellished with a rude engraving of the ancient Manor House, from his waistcoat pocket. 'It immensely adds to the zest of an investigation, my dear Mr Mac, when one is in conscious sympathy with the historical atmosphere of one's surroundings. Don't look so impatient, for I assure you that even so bald an account as this raises some sort of picture of the past in one's mind. Permit me to give you a sample. "Erected in the fifth year of the reign of James I, and standing upon the site of a much older building, the Manor House of Birlstone presents one of the finest surviving examples of the moated Jacobean residence –"'

'You are making fools of us, Mr Holmes.'

'Tut, tut, Mr Mac! – the first sign of temper I have detected in you. Well, I won't read it verbatim, since you feel so strongly upon the subject. But when I tell you that there is some account of the taking of the place by a Parliamentary colonel in 1644, of the concealment of Charles for several days in the course of the Civil War, and finally of a visit there by the second George, you will admit that there are various associations of interest connected with this ancient house.'

'I don't doubt it, Mr Holmes, but that is no business of ours.'

'Is it not? Is it not? Breadth of view, my dear Mr Mac, is one of the essentials of our profession. The interplay of ideas and the oblique uses of knowledge are often of extraordinary interest. You will excuse these remarks from one who, though a mere connoisseur of crime, is still rather older and perhaps more experienced than yourself.'

'I'm the first to admit that,' said the detective, heartily. 'You get to your point, I admit, but you have such a deuced round-the-corner way of doing it.'

'Well, well, I'll drop past history and get down to present-day facts. I called last night, as I have already said, at the Manor House. I did not see either Mr Barker or Mrs Douglas. I saw no necessity to disturb them, but I was pleased to hear that the lady was not visibly pining and that she had partaken of an excellent dinner. My visit was specially made to the good Mr Ames, with whom I exchanged some amiabilities which culminated in his allowing me, without reference to anyone else, to sit alone for a time in the study.'

'What! With that!' I ejaculated.

'No, no; everything is now in order. You gave permission for that, Mr Mac, as I am informed. The room was in its normal state, and in it I passed an instructive quarter of an hour.'

'What were you doing?'

'Well, not to make a mystery of so simple a matter, I was looking for the missing dumb-bell. It has always bulked rather large in my estimate of the case. I ended by finding it.'

'Where?'

'Ah! There we come to the edge of the unexplored. Let me go a little farther, a very little farther, and I will promise that you shall share everything that I know.'

'Well, we're bound to take you on your own terms,' said the inspector; 'but when it comes to telling us to abandon the case – Why, in the name of goodness, should we abandon the case?'

'For the simple reason, my dear Mr Mac, that you have not got the first idea what it is that you are investigating.'

'We are investigating the murder of Mr John Douglas, of Birlstone Manor.'

'Yes, yes; so you are. But don't trouble to trace the mysterious gentleman upon the bicycle. I assure you that it won't help you.'

'Then what do you suggest that we do?'

'I will tell you exactly what to do, if you will do it.'

'Well, I'm bound to say I've always found you had reason behind all your queer ways. I'll do what you advise.'

'And you, Mr White Mason?'

The country detective looked helplessly from one to the other. Mr Holmes and his methods were new to him.

'Well, if it is good enough for the inspector it is good enough for me,' he said, at last.

'Capital!' said Holmes. 'Well, then, I should recommend a nice, cheery, country walk for both of you. They tell me that the views from Birlstone Ridge over the Weald are very remarkable. No doubt lunch could be got at some suitable hostelry, though my ignorance of the country prevents me from recommending one. In the evening, tired but happy –'

'Man, this is getting past a joke!' cried MacDonald, rising angrily from his chair.

'Well, well, spend the day as you like,' said Holmes, patting him cheerfully on the shoulder. 'Do what you like and go where you will, but meet me here before dusk without fail – without fail, Mr Mac.'

'That sounds more like sanity.'

'All of it was excellent advice, but I don't insist, so long as you are here when I need you. But now, before we part, I want you to write a note to Mr Barker.'

'Well?'

'I'll dictate it, if you like. Ready?

' "Dear sir, – It has struck me that it is our duty to drain the moat, in the hope that we may find some –" '

'It's impossible,' said the inspector; 'I've made inquiry.'

'Tut, tut, my dear sir! Do, please, do what I ask you.'

'Well, go on.'

' "– in the hope that we may find something which may bear upon our investigation. I have made arrangements, and the workmen will be at work early tomorrow morning diverting the stream –" '

'Impossible!'

' "– diverting the stream, so I thought it best to explain matters beforehand." Now sign that, and send it by hand about four o'clock. At that hour we shall meet again in this room. Until then we can each do what we like, for I can assure you that this inquiry has come to a definite pause.'

Evening was drawing in when we reassembled. Holmes was very serious in his manner, myself curious, and the detectives obviously critical and annoyed.

'Well, gentlemen,' said my friend, gravely, 'I am asking you now to put everything to the test with me, and you will judge for yourselves whether the observations which I have made justify the conclusions to which I have come. It is a chill evening, and I do not know how long our expedition may last, so I beg that you will wear your warmest coats. It is of the first importance that we should be in our places before it grows dark, so, with your permission, we will get started at once.'

We passed along the outer bounds of the Manor House park until we came to a place where there was a gap in the rails which fenced it. Through this we slipped, and then, in the gathering gloom, we followed Holmes until we had reached a shrubbery which lies nearly opposite to the main door and the drawbridge. The latter had not been raised. Holmes crouched down behind the screen of laurels, and we all three followed his example.

'Well, what are we to do now?' asked MacDonald, with some gruffness.

'Possess our souls in patience and make as little noise as possible,' Holmes answered.

'What are we here for at all? I really think that you might treat us with more frankness.'

Holmes laughed.

'Watson insists that I am the dramatist in real life,' said he. 'Some touch of the artist wells up within me and calls insistently for a well-staged performance. Surely our profession, Mr Mac, would be a drab and sordid one if we did not sometimes set the scene so as to glorify our results. The blunt accusation, the brutal tap upon the shoulder – what can one make of such a *dénouement*? But the quick inference, the subtle trap, the clever forecast of coming events, the triumphant vindication of bold theories – are these not the pride and the justification of our life's work? At the present moment you thrill with the glamour of the situation and the anticipation of the hunter. Where would be that thrill if I had been as definite as a time-table? I only ask a little patience, Mr Mac, and all will be clear to you.'

'Well, I hope the pride and justification and the rest of it will come before we all get our death of cold,' said the London detective, with comic resignation.

We all had good reason to join in the aspiration, for our vigil was a long and bitter one. Slowly the shadows darkened over the long sombre face of the old house. A cold, damp reek from the moat chilled us to the bones and set our teeth chattering. There was a single lamp over the gateway and a steady globe of light in the fatal study. Everything else was dark and still.

'How long is this to last?' asked the inspector, suddenly. 'And what is it we are watching for?'

'I have no more notion than you how long it is to last,' Holmes answered with some asperity. 'If criminals would always schedule their movements like railway trains it would certainly be more convenient for all of us. As to what it is we – Well, *that's* what we are watching for.'

As he spoke the bright yellow light in the study was obscured by somebody passing to and fro before it. The laurels among which we lay were immediately opposite the window and not more than a hundred feet from it. Presently it was thrown open with a whining of hinges, and we could dimly see the dark outline of a man's head and shoulders looking out into the gloom. For some minutes he peered forth, in a furtive, stealthy fashion, as one who wishes to be assured that he is unobserved. Then he leaned forward, and in the intense silence we were aware of the soft lapping of agitated water. He seemed to be stirring up the moat with something which he held in his hand. Then suddenly he hauled something in as a fisherman lands a fish – some large, round object which obscured the light as it was dragged through the open casement.

'Now!' cried Holmes. 'Now!'

We were all upon our feet, staggering after him with our stiffened limbs, whilst he, with one of those out-flames of nervous energy which could make him on occasion both the most active and the strongest man that I have ever known, ran swiftly across the bridge and rang violently at the bell. There was the rasping of bolts from the other side, and the amazed Ames stood in the entrance. Holmes brushed him aside without a word and, followed by all of us, rushed into the room which had been occupied by the man whom we had been watching.

The oil lamp on the table represented the glow which we had seen from outside. It was now in the hand of Cecil Barker, who held it towards us as we entered. Its light shone upon his strong, resolute, clean-shaven face and his menacing eyes.

'What the devil is the meaning of all this?' he cried. 'What are you after, anyhow?'

Holmes took a swift glance round and then pounced upon a sodden bundle tied together with cord which lay where it had been thrust under the writing-table.

'This is what we are after, Mr Barker. This bundle, weighted with a dumb-bell, which you have just raised from the bottom of the moat.'

Barker stared at Holmes with amazement in his face.

'How in thunder came you to know anything about it?' he asked.

'Simply that I put it there.'

'You put it there! You!'

'Perhaps I should have said "replaced it there",' said Holmes. 'You will remember, Inspector MacDonald, that I was somewhat struck by the absence of a dumb-bell. I drew your attention to it, but with the pressure of other events you had hardly the time to give it the consideration which would have enabled you to draw deductions from it. When water is near and a weight is missing it is not a very far-fetched supposition that something has been sunk in the water. The idea was at least worth testing, so with the help of Ames, who admitted me to the room, and the crook of Dr Watson's umbrella, I was able last night to fish up and inspect this bundle. It was of the first importance, however, that we should be able to prove who placed it there. This we accomplished by the very obvious device of announcing that the moat would be dried tomorrow, which had, of course, the effect that whoever had hidden the bundle would most certainly withdraw it the moment that darkness enabled him to do so. We have no fewer than four witnesses as to who it was who took advantage of the opportunity, and so, Mr Barker, I think the word lies now with you.'

Sherlock Holmes put the sopping bundle upon the table beside the lamp and undid the cord which bound it. From within he extracted a dumb-bell, which he tossed down to its fellow in the corner. Next he drew forth a pair of boots. 'American, as you perceive,' he remarked, pointing to the toes. Then he laid upon the table a long, deadly, sheathed knife. Finally he unravelled a bundle of clothing, comprising a complete set of under-clothes, socks, a grey tweed suit, and a short yellow overcoat.

'The clothes are commonplace,' remarked Holmes, 'save only the overcoat, which is full of suggestive touches.' He held it tenderly towards the light, whilst his long, thin fingers flickered over it. 'Here, as you perceive, is the inner pocket prolonged into the lining in such a fashion as to give ample space for the truncated fowling-piece. The tailor's tab is on the neck – Neale, Outfitter, Vermissa, USA. I have spent an instructive afternoon in the rector's library, and have enlarged my knowledge by adding the fact that Vermissa is a flourishing little town at the head of one of the best-known coal and iron valleys in the United States. I have some recollection, Mr Barker, that you associated the coal districts with Mr Douglas's first wife, and it would surely not be too far-fetched an inference that the V. V. upon the card by the dead body might stand for Vermissa Valley, or that this very valley, which sends forth emissaries of murder, may be that Valley of Fear of which we have heard. So much is fairly clear. And now, Mr Barker, I seem to be standing rather in the way of your explanation.'

It was a sight to see Cecil Barker's expressive face during this exposition of the great detective. Anger, amazement, consternation, and indecision swept over it in turn. Finally he took refuge in a somewhat acid irony.

'You know such a lot, Mr Holmes, perhaps you had better tell us some more,' he sneered.

'I have no doubt that I could tell you a great deal more, Mr Barker, but it would come with a better grace from you.'

'Oh, you think so, do you? Well, all I can say is that if there's any secret here it is not my secret, and I am not the man to give it away.'

'Well, if you take that line, Mr Barker,' said the inspector, quietly, 'we must just keep you in sight until we have the warrant and can hold you.'

'You can do what you damn well please about that,' said Barker, defiantly.

The proceedings seemed to have come to a definite end so far as he was concerned, for one had only to look at that granite face to realize that no *peine forte et dure* would ever force him to plead against his will. The deadlock was broken, however, by a woman's voice. Mrs Douglas had been standing listening at the half-opened door, and now she entered the room.

'You have done enough for us, Cecil,' said she. 'Whatever comes of it in the future, you have done enough.'

'Enough and more than enough,' remarked Sherlock Holmes, gravely. 'I have every sympathy with you, madam, and I should strongly urge you to have some confidence in the common sense of our jurisdiction and to take the police voluntarily into your complete confidence. It may be that I am myself at fault for not following up the hint which you conveyed to me through my friend, Dr Watson, but at that time I had every reason to believe that you were directly concerned in the crime. Now I am assured that this is not so. At the same time, there is much that is unexplained, and I should strongly recommend that you ask *Mr Douglas* to tell us his own story.'

Mrs Douglas gave a cry of astonishment at Holmes's words.

The detectives and I must have echoed it, when we were aware of a man who seemed to have emerged from the wall, and who advanced now from the gloom of the corner in which he had appeared. Mrs Douglas turned, and in an instant her arms were round him. Barker had seized his outstretched hand.

'It's best this way, Jack,' his wife repeated. 'I am sure that it is best.'

'Indeed, yes, Mr Douglas,' said Sherlock Holmes. 'I am sure that you will find it best.'

The man stood blinking at us with the dazed look of one who comes from the dark into the light. It was a remarkable face – bold grey eyes, a strong, short-clipped, grizzled moustache, a square, projecting chin, and a humorous mouth. He took a good look at us all, and then, to my amazement, he advanced to me and handed me a bundle of paper.

'I've heard of you,' said he, in a voice which was not quite English and not quite American, but was altogether mellow and pleasing. 'You are the historian of this bunch. Well, Dr Watson, you've never had such a story as that pass through your hands before, and I'd lay my last dollar on that. Tell it your own way, but there are the facts, and you can't miss the public so long as you have those. I've been cooped up two days, and I've spent the daylight hours – as much daylight as I could get in that rat-trap – in putting the thing into words. You're welcome to them – you and your public. There's the story of the Valley of Fear.'

'That's the past, Mr Douglas,' said Sherlock Holmes, quietly. 'What we desire now is to hear your story of the present.'

'You'll have it, sir,' said Douglas. 'Can I smoke as I talk? Well, thank you, Mr Holmes; you're a smoker yourself, if I remember right, and you'll guess what it is to be sitting for two days with tobacco in your pocket and afraid that the smell will give you away.' He leaned against the mantelpiece and sucked at the cigar which Holmes had handed him. 'I've heard of you, Mr Holmes; I never guessed that I would meet you. But before you are through with that' – he nodded at my papers – 'you will say I've brought you something fresh.'

Inspector MacDonald had been staring at the newcomer with the greatest amazement.

'Well, this fairly beats me!' he cried at last. 'If you are Mr John Douglas, of Birlstone Manor, then whose death have we been investigating for these two days, and where in the world have you sprung from now? You seemed to me to come out of the floor like a Jack-in-the-box.'

'Ah, Mr Mac,' said Holmes, shaking a reproving forefinger, 'you would not read that excellent local compilation which described the concealment of King Charles. People did not hide in those days without reliable hiding-places, and the hiding-place that has once been used may be again. I had persuaded myself that we should find Mr Douglas under this roof.'

'And how long have you been playing this trick upon us, Mr Holmes?' said the inspector, angrily. 'How long have you allowed us to waste ourselves upon a search that you knew to be an absurd one?'

'Not one instant, my dear Mr Mac. Only last night did I form my views of the case. As they could not be put to the proof until this evening, I invited you and your colleague to take a holiday for the day. Pray, what more could I do? When I found the suit of clothes in the moat it at once became apparent to me that the body we had found could not have been the body of Mr John Douglas at all, but must be that of the bicyclist from Tunbridge Wells. No other conclusion was possible. Therefore I had to determine where Mr John Douglas himself could be, and the balance of probability was that, with the connivance of his wife and his friend, he was concealed in a house which had such conveniences for a fugitive, and awaiting quieter times, when he could make his final escape.'

'Well, you figured it out about right,' said Mr Douglas, approvingly. 'I thought I'd dodge your British law, for I was not sure how

I stood under it, and also I saw my chance to throw these hounds once for all off my track. Mind you, from first to last I have done nothing to be ashamed of, and nothing that I would not do again, but you'll judge that for yourselves when I tell you my story. Never mind warning me, inspector; I'm ready to stand pat upon the truth.

'I'm not going to begin at the beginning. That's all there' – he indicated my bundle of papers – 'and a mighty queer yarn you'll find it. It all comes down to this: that there are some men that have good cause to hate me and would give their last dollar to know that they had got me. So long as I am alive and they are alive, there is no safety in this world for me. They hunted me from Chicago to California; then they chased me out of America; but when I married and settled down in this quiet spot I thought my last years were going to be peaceable. I never explained to my wife how things were. Why should I pull her into it? She would never have a quiet moment again, but would be always imagining trouble. I fancy she knew something, for I may have dropped a word here or a word there – but until yesterday, after you gentlemen had seen her, she never knew the rights of the matter. She told you all she knew, and so did Barker here, for on the night when this thing happened there was mighty little time for explanations. She knows everything now, and I would have been a wiser man if I had told her sooner. But it was a hard question, dear' – he took her hand for an instant in his own – 'and I acted for the best.

'Well, gentlemen, the day before these happenings I was over in Tunbridge Wells and I got a glimpse of a man in the street. It was only a glimpse, but I have a quick eye for these things, and I never doubted who it was. It was the worst enemy I had among them all – one who has been after me like a hungry wolf after a caribou all these years. I knew there was trouble coming, and I came home and made ready for it. I guessed I'd fight through it all right on my own. There was a time when my luck was the talk of the whole United States. I never doubted that it would be with me still.

'I was on my guard all that next day and never went out into the park. It's as well, or he'd have had the drop on me with that buck-shot gun of his before ever I could draw on him. After the bridge was up – my mind was always more restful when that bridge was up in the evenings – I put the thing clear out of my head. I never figured on his getting into the house and waiting for me. But when I made my round in my dressing-gown, as my habit was, I had no sooner entered the study than I scented danger. I guess when a man has had dangers in his life – and I've had more than most in my time – there is a kind of sixth sense that waves the red flag. I saw the signal clear enough, and yet I couldn't tell you why. Next instant I spotted a boot under the window curtain, and then I saw why plain enough.

'I'd just the one candle that was in my hand, but there was a good light from the hall lamp through the open door. I put down the candle and jumped for a hammer that I'd left on the mantel. At the same moment he sprang at me. I saw the glint of a knife and I lashed at him with the hammer. I got him somewhere, for the knife tinkled down on the floor. He dodged round the table as quick as an eel, and a moment later he'd got his gun from under his coat. I heard him cock it, but I had got hold of it before he could fire. I had it by the barrel, and we wrestled for it all ends up for a minute or more. It was death to the man that lost his grip. He never lost his grip, but he got it butt downwards for a moment too long. Maybe it was I that pulled the trigger. Maybe we just jolted it off between us. Anyhow, he got both barrels in the face, and there I was, staring down at all that was left of Ted Baldwin. I'd recognized him in the township and again when he sprang for me, but his own mother wouldn't recognize him as I saw him then. I'm used to rough work, but I fairly turned sick at the sight of him.

'I was hanging on to the side of the table when Barker came

hurrying down. I heard my wife coming, and I ran to the door and stopped her. It was no sight for a woman. I promised I'd come to her soon. I said a word or two to Barker – he took it all in at a glance – and we waited for the rest to come along. But there was no sign of them. Then we understood that they could hear nothing, and that all that had happened was only known to ourselves.

'It was at that instant that the idea came to me. I was fairly dazzled by the brilliancy of it. The man's sleeve had slipped up and there was the branded mark of the Lodge upon his forearm. See here.'

The man whom we knew as Douglas turned up his own coat and cuff to show a brown triangle within a circle exactly like that which we had seen upon the dead man.

'It was the sight of that which started me on to it. I seemed to see it all clear at a glance. There was his height and hair and figure about the same as my own. No one could swear to his face, poor devil! I brought down this suit of clothes, and in a quarter of an hour Barker and I had put my dressing-gown on him and he lay as you found him. We tied all his things into a bundle, and I weighted them with the only weight I could find and slung them through the window. The card he had meant to lay upon my body was lying beside his own. My rings were put on his finger, but when it came to the wedding-ring' – he held out his muscular hand – 'you can see for yourselves that I had struck my limit. I have not moved it since the day I was married, and it would have taken a file to get it off. I don't know, anyhow, that I would have cared to part with it, but if I had wanted to I couldn't. So we just had to leave the detail to take care of itself. On the other hand, I brought a bit of plaster down and put it where I am wearing one myself at this instant. You slipped up there, Mr Holmes, clever as you are, for if you had chanced to take off that plaster you would have found no cut underneath it.

'Well, that was the situation. If I could lie low for a while and then get away where I would be joined by my wife, we would have a chance at last of living at peace for the rest of our lives. These devils would give me no rest so long as I was above-ground but if they saw in the papers that Baldwin had got his man there would be an end of all my troubles. I hadn't much time to make it clear to Barker and to my wife, but they understood enough to be able to help me. I knew all about this hiding-place, so did Ames, but it never entered his head to connect it with the matter. I retired into it, and it was up to Barker to do the rest.

'I guess you can fill in for yourselves what he did. He opened the window and made the mark on the sill to give an idea of how the murderer escaped. It was a tall order, that, but as the bridge was up there was no other way. Then, when everything was fixed, he rang the bell for all he was worth. What happened afterwards you know – and so, gentlemen, you can do what you please, but I've told you the truth and the whole truth, so help me, God! What I ask you now is, how do I stand by the English law?'

There was a silence, which was broken by Sherlock Holmes.

'The English law is, in the main, a just law. You will get no worse than your deserts from it. But I would ask you how did this man know that you lived here, or how to get into your house, or where to hide to get you?'

'I know nothing of this.'

Holmes's face was very white and grave.

'The story is not over yet, I fear,' said he. 'You may find worse dangers than the English law, or even than your enemies from America. I see trouble before you, Mr Douglas. You'll take my advice and still be on your guard.'

And now, my long-suffering readers, I will ask you to come away with me for a time, far from the Sussex Manor House of Birlstone, and far also from the year of grace in which we made our eventful journey which ended with the strange story of the man who had been known as John Douglas. I wish you to journey back some twenty years in time, and westward some thousands of miles in space, that I may lay before you a singular and a terrible narrative – so singular and so terrible that you may find it hard to believe that, even as I tell it, even so did it occur. Do not think that I intrude one story before another is finished. As you read on you will find that this is not so. And when I have detailed those distant events and you have solved this mystery of the past we shall meet once more in those rooms in Baker Street where this, like so many other wonderful happenings, will find its end.

PART TWO
The Scowrers

Chapter One

The Man

It was the fourth of February in the year 1875. It had been a severe winter, and the snow lay deep in the gorges of the Gilmerton Mountains. The steam plough had, however, kept the railtrack open, and the evening train which connects the long line of coal-mining and iron-working settlements was slowly groaning its way up the steep gradients which lead from Stagville on the plain to Vermissa, the central township which lies at the head of the Vermissa Valley. From this point the track sweeps downwards to Barton's Crossing, Helmdale, and the purely agricultural country of Merton. It was a single-track railroad, but at every siding, and they were numerous, long lines of trucks piled with coal and with iron ore told of the hidden wealth which had brought a rude population and a bustling life to this most desolate corner of the United States of America.

For desolate it was. Little could the first pioneer who had traversed it have ever imagined that the fairest prairies and the most lush water-pastures were valueless compared with this gloomy land of black crag and tangled forest. Above the dark and often scarcely penetrable woods upon their sides, the high, bare crowns of the mountains, white snow and jagged rock, towered upon either flank, leaving a long, winding, tortuous valley in the centre. Up this the little train was slowly crawling.

The oil lamps had just been lit in the leading passenger-car, a long, bare carriage in which some twenty or thirty people were seated. The greater number of these were workmen returning from their day's toil in the lower portion of the valley. At least a dozen, by their grimed faces and the safety lanterns which they carried, proclaimed themselves as miners. These sat smoking in a group, and conversed in low voices, glancing occasionally at two men on the opposite side of the car, whose uniform and badges showed them to be policemen. Several women of the labouring class, and one or two travellers who might have been small local storekeepers, made up the rest of the company, with the exception of one young man in a corner by himself. It is with this man that we are concerned. Take a good look at him, for he is worth it.

He is a fresh-complexioned, middle-sized young man, not far, one would guess, from his thirtieth year. He has large, shrewd, humorous grey eyes which twinkle inquiringly from time to time as he looks round through his spectacles at the people about him. It is easy to see that he is of a sociable and possibly simple disposition, anxious to be friendly to all men. Anyone could pick him at once as gregarious in his habits and communicative in his nature, with a quick wit and a ready smile. And yet the man who studied him more closely might discern a certain firmness of jaw and grim tightness about the lips which would warn him that there were depths beyond, and that this pleasant, brown-haired young Irishman might conceivably leave his mark for good or evil upon any society to which he was introduced.

Having made one or two tentative remarks to the nearest miner, and received only short gruff replies, the traveller resigned himself to uncongenial silence, staring moodily out of the window at the fading landscape. It was not a cheering prospect. Through the growing gloom there pulsed the red glow of the furnaces on the sides of the hills. Great heaps of slag and dumps of cinders loomed up on each side, with the high shafts of the collieries towering above them. Huddled groups of mean wooden houses, the windows of which were beginning to outline themselves in light, were scattered here and there along the line, and the frequent halting-places were crowded with their swarthy inhabitants. The iron and coal valleys of the Vermissa district were no resorts for the leisured or the cultured.

Everywhere there were stern signs of the crudest battle of life, the rude work to be done, and the rude, strong workers who did it.

The young traveller gazed out into this dismal country with a face of mingled repulsion and interest, which showed that the scene was new to him. At intervals he drew from his pocket a bulky letter to which he referred, and on the margins of which he scribbled some notes. Once from the back of his waist he produced something which one would hardly have expected to find in the possession of so mild-mannered a man. It was a navy revolver of the largest size. As he turned it slantwise to the light, the glint upon the rims of the copper shells within the drum showed that it was fully loaded. He quickly restored it to his secret pocket, but not before it had been observed by a working man who had seated himself upon the adjoining bench.

'Halloa, mate!' said he. 'You seem heeled and ready.'

The young man smiled with an air of embarrassment.

'Yes,' said he; 'we need them sometimes in the place I come from.'

'And where may that be?'

'I'm last from Chicago.'

'A stranger in these parts?'

'Yes.'

'You may find you need it here,' said the workman.

'Ah! Is that so?' The young man seemed interested.

'Have you heard nothing of doings hereabouts?'

'Nothing out of the way.'

'Why, I thought the country was full of it. You'll hear quick enough. What made you come here?'

'I heard there was always work for a willing man.'

'Are you one of the Labour Union?'

'Sure.'

'Then you'll get your job, I guess. Have you any friends?'

'Not yet, but I have the means of making them.'

'How's that, then?'

'I am one of the Ancient Order of Freemen. There's no town without a lodge, and where there is a lodge I'll find my friends.'

The remark had a singular effect upon his companion. He glanced round suspiciously at the others in the car. The miners were still whispering among themselves. The two police officers were dozing. He came across, seated himself close to the young traveller, and held out his hand.

'Put it there,' he said.

A hand-grip passed between the two.

'I see you speak the truth. But it's well to make certain.'

He raised his right hand to his right eyebrow. The traveller at once raised his left hand to his left eyebrow.

'Dark nights are unpleasant,' said the workman.

'Yes, for strangers to travel,' the other answered.

'That's good enough. I'm Brother Scanlan, Lodge 341, Vermissa Valley. Glad to see you in these parts.'

'Thank you. I'm Brother John McMurdo, Lodge 29, Chicago. Bodymaster, J. H. Scott. But I am in luck to meet a brother so early.'

'Well, there are plenty of us about. You won't find the Order more flourishing anywhere in the States than right here in Vermissa Valley. But we could do with some lads like you. I can't understand a spry man of the Labour Union finding no work to do in Chicago.'

'I found plenty of work to do,' said McMurdo.

'Then why did you leave?'

McMurdo nodded towards the policemen and smiled.

'I guess those chaps would be glad to know,' he said.

Scanlan groaned sympathetically.

'In trouble?' he asked in a whisper.

'Deep.'

'A penitentiary job?'

'And the rest.'

'Not a killing?'

'It's early days to talk of such things,' said McMurdo, with the air of a man who had been surprised into saying more than he intended. 'I've my own good reason for leaving Chicago, and let that be enough for you. Who are you that you should take it on yourself to ask such things?'

His grey eyes gleamed with sudden and dangerous anger from behind his glasses.

'All right, mate. No offence meant. The boys will think none the worse of you whatever you may have done. Where are you bound for now?'

'To Vermissa.'

'That's the third halt down the line. Where are you staying?'

McMurdo took out an envelope and held it close to the murky oil lamp.

'Here is the address – Jacob Shafter, Sheridan Street. It's a boarding-house that was recommended by a man I knew in Chicago.'

'Well, I don't know it, but Vermissa is out of my beat. I live at Hobson's Patch, and that's here where we are drawing up. But, say, there's one bit of advice I'll give you before we part. If you're in trouble in Vermissa, go straight to the Union House and see Boss McGinty. He is the bodymaster of Vermissa Lodge, and nothing can happen in these parts unless Black Jack McGinty wants it. So long, mate. Maybe we'll meet in Lodge one of these evenings. But mind my words; if you are in trouble go to Boss McGinty.'

Scanlan descended, and McMurdo was left once again to his thoughts. Night had now fallen, and the flames of the frequent furnaces were roaring and leaping in the darkness. Against their lurid background dark figures were bending and straining, twisting, and turning, with the motion of winch or of windlass, to the rhythm of an eternal clank and roar.

'I guess hell must look something like that,' said a voice.

McMurdo turned and saw that one of the policemen had shifted in his seat and was staring out into the fiery waste.

'For that matter,' said the other policeman, 'I allow that hell must *be* something like that. If there are worse devils down yonder than some we could name, it's more than I'd expect. I guess you are new to this part, young man?'

'Well, what if I am?' McMurdo answered, in a surly voice.

'Just this, mister; that I should advise you to be careful in choosing your friends. I don't think I'd begin with Mike Scanlan or his gang if I were you.'

'What in thunder is it to you who are my friends?' roared McMurdo, in a voice which brought every head in the carriage round to witness the altercation. 'Did I ask you for your advice, or did you think me such a sucker that I couldn't move without it? You speak when you are spoken to, and by the Lord you'd have to wait a long time if it was me!'

He thrust out his face, and grinned at the patrolmen like a snarling dog.

The two policemen, heavy, good-natured men, were taken aback by the extraordinary vehemence with which their friendly advances had been rejected.

'No offence, stranger,' said one. 'It was a warning for your own good, seeing that you are, by your own showing, new to the place.'

'I'm new to the place, but I'm not new to you and your kind,' cried McMurdo, in a cold fury. 'I guess you're the same in all places, shoving your advice in when nobody asks for it.'

'Maybe we'll see more of you before very long,' said one of the patrolmen, with a grin. 'You're a real handpicked one, if I am a judge.'

'I was thinking the same,' remarked the other. 'I guess we may meet again.'

'I'm not afraid of you, and don't you think it,' cried McMurdo. 'My name's Jack McMurdo – see? If you want me you'll find me at Jacob Shafter's, at Sheridan Street, Vermissa, so I'm not hiding from you, am I? Day or night I dare to look the like of you in the face. Don't make any mistake about that.'

There was a murmur of sympathy and admiration from the miners at the dauntless demeanour of the newcomer, while the two policemen shrugged their shoulders and renewed a conversation between themselves. A few minutes later the train ran into the ill-lit depot and there was a general clearing, for Vermissa was far the largest township on the line. McMurdo picked up his leather grip-sack, and was about to start off into the darkness when one of the miners accosted him.

'By gosh, mate, you know how to speak to the cops,' he said, in a voice of awe. 'It was grand to hear you. Let me carry your grip-sack and show you the road. I'm passing Shafter's on the way to my own shack.'

There was a chorus of friendly 'Good nights' from the other miners as they passed from the platform. Before ever he had set foot in it, McMurdo the turbulent had become a character in Vermissa.

The country had been a place of terror, but the township was in its way even more depressing. Down that long valley there was at least a certain gloomy grandeur in the huge fires and the clouds of drifting smoke, while the strength and industry of man found fitting monuments in the hills which he had spilled by the side of his monstrous excavations. But the town showed a dead level of mean ugliness and squalor. The broad street was churned up by the traffic into a horrible rutted paste of muddy snow. The sidewalks were narrow and uneven. The numerous gas-lamps served only to show more clearly a long line of wooden houses, each with its veranda facing the street, unkempt and dirty. As they approached the centre of the town, the scene was brightened by a row of well-lit stores, and even more by a cluster of liquor saloons and gaming-houses, in which the miners spent their hard-earned but generous wages.

'That's the Union House,' said the guide, pointing to one sal-oon which rose almost to the dignity of being an hotel. 'Jack McGinty is the Boss there.'

'What sort of a man is he?' asked McMurdo.

'What! Have you never heard of the Boss?'

'How could I have heard of him when you know that I am a stranger in these parts?'

'Well, I thought his name was known right across the Union. It's been in the papers often enough.'

'What for?'

'Well' – the miner lowered his voice – 'over the affairs.'

'What affairs?'

'Good Lord, mister, you are queer goods, if I may say it with-out offence. There's only one set of affairs that you'll hear of in these parts, and that's the affairs of the Scowrers.'

'Why, I seem to have read of the Scowrers in Chicago. A gang of murderers, are they not?'

'Hush, on your life!' cried the miner, standing still in his alarm, and gazing in amazement at his companion. 'Man, you won't live long in these parts if you speak in the open street like that. Many a man has had the life beaten out of him for less.'

'Well, I know nothing about them. It's only what I have read.'

'And I'm not saying that you have not read the truth.' The man looked nervously round him as he spoke, peering into the shadows as if he feared to see some lurking danger. 'If killing is murder, then God knows there is murder and to spare. But don't you dare breathe the name of Jack McGinty in connection with it, stranger, for every whisper goes back to him, and he is not one that is likely to let it pass. Now, that's the house you're after – that one standing back from the street. You'll find old Jacob Shafter that runs it as honest a man as lives in this township.'

'I thank you,' said McMurdo, and shaking hands with his new acquaintance he plodded, his grip-sack in his hand, up the path which led to the dwelling-house, at the door of which he gave a resounding knock. It was opened at once by someone very different from what he had expected.

It was a woman, young and singularly beautiful. She was of the Swedish type, blonde and fair-haired, with the piquant contrast of a pair of beautiful dark eyes, with which she surveyed the stranger with surprise and a pleasing embarrassment which brought a wave of colour over her pale face. Framed in the bright light of the open doorway, it seemed to McMurdo that he had never seen a more beautiful picture, the more attractive for its contrast with the sordid and gloomy surroundings. A lovely violet growing upon one of those black slag-heaps of the mines would not have seemed more surprising. So entranced was he that he stood staring without a word, and it was she who broke the silence.

'I thought it was father,' said she, with a pleasing little touch of a Swedish accent. 'Did you come to see him? He is down town. I expect him back every minute.'

McMurdo continued to gaze at her in open admiration until her eyes dropped in confusion before this masterful visitor.

'No, miss,' he said at last; 'I'm in no hurry to see him. But your house was recommended to me for board. I thought it might suit me, and now I know it will.'

'You are quick to make up your mind,' said she, with a smile.

'Anyone but a blind man could do as much,' the other answered.

She laughed at the compliment.

'Come right in, sir,' she said. 'I'm Miss Ettie Shafter, Mr Shafter's daughter. My mother's dead, and I run the house. You can sit down by the stove in the front room until father comes along. Ah, here he is; so you can fix things with him right away.'

A heavy, elderly man came plodding up the path. In a few words McMurdo explained his business. A man of the name of Murphy had given him the address in Chicago. He in turn had had it from someone else. Old Shafter was quite ready. The stranger made no bones about terms, agreed at once to every condition, and was apparently fairly flush of money. For twelve dollars a week, paid in advance, he was to have board and lodging. So it was that McMurdo, the self-confessed fugitive from justice, took up his abode under the roof of the Shafters, the first step which was to lead to so long and dark a train of events, ending in a far distant land.

Chapter Two

The Bodymaster

McMurdo was a man who made his mark quickly. Wherever he was the folk around soon knew it. Within a week he had become infinitely the most important person at Shafter's. There were ten or a dozen boarders there, but they were honest foremen or commonplace clerks from the stores, of a very different calibre to the young Irishman. Of an evening when they gathered together his joke was always the readiest, his conversation the brightest, and his song the best. He was a born boon companion, with a magnetism which drew good humour from all around him. And yet he showed again and again, as he had shown in the railway-carriage, a capacity for sudden, fierce anger which compelled the respect and even fear of those who met him. For the law, too, and all connected with it, he exhibited a bitter contempt which delighted some and alarmed others of his fellow-boarders.

From the first he made it evident, by his open admiration, that the daughter of the house had won his heart from the instant that he had set eyes upon her beauty and her grace. He was no backward suitor. On the second day he told her that he loved her, and from then onwards he repeated the same story with an absolute disregard of what she might say to discourage him.

'Someone else!' he would cry. 'Well, the worse luck for someone else! Let him look out for himself! Am I to lose my life's chance and all my heart's desire for someone else? You can keep on saying "No", Ettie! The day will come when you will say "Yes", and I'm young enough to wait.'

He was a dangerous suitor, with his glib Irish tongue and his pretty, coaxing ways. There was about him also that glamour of experience and of mystery which attracts a woman's interest and finally her love. He could talk of the sweet valleys of County Monaghan from which he came, of the lovely distant island, the low hills and green meadows of which seemed the more beautiful when imagination viewed them from this place of grime and snow. Then he was versed in the life of the cities of the North, of Detroit and the lumber-camps of Michigan, of Buffalo, and finally of Chicago, where he had worked in a saw-mill. And afterwards came the hint of romance, the feeling that strange things had happened to him in that great city, so strange and so intimate that they might not be spoken of. He spoke wistfully of a sudden leaving, a breaking of old ties, a flight into a strange world ending in this dreary valley, and Ettie listened, her dark eyes gleaming with pity and with sympathy – those two qualities which may turn so rapidly and so naturally to love.

McMurdo had obtained a temporary job as a book-keeper, for he was a well-educated man. This kept him out most of the day, and he had not found occasion yet to report himself to the head of the Lodge of the Ancient Order of Freemen. He was reminded of his omission, however, by a visit one evening from Mike Scanlan, the fellow-member whom he had met in the train. Scanlan, a small, sharp-faced, nervous, black-eyed man, seemed glad to see him once more. After a glass or two of whisky, he broached the object of his visit.

'Say, McMurdo,' said he, 'I remembered your address, so I made bold to call. I'm surprised that you've not reported to the bodymaster. What's amiss that you've not seen Boss McGinty yet?'

'Well, I had to find a job. I have been busy.'

'You must find time for him if you have none for anything else. Good Lord, man, you're mad not to have been down to the Union House and registered your name the first morning after you came here! If you fall foul of him – well, you *mustn't* – that's all!'

McMurdo showed mild surprise.

'I've been a member of Lodge for over two years, Scanlan, but I never heard that duties were so pressing as all that.'

'Maybe not in Chicago!'

'Well, it's the same society here.'

'Is it?' Scanlan looked at him long and fixedly. There was something sinister in his eyes.

'Is it not?'

'You'll tell me that in a month's time. I hear you had a talk with the patrolmen after I left the train.'

'How did you know that?'

'Oh, it got about – things do get about for good and for bad in this district.'

'Well, yes. I told the hounds what I thought of them.'

'By the Lord, you'll be a man after McGinty's heart!'

'What – does he hate the police, too?'

Scanlan burst out laughing.

'You go and see him, my lad,' said he, as he took his leave. 'It's not the police, but you, that he'll hate if you don't! Now, take a friend's advice and go at once!'

It chanced that on the same evening McMurdo had another more pressing interview which urged him in the same direction. It may have been that his attentions to Ettie had been more evident than before, or that they had gradually obtruded themselves into the slow mind of his good Swedish host; but, whatever the cause, the boarding-house keeper beckoned the young man into his private room and started on to the subject without any circumlocution.

'It seems to me, mister,' said he, 'dat you are gettin' set on my Ettie. Ain't dat so, or am I wrong?'

'Yes, that is so,' the young man answered.

'Well, I vant to tell you right now dat it ain't no manner of use. There's someone slipped in afore you.'

'She told me so.'

'Well, you can lay dat she told you truth! But did she tell you who it vas?'

'No; I asked her, but she would not tell.'

'I dare say not, the leetle baggage. Perhaps she did not vish to vrighten you avay.'

'Frighten!' McMurdo was on fire in a moment.

'Ah, yes, my vriend! You need not be ashamed to be vrightened of him. It is Teddy Baldwin.'

'And who the devil is he?'

'He is a Boss of Scowrers.'

'Scowrers! I've heard of them before. It's Scowrers here and Scowrers there, and always in a whisper! What are you all afraid of? Who *are* the Scowrers?'

The boarding-house keeper instinctively sank his voice, as everyone did who talked about the terrible society.

'The Scowrers,' said he, 'are the Ancient Order of Freemen.'

The young man started.

'Why, I am a member of that Order myself.'

'You! I would never have had you in my house if I had known it – not if you vere to pay me a hundred dollar a veek.'

'What's amiss with the Order? It's for charity and good-fellowship. The rules say so.'

'Maybe in some places. Not here!'

'What is it here?'

'It's a murder society, dat's vat it is.'

McMurdo laughed incredulously.

'How do you prove that?' he asked.

'Prove it! Are there not vifty murders to prove it? Vat about Milman and Van Shorst, and the Nicholson vamily, and old Mr Hyam, and little Billy James, and the others? Prove it! Is dere a man or a voman in dis valley dat does not know it?'

'See here!' said McMurdo, earnestly. 'I want you to take back what you've said or else to make it good. One or the other you must do before I quit this room. Put yourself in my place. Here am I, a stranger in the town. I belong to a society that I know only as an innocent one. You'll find it through the length and breadth of the States, but always as an innocent one. Now, when I am counting upon joining it here, you tell me that it is the same as a murder society called the "Scowrers". I guess you owe me either an apology or else an explanation, Mr Shafter.'

'I can but tell you vat the whole vorld knows, mister. The bosses of the one are the bosses of the other. If you offend the one it is the other dat vill strike you. We have proved it too often.'

'That's just gossip! I want proof!' said McMurdo.

'If you live here long you vill get your proof. But I vorget dat you are yourself one of dem. You vill soon be as bad as the rest. But you vill find other lodgings, mister. I cannot have you here. Is it not bad enough dat one of these people come courting my Ettie, and dat I dare not turn him down, but dat I should have another for my boarder? Yes, indeed, you shall not sleep here after tonight!'

So McMurdo found himself under sentence of banishment both from his comfortable quarters and from the girl whom he loved. He found her alone in the sitting-room that same evening, and he poured his troubles into her ear.

'Sure, your father is after giving me notice,' he said. 'It's little I would care if it was just my room; but indeed, Ettie, though it's only a week that I've known you, you are the very breath of life to me, and I can't live without you.'

'Oh, hush, Mr McMurdo! Don't speak so!' said the girl. 'I have told you, have I not, that you are too late? There is another, and if I have not promised to marry him at once, at least I can promise no one else.'

'Suppose I had been first, Ettie, would I have had a chance?'

The girl sank her face into her hands.

'I wish to Heaven that you *had* been first,' she sobbed.

McMurdo was down on his knees before her in an instant.

'For God's sake, Ettie, let it stand at that!' he cried. 'Will you ruin your life and my own for the sake of this promise? Follow your heart, acushla! 'Tis a safer guide than any promise given before you knew what it was that you were saying.'

He had seized Ettie's white hand between his own strong brown ones.

'Say that you will be mine and we will face it out together.'

'Not here?'

'Yes, here.'

'No, no, Jack!' His arms were round her now. 'It could not be here. Could you take me away?'

A struggle passed for a moment over McMurdo's face, but it ended by setting like granite.

'No, here,' he said. 'I'll hold you against the world, Ettie, right here where we are!'

'Why should we not leave together?'

'No, Ettie, I can't leave here.'

'But why?'

'I'd never hold my head up again if I felt that I had been driven out. Besides, what is there to be afraid of? Are we not free folk in a free country? If you love me and I you, who will dare to come between?'

'You don't know, Jack. You've been here too short a time. You don't know this Baldwin. You don't know McGinty and his Scowrers.'

'No, I don't know them, and I don't fear them, and I don't believe in them!' said McMurdo. 'I've lived among rough men, my darling, and instead of fearing them it has always ended that they have feared me – always, Ettie. It's mad on the face of it! If these men, as your father says, have done crime after crime in the valley, and if every one knows them by name, how comes it that none are brought to justice? You answer me that, Ettie!'

'Because no witness dares to appear against them. He would not live a month if he did. Also because they have always their own men to swear that the accused one was far from the scene of the crime. But surely, Jack, you must have read all this! I had understood that every paper in the States was writing about it.'

'Well, I have read something, it is true, but I had thought it was a story. Maybe these men have some reason in what they do. Maybe they are wronged and have no other way to help themselves.'

'Oh, Jack, don't let me hear you speak so! That is how he speaks – the other one!'

'Baldwin – he speaks like that, does he?'

'And that is why I loathe him so. Oh, Jack, now I can tell you the truth, I loathe him with all my heart; but I fear him also. I fear him for myself, but, above all, I fear him for Father. I know that some great sorrow would come upon us if I dared to say what I really felt. That is why I have put him off with half-promises. It was in real truth our only hope. But if you would fly with me, Jack, we could take Father with us and live for ever far from the power of these wicked men.'

Again there was a struggle upon McMurdo's face, and again it set like granite.

'No harm shall come to you, Ettie – nor to your father either. As to wicked men, I expect you may find that I am as bad as the worst of them before we're through.'

'No, no, Jack! I would trust you anywhere.'

McMurdo laughed bitterly.

'Good Lord, how little you know of me! Your innocent soul, my darling, could not even guess what is passing in mine. But, halloa, who's the visitor?'

The door had opened suddenly and a young fellow came swaggering in with the air of one who is the master. He was a handsome, dashing young man of about the same age and build as McMurdo himself. Under his broad-brimmed black felt hat, which he had not troubled to remove, a handsome face, with fierce, domineering eyes and curved hawkbill of a nose, looked savagely at the pair who sat by the stove.

Ettie had jumped to her feet, full of confusion and alarm.

'I'm glad to see you, Mr Baldwin,' said she. 'You're earlier than I had thought. Come and sit down.'

Baldwin stood with his hands on his hips looking at McMurdo. 'Who is this?' he asked, curtly.

'It's a friend of mine, Mr Baldwin – a new boarder here. Mr McMurdo, can I introduce you to Mr Baldwin?'

The young men nodded in a surly fashion to each other.

'Maybe Miss Ettie has told you how it is with us?' said Baldwin.

'I didn't understand that there was any relation between you.'

'Did you not? Well, you can understand it now. You can take it from me that this young lady is mine, and you'll find it a very fine evening for a walk.'

'Thank you, I am in no humour for a walk.'

'Are you not?' The man's savage eyes were blazing with anger. 'Maybe you are in a humour for a fight, Mr Boarder?'

'That I am,' cried McMurdo, springing to his feet. 'You never said a more welcome word.'

'For God's sake, Jack! Oh, for God's sake!' cried poor, distracted Ettie. 'Oh, Jack, Jack, he will do you a mischief!'

'Oh, it's "Jack", is it!' said Baldwin, with an oath. 'You've come to that already, have you?'

'Oh, Ted, be reasonable – be kind! For my sake, Ted, if ever you loved me, be great-hearted and forgiving!'

'I think, Ettie, that if you were to leave us alone we could get this thing settled,' said McMurdo, quietly. 'Or maybe, Mr Baldwin, you will take a turn down the street with me. It's a fine evening, and there's some open ground beyond the next block.'

'I'll get even with you without needing to dirty my hands,' said his enemy. 'You'll wish you had never set foot in this house before I am through with you.'

'No time like the present,' cried McMurdo.

'I'll choose my own time, mister. You can leave the time to me.

See here!' He suddenly rolled up his sleeve and showed upon his forearm a peculiar sign which appeared to have been branded there. It was a circle with a triangle within it. 'D'you know what that means?'

'I neither know nor care!'

'Well, you will know. I'll promise you that. You won't be much older either. Perhaps Miss Ettie can tell you something about it. As to you, Ettie, you'll come back to me on your knees. D'ye hear, girl? On your knees! And then I'll tell you what your punishment may be. You've sowed – and, by the Lord, I'll see that you reap!' He glared at them both in fury. Then he turned upon his heel, and an instant later the outer door had banged behind him.

For a few moments McMurdo and the girl stood in silence. Then she threw her arms around him.

'Oh, Jack, how brave you were! But it is no use – you must fly! Tonight – Jack – tonight! It's your only hope. He will have your life. I read it in his horrible eyes. What chance have you against a dozen of them, with Boss McGinty and all the power of the Lodge behind them?'

McMurdo disengaged her hands, kissed her, and gently pushed her back into a chair.

'There, acushla, there! Don't be disturbed or fear for me. I'm a Freeman myself. I'm after telling your father about it. Maybe I am no better than the others, so don't make a saint of me. Perhaps you hate me, too, now that I've told you as much.'

'Hate you, Jack! While life lasts I could never do that. I've heard that there is no harm in being a Freeman anywhere but here, so why should I think the worse of you for that? But if you are a Freeman, Jack, why should you not go down and make a friend of Boss McGinty? Oh, hasten, Jack, hasten! Get your word in first, or the hounds will be on your trail.'

'I was thinking the same thing,' said McMurdo. 'I'll go right now and fix it. You can tell your father that I'll sleep here tonight and find some other quarters in the morning.'

The bar of McGinty's saloon was crowded as usual, for it was the favourite lounge of all the rougher elements of the town. The man was popular, for he had a rough, jovial disposition which formed a mask, covering a great deal which lay behind it. But, apart from this popularity, the fear in which he was held throughout the township, and, indeed, down the whole thirty miles of the valley and past the mountains upon either side of it, was enough in itself to fill his bar, for none could afford to neglect his goodwill.

Besides those secret powers which it was universally believed that he exercised in so pitiless a fashion, he was a high public official, a municipal councillor, and a commissioner for roads, elected to the office through the votes of the ruffians who in turn expected to receive favours at his hands. Rates and taxes were enormous, the public works were notoriously neglected, the accounts were slurred over by bribed auditors, and the decent citizen was terrorized into paying public blackmail, and holding his tongue lest some worse thing befall him. Thus it was that, year by year, Boss McGinty's diamond pins became more obtrusive, his gold chains more weighty across a more gorgeous vest, and his saloon stretched farther and farther, until it threatened to absorb one whole side of the Market Square.

McMurdo pushed open the swinging door of the saloon and made his way amid the crowd of men within, through an atmosphere which was blurred with tobacco smoke and heavy with the smell of spirits. The place was brilliantly lighted, and the huge, heavily gilt mirrors upon every wall reflected and multiplied the garish illumination. There were several bartenders in their shirtsleeves hard at work, mixing drinks for the loungers who fringed the broad, heavily metalled counter. At the far end, with his body resting upon the bar, and a cigar stuck at an acute angle from the corner of his mouth, there stood a tall, strong, heavily built man, who could be none other than the famous McGinty himself. He was a black-maned giant, bearded to the cheek-bones, and with a shock of raven hair which fell to his collar. His complexion was as swarthy as that of an Italian, and his eyes were of a strange, dead black, which, combined with a slight squint, gave them a particularly sinister appearance. All else in the man, his noble proportions, his fine features, and his frank bearing, fitted in with that jovial man-to-man manner which he affected. Here, one would say, is a bluff, honest fellow, whose heart would be sound, however rude his outspoken words might seem. It was only when those dead, dark eyes, deep and remorseless, were turned upon a man that he shrank within himself, feeling that he was face to face with an infinite possibility of latent evil, with a strength and courage and cunning behind it which made it a thousand times more deadly.

Having had a good look at his man, McMurdo elbowed his way forward with his usual careless audacity, and pushed himself through the little group of courtiers who were fawning upon the powerful Boss, laughing uproariously at the smallest of his jokes. The young stranger's bold grey eyes looked back fearlessly through their glasses at the deadly black ones which turned sharply upon him.

'Well, young man, I can't call your face to mind.'

'I'm new here, Mr McGinty.'

'You are not so new that you can't give a gentleman his proper title.'

'He's Councillor McGinty, young man,' said a voice from the group.

'I'm sorry, Councillor. I'm strange to the ways of the place. But I was advised to see you.'

'Well, you see me. This is all there is. What d'you think of me?'

'Well, it's early days. If your heart is as big as your body, and your soul as fine as your face, then I'd ask for nothing better,' said McMurdo.

'By gosh, you've got an Irish tongue in your head, anyhow,' cried the saloon-keeper, not quite certain whether to humour this audacious visitor or to stand upon his dignity. 'So you are good enough to pass my appearance?'

'Sure,' said McMurdo.

'And you were told to see me?'

'I was.'

'And who told you?'

'Brother Scanlan, of Lodge 341, Vermissa. I drink your health, Councillor, and to our better acquaintance.' He raised a glass with which he had been served to his lips and elevated his little finger as he drank it.

McGinty, who had been watching him narrowly, raised his thick black eyebrows.

'Oh, it's like that, is it?' said he. 'I'll have to look a bit closer into this, Mister –'

'McMurdo.'

'A bit closer, Mr McMurdo, for we don't take folk on trust in these parts, nor believe all we're told neither. Come in here for a moment, behind the bar.'

There was a small room there lined round with barrels. McGinty carefully closed the door, and then seated himself on one of them, biting thoughtfully on his cigar, and surveying his companion with those disquieting eyes. For a couple of minutes he sat in complete silence.

McMurdo bore the inspection cheerfully, one hand in his coat-pocket, the other twisting his brown moustache. Suddenly McGinty stooped and produced a wicked-looking revolver.

'See here, my joker,' said he; 'if I thought you were playing any game on us, it would be a short shrift for you.'

'This is a strange welcome,' McMurdo answered, with some dignity, 'for the bodymaster of a Lodge of Freemen to give to a strange brother.'

'Aye, but it's just that same that you have to prove,' said McGinty, 'and God help you if you fail. Where were you made?'

'Lodge 29, Chicago.'

'When?'

'June 24th, 1872.'

'What bodymaster?'

'James H. Scott.'

'Who is your district ruler?'

'Bartholomew Wilson.'

'Hum! You seem glib enough in your tests. What are you doing here?'

'Working, the same as you, but a poorer job.'

'You have your back answer quick enough.'

'Yes, I was always quick of speech.'

'Are you quick of action?'

'I have had that name among those who knew me best.'

'Well, we may try you sooner than you think. Have you heard anything of the Lodge in these parts?'

'I've heard that it takes a man to be a brother.'

'True for you, Mr McMurdo. Why did you leave Chicago?'

'I'm hanged if I tell you that.'

McGinty opened his eyes. He was not used to being answered in such fashion, and it amused him.

'Why won't you tell me?'

'Because no brother may tell another a lie.'

'Then the truth is too bad to tell?'

'You can put it that way if you like.'

'See here, mister; you can't expect me, as bodymaster, to pass into the Lodge a man for whose past he can't answer.'

McMurdo looked puzzled. Then he took a worn newspaper cutting from an inner pocket.

'You wouldn't squeal on a fellow?' said he.

'I'll wipe my hand across your face if you say such words to me,' cried McGinty, hotly.

'You are right, Councillor,' said McMurdo, meekly. 'I should apologize. I spoke without thought. Well, I know that I am safe in your hands. Look at that cutting.'

The Valley of Fear

McGinty glanced his eyes over the account of the shooting of one Jonas Pinto, in the Lake Saloon, Market Street, Chicago, in the New Year week of '74.

'Your work?' he asked, as he handed back the paper.

McMurdo nodded.

'Why did you shoot him?'

'I was helping Uncle Sam to make dollars. Maybe mine were not as good gold as his, but they looked as well and were cheaper to make. This man Pinto helped me to shove the queer –'

'To do what?'

'Well, it means to pass the dollars out into circulation. Then he said he would split. Maybe he did split. I didn't wait to see. I just killed him and lighted out for the coal country.'

'Why the coal country?'

''Cause I'd read in the papers that they weren't too particular in those parts.'

McGinty laughed.

'You were first a coiner and then a murderer, and you came to these parts because you thought you'd be welcome?'

'That's about the size of it,' McMurdo answered.

'Well, I guess you'll go far. Say, can you make those dollars yet?'

McMurdo took half a dozen from his pocket. 'Those never passed the Washington mint,' said he.

'You don't say!' McGinty held them to the light in his enormous hand, which was as hairy as a gorilla's. 'I can see no difference! Gosh, you'll be a mighty useful brother, I'm thinking. We can do with a bad man or two amongst us, friend McMurdo, for there are times when we have to take our own part. We'd soon be against the wall if we didn't shove back at those that were pushing us.'

'Well, I guess I'll do my share of shoving with the rest of the boys.'

'You seem to have a good nerve. You didn't flinch when I put this pistol on you.'

'It was not me that was in danger.'

'Who, then?'

'It was you, Councillor.' McMurdo drew a cocked pistol from the side-pocket of his pea-jacket. 'I was covering you all the time. I guess my shot would have been as quick as yours.'

McGinty flushed an angry red and then burst into a roar of laughter.

'By gosh!' said he. 'Say, we've had no such holy terror come to hand this many a year. I reckon the Lodge will learn to be proud of you. Well, what the deuce do you want? And can't I speak alone with a gentleman for five minutes but you must butt in upon us?'

The bar-tender stood abashed.

'I'm sorry, Councillor, but it's Mr Ted Baldwin. He says he must see you this very minute.'

The message was unnecessary, for the set, cruel face of the man himself was looking over the servant's shoulder. He pushed the bar-tender out and closed the door on him.

'So,' said he, with a furious glance at McMurdo, 'you got here first, did you? I've a word to say to you, Councillor, about this man.'

'Then say it here and now, before my face,' cried McMurdo.

'I'll say it at my own time, in my own way.'

'Tut, tut!' said McGinty, getting off his barrel. 'This will never do. We have a new brother here, Baldwin, and it's not for us to greet him in such a fashion. Hold out your hand, man, and make it up.'

'Never!' cried Baldwin, in a fury.

'I've offered to fight him if he thinks I have wronged him,' said McMurdo. 'I'll fight him with fists, or, if that won't satisfy him, I'll fight him any other way he chooses. Now I'll leave it to you, Councillor, to judge between us as a bodymaster should.'

'What is it, then?'

'A young lady. She's free to choose for herself.'

'Is she?' cried Baldwin.

'As between two brothers of the Lodge, I should say that she was,' said the Boss.

'Oh, that's your ruling, is it?'

'Yes, it is, Ted Baldwin,' said McGinty, with a wicked stare. 'Is it you that would dispute it?'

'You would throw over one that has stood by you this five years in favour of a man that you never saw before in your life? You're not bodymaster for life, Jack McGinty, and, by God, when next it comes to a vote –'

The Councillor sprang at him like a tiger. His hand closed round the other's neck and he hurled him back across one of the barrels. In his mad fury he would have squeezed the life out of him if McMurdo had not interfered.

'Easy, Councillor! For Heaven's sake, go easy!' he cried, as he dragged him back.

McGinty released his hold, and Baldwin, cowed and shaken, gasping for breath, and shivering in every limb as one who has looked over the very edge of death, sat up on the barrel over which he had been hurled.

'You've been asking for it this many a day, Ted Baldwin. Now you've got it,' cried McGinty, his huge chest rising and falling. 'Maybe you think if I were voted down from bodymaster you would find yourself in my shoes. It's for the Lodge to say that. But so long as I am the chief, I'll have no man lift his voice against me or my rulings.'

'I have nothing against you,' mumbled Baldwin, feeling his throat.

'Well, then,' cried the other, relapsing in a moment into a bluff joviality, 'we are all good friends again, and there's an end of the matter.'

He took a bottle of champagne down from the shelf and twisted out the cork.

'See now,' he continued, as he filled three high glasses, 'let us drink the quarrelling toast of the Lodge. After that, as you know, there can be no bad blood between us. Now, then, the left hand on the apple of my throat, I say to you, Ted Baldwin, what is the offence, sir?'

'The clouds are heavy,' answered Baldwin.

'But they will for ever brighten.'

'And this I swear.'

The men drank their wine, and the same ceremony was performed between Baldwin and McMurdo.

'There,' cried McGinty, rubbing his hands, 'that's the end of the black blood. You come under Lodge discipline if it goes farther, and that's a heavy hand in these parts, as Brother Baldwin knows, and as you will very soon find out, Brother McMurdo, if you ask for trouble.'

'Faith, I'd be slow to do that,' said McMurdo. He held out his hand to Baldwin. 'I'm quick to quarrel and quick to forgive. It's my hot Irish blood, they tell me. But it's over for me, and I bear no grudge.'

Baldwin had to take the proffered hand, for the baleful eye of the terrible Boss was upon him. But his sullen face showed how little the words of the other had moved him.

McGinty clapped them both on the shoulders.

'Tut! These girls, these girls!' he cried. 'To think that the same petticoats should come between two of my boys. It's the devil's own luck. Well, it's the colleen inside of them that must settle the question, for it's outside the jurisdiction of a bodymaster, and the Lord be praised for that. We have enough on us, without the women as well. You'll have to be affiliated to Lodge 341, Brother McMurdo. We have our own ways and methods, different to Chicago. Saturday night is our meeting, and if you come then we'll make you free for ever of the Vermissa Valley.'

Chapter Three

Lodge 341, Vermissa

On the day following the evening which had contained so many exciting events McMurdo moved his lodgings from old Jacob Shafter's and took up his quarters at the Widow MacNamara's, on the extreme outskirts of the town. Scanlan, his original acquaintance aboard the train, had occasion shortly afterwards to move into Vermissa, and the two lodged together. There was no other boarder, and the hostess was an easy-going old Irishwoman who left them to themselves, so that they had a freedom for speech and action welcome to men who had secrets in common. Shafter had relented to the extent of letting McMurdo come to his meals there when he liked, so that his intercourse with Ettie was by no means broken. On the contrary, it drew closer and more intimate as the weeks went by. In his bedroom at his new abode McMurdo felt it to be safe to take out the coining moulds, and under many a pledge of secrecy a number of the brothers from the Lodge were allowed to come in and see them, each of them carrying away in his pocket some examples of the false money, so cunningly struck that there was never the slightest difficulty or danger in passing it. Why, with such a wonderful art at his command, McMurdo should condescend to work at all was a perpetual mystery to his companions, though he made it clear to any one who asked him that if he lived without any visible means it would very quickly bring the police on his track.

One policeman was, indeed, after him already, but the incident, as luck would have it, did the adventurer a great deal more good than harm. After the first introduction there were few evenings when he did not find his way to McGinty's saloon, there to make closer acquaintance with 'the boys', which was the jovial title by which the dangerous gang who infested the place were known to each other. His dashing manner and fearlessness of speech made him a favourite with them all, while the rapid and scientific way in which he polished off his antagonist in an 'all in' bar-room scrap earned the respect of that rough community. Another incident, however, raised him even higher in their estimation.

Just at the crowded hour one night the door opened and a man entered with the quiet blue uniform and peaked cap of the Coal and Iron Police. This was a special body raised by the railways and colliery owners to supplement the efforts of the ordinary civil police, who were perfectly helpless in the face of the organized ruffianism which terrorized the district. There was a hush as he entered, and many a curious glance was cast at him, but the relations between policemen and criminals are peculiar in the States, and McGinty himself, standing behind the counter, showed no surprise when the inspector enrolled himself among his customers.

'A straight whisky, for the night is bitter,' said the police-officer. 'I don't think we have met before, Councillor?'

'You'll be the new captain?' said McGinty.

'That's so. We're looking to you, Councillor, and to the other leading citizens, to help us in upholding law and order in this township. Captain Marvin is my name – of the Coal and Iron.'

'We'd do better without you, Captain Marvin,' said McGinty, coldly. 'For we have our own police of the township, and no need for any imported goods. What are you but the paid tool of the men of capital, hired by them to club or to shoot your poorer fellow-citizens?'

'Well, well, we won't argue about that,' said the police-officer, good-humouredly. 'I expect we all do our duty same as we see it, but we can't all see it the same.' He had drunk off his glass and had turned to go, when his eyes fell upon the face of Jack McMurdo, who was scowling at his elbow. 'Halloa! halloa!' he cried, looking him up and down. 'Here's an old acquaintance.'

McMurdo shrank away from him.

'I was never a friend to you nor any other cursed copper in my life,' said he.

'An acquaintance isn't always a friend,' said the police captain, grinning. 'You're Jack McMurdo of Chicago, right enough, and don't deny it.'

McMurdo shrugged his shoulders.

'I'm not denying it,' said he. 'D'ye think I'm ashamed of my own name?'

'You've got good cause to be, anyhow.'

'What the devil d'you mean by that?' he roared, with his fists clenched.

'No, no, Jack; bluster won't do with me. I was an officer in Chicago before ever I came to this darned coal-bunker, and I know a Chicago crook when I see one.'

McMurdo's face fell.

'Don't tell me that you're Marvin of the Chicago Central!' he cried.

'Just the same old Teddy Marvin at your service. We haven't forgotten the shooting of Jonas Pinto up there.'

'I never shot him.'

'Did you not? That's good impartial evidence, ain't it? Well, his death came in uncommon handy for you, or they would have had you for shoving the queer. Well, we can let that be bygones, for, between you and me – and perhaps I'm going farther than my duty in saying it – they could get no clear case against you, and Chicago's open to you tomorrow.'

'I'm very well where I am.'

'Well, I've given you the office, and you're a sulky dog not to thank me for it.'

'Well, I suppose you mean well, and I do thank you,' said McMurdo, in no very gracious manner.

'It's mum with me so long as I see you living on the straight,' said the captain. 'But, by gum, if you get off on the cross after this it's another story! So good night to you – and good night, Councillor.'

He left the bar-room, but not before he had created a local hero. McMurdo's deeds in far Chicago had been whispered before. He had put off all questions with a smile as one who did not wish to have greatness thrust upon him. But now the thing was officially confirmed. The bar-loafers crowded round him and shook him heartily by the hand. He was free of the community from that time on. He could drink hard and show little trace of it, but that evening, had his mate Scanlan not been at hand to lead him home, the fêted hero would surely have spent his night under the bar.

On a Saturday night McMurdo was introduced to the Lodge. He had thought to pass in without ceremony as being an initiate of Chicago; but there were particular rites in Vermissa of which they were proud, and these had to be undergone by every postulant. The assembly met in a large room reserved for such purposes at the Union House. Some sixty members assembled at Vermissa, but that by no means represented the full strength of the organization, for there were several other lodges in the valley, and others across the mountains on either side, who exchanged members when any serious business was afoot, so that a crime might be done by men who were strangers to the locality. Altogether, there were not fewer than five hundred scattered over the coal district.

In the bare assembly room the men were gathered round a long table. At the side was a second one laden with bottles and glasses, on which some members of the company were already turning their eyes. McGinty sat at the head with a flat black velvet cap upon his shock of tangled black hair and a coloured purple stole round his neck, so that he seemed to be a priest presiding over some diabolical ritual. To right and left of him were the higher Lodge officials, the cruel, handsome face of Ted Baldwin among them. Each of these wore some scarf or medallion as emblem of his office. They were, for the most part, men of mature age, but the rest of the company consisted of young fellows from eighteen to twenty-five, the ready and capable agents who carried out the commands of their seniors. Among the older men were many whose features showed the tigerish, lawless souls within, but looking at the rank and file it was difficult to believe that these eager and open-faced young fellows were in very truth a dangerous gang of murderers, whose minds had suffered such complete moral perversion that they took a horrible pride in their proficiency at the business, and looked with the deepest respect at the man who had the reputation for making what they called a 'clean job'. To their contorted natures it had become a spirited and chivalrous thing to volunteer for service against some man who had never injured them, and whom, in many cases, they had never seen in their lives. The crime committed, they quarrelled as to who had actually struck the fatal blow, and amused each other and the company by describing the cries and contortions of the murdered man. At first they had shown some secrecy in their arrangements, but at the time which this narrative describes their proceedings were extraordinarily open, for the repeated failures of the law had proved to them that, on the one hand, no one would dare to witness against them, and, on the other, they had an unlimited number of staunch witnesses upon whom they could call, and a well-filled treasure chest from which they could draw the funds to engage the best legal talent in the State. In ten long years of outrage there had been no single conviction, and the only danger that ever threatened the Scowrers lay in the victim himself, who, however outnumbered and taken by surprise, might, and occasionally did, leave his mark upon his assailants.

McMurdo had been warned that some ordeal lay before him, but no one would tell him in what it consisted. He was led now into an outer room by two solemn brothers. Through the plank partition he could hear the murmur of many voices from the assembly within. Once or twice he caught the sound of his own name, and he knew that they were discussing his candidature. Then there entered an inner guard, with a green and gold sash across his chest.

'The bodymaster orders that he shall be trussed, blinded, and entered,' said he. The three of them then removed his coat, turned up the sleeve of his right arm, and finally passed a rope round above the elbows and made it fast. They next placed a thick black cap right over his head and the upper part of his face, so that he could see nothing. He was then led into the assembly hall.

It was pitch-dark and very oppressive under his hood. He heard the rustle and murmur of the people round him, and then the voice of McGinty sounded, dull and distant, through the covering of his ears.

'John McMurdo,' said the voice, 'are you already a member of the Ancient Order of Freemen?'

He bowed in assent.

'Is your Lodge No. 29, Chicago?'

He bowed again.

'Dark nights are unpleasant,' said the voice.

'Yes, for strangers to travel,' he answered.

'The clouds are heavy.'

'Yes; a storm is approaching.'

'Are the brethren satisfied?' asked the bodymaster.

There was a general murmur of assent.

'We know, brother, by your sign and by your countersign, that you are indeed one of us,' said McGinty. 'We would have you know, however, that in this county and in other counties of these parts we have certain rites, and also certain duties of our own, which call for good men. Are you ready to be tested?'

'I am.'

'Are you of stout heart?'

'I am.'

'Take a stride forward to prove it.'

As the words were said he felt two hard points in front of his eyes, pressing upon them so that it appeared as if he could not move forward without a danger of losing them. None the less, he nerved himself to step resolutely out, and as he did so the pressure melted away. There was a low murmur of applause.

'He is of stout heart,' said the voice. 'Can you bear pain?'

'As well as another,' he answered.

'Test him!'

It was all he could do to keep himself from screaming out, for an agonizing pain shot through his forearm. He nearly fainted at the sudden shock of it, but he bit his lip and clenched his hands to hide his agony.

'I can take more than that,' said he.

This time there was loud applause. A finer first appearance had never been made in the Lodge. Hands clapped him on the back, and the hood was plucked from his head. He stood blinking and smiling amid the congratulations of the brothers.

'One last word, Brother McMurdo,' said McGinty. 'You have already sworn the oath of secrecy and fidelity, and you are aware that the punishment for any breach of it is instant and inevitable death?'

'I am,' said McMurdo.

'And you accept the rule of the bodymaster for the time being under all circumstances?'

'I do.'

'Then, in the name of Lodge 341, Vermissa, I welcome you to its privileges and debates. You will put the liquor on the table, Brother Scanlan, and we will drink to our worthy brother.'

McMurdo's coat had been brought to him, but before putting it on he examined his right arm, which still smarted heavily.

There, on the flesh of the forearm, was a clear-cut circle with a triangle within it, deep and red, as the branding-iron had left it. One or two of his neighbours pulled up their sleeves and showed their own Lodge marks.

'We've all had it,' said one, 'but not all as brave as you over it.'

'Tut! It was nothing,' said he, but it burned and ached all the same.

When the drinks which followed the ceremony of initiation had all been disposed of, the business of the Lodge proceeded. McMurdo, accustomed only to the prosaic performances of Chicago, listened with open ears, and more surprise than he ventured to show, to what followed.

'The first business on the agenda paper,' said McGinty, 'is to read the following letter from Division Master Windle, of Merton County, Lodge 249. He says:

"Dear Sir, – There is a job to be done on Andrew Rae, of Rae and Sturmash, coal-owners near this place. You will remember that your Lodge owes us a return, having had the services of two brethren in the matter of the patrolman last fall. If you will send two good men they will be taken charge of by Treasurer Higgins of this Lodge, whose address you know. He will show them when to act and where. – Yours in freedom. J. W. Windle, D.M.A.O.F."

Windle has never refused us when we have had occasion to ask for the loan of a man or two, and it is not for us to refuse him.' McGinty paused and looked round the room with his dull, malevolent eyes. 'Who will volunteer for the job?'

Several young fellows held up their hands. The bodymaster looked at them with an approving smile.

'You'll do, Tiger Cormac. If you handle it as well as you did the last you won't be amiss. And you, Wilson.'

'I've no pistol,' said the volunteer, a mere boy in his teens.

'It's your first, is it not? Well, you have to be blooded some time. It will be a great start for you. As to the pistol, you'll find it waiting for you, or I'm mistaken. If you report yourselves on Monday it will be time enough. You'll get a great welcome when you return.'

'Any reward this time?' asked Cormac, a thick-set, dark-faced, brutal-looking young man, whose ferocity had earned him the nickname of 'Tiger'.

'Never mind the reward. You just do it for the honour of the thing. Maybe when it is done there will be a few odd dollars at the bottom of the box.'

'What has the man done?' asked young Wilson.

'Sure, it's not for the likes of you to ask what the man has done. He has been judged over there. That's no business of ours. All we have to do is to carry it out for them, same as they would for us. Speaking of that, two brothers from the Merton Lodge are coming over to us next week to do some business in this quarter.'

'Who are they?' asked someone.

'Faith, it is wiser not to ask. If you know nothing you can testify nothing, and no trouble can come of it. But they are men who will make a clean job when they are about it.'

'And time, too!' cried Ted Baldwin. 'Folk are getting out of hand in these parts. It was only last week that three of our men were turned off by Foreman Blaker. It's been owing him a long time, and he'll get it full and proper.'

'Get what?' McMurdo whispered to his neighbour.

'The business end of a buck-shot cartridge,' cried the man, with the loud laugh. 'What think you of our ways, brother?'

McMurdo's criminal soul seemed to have already absorbed the spirit of the vile association of which he was now a member.

'I like it well,' said he. ''Tis a proper place for a lad of mettle.'

Several of those who sat around heard his words and applauded them.

'What's that?' cried the black-maned bodymaster, from the end of the table.

'"Tis our new brother, sir, who finds our ways to his taste.'

McMurdo rose to his feet for an instant.

'I would say, Worshipful Master, that if a man should be wanted I should take it as an honour to be chosen to help the Lodge.'

There was great applause at this. It was felt that a new sun was pushing its rim above the horizon. To some of the elders it seemed that the progress was a little too rapid.

'I would move,' said the secretary, Harraway, a vulture-faced old greybeard who sat near the chairman, 'that Brother McMurdo should wait until it is the good pleasure of the Lodge to employ him.'

'Sure, that was what I meant. I'm in your hands,' said McMurdo.

'Your time will come, brother,' said the chairman. 'We have marked you down as a willing man, and we believe that you will do good work in these parts. There is a small matter tonight in which you may take a hand, if it so please you.'

'I will wait for something that is worth while.'

'You can come tonight, anyhow, and it will help you to know what we stand for in this community. I will make the announcement later. Meanwhile' – he glanced at his agenda paper – 'I have one or two more points to bring before the meeting. First of all, I will ask the treasurer as to our bank balance. There is the pension to Jim Carnaway's widow. He was struck down doing the work of the Lodge, and it is for us to see that she is not the loser.'

'Jim was shot last month when they tried to kill Chester Wilcox, of Marley Creek,' McMurdo's neighbour informed him.

'The funds are good at the moment,' said the treasurer, with the bank-book in front of him. 'The firms have been generous of late. Max Linder and Co. paid five hundred to be left alone. Walker Brothers sent in a hundred, but I took it on myself to return it and ask for five. If I do not hear by Wednesday their winding gear may get out of order. We had to burn their breaker last year before they became reasonable. Then the West Section Coaling Company has paid its annual contribution. We have enough in hand to meet any obligations.'

'What about Archie Swindon?' asked a brother.

'He has sold out and left the district. The old devil left a note for us to say that he had rather be a free crossing-sweeper in New York than a large mine-owner under the power of a ring of blackmailers. By gosh, it was as well that he made a break for it before the note reached us! I guess he dare not show his face in this valley again.'

An elderly, clean-shaven man, with a kindly face and a good brow, rose from the end of the table which faced the chairman.

'Mr Treasurer,' he asked, 'may I ask who has bought the property of this man that we have driven out of the district?'

'Yes, Brother Morris. It has been bought by the State and Merton County Railroad Company.'

'And who bought the mines of Todman and of Lee that came into the market in the same way last year?'

'The same company, Brother Morris.'

'And who bought the ironworks of Manson and of Shuman and of Van Deher and of Atwood, which have all been given up of late?'

'They were all bought by the West Gilmerton General Mining Company.'

'I don't see, Brother Morris,' said the chairman, 'that it matters a nickel to us who buys them, since they can't carry them out of the district.'

'With all respect to you, Worshipful Master, I think that it may matter very much to us. This process has been going on now for ten long years. We are gradually driving all the small men out of trade. What is the result? We find in their places great companies like the Railroad or the General Iron, who have their directors in New York or Philadelphia, and care nothing for our threats. We can take it out of their local bosses, but it only means that others will be sent in their stead. And we are making it dangerous for ourselves. The small men could not harm us. They had not the money nor the power. So long as we did not squeeze them too dry, they would stay on under our power. But if these big companies find that we stand between them and their profits, they will spare no pains and no expense to hunt us down and bring us to court.'

There was a hush at these ominous words, and every face darkened as gloomy looks were exchanged. So omnipotent and unchallenged had they been that the very thought that there was possible retribution in the background had been banished from their minds. And yet the idea struck a chill to the most reckless of them.

'It is my advice,' the speaker continued, 'that we bear less heavily upon the small men. On the day that they have all been driven out the power of this society will have been broken.'

Unwelcome truths are not popular. There were angry cries as the speaker resumed his seat. McGinty rose with gloom upon his brow.

'Brother Morris,' said he, 'you were always a croaker. So long as the members of the Lodge stand together there is no power in this United States that can touch them. Sure, have we not tried it often enough in the law courts? I expect the big companies will find it easier to pay than to fight, same as the little companies do. And now, brethren' – McGinty took off his black velvet cap and his stole as he spoke – 'this Lodge has finished its business for the evening save for one small matter which may be mentioned when we are parting. The time has now come for fraternal refreshment and for harmony.'

Strange indeed is human nature. Here were these men to whom murder was familiar, who again and again had struck down the father of the family, some man against whom they had no personal feeling, without one thought of compunction or of compassion for his weeping wife or helpless children, and yet the tender or pathetic in music could move them to tears. McMurdo had a fine tenor voice, and if he had failed to gain the goodwill of the Lodge before, it could no longer have been withheld after he had thrilled them with 'I'm Sitting on the Stile, Mary', and 'On the Banks of Allan Water'. In his very first night the new recruit had made himself one of the most popular of the brethren, marked already for advancement and high office. There were other qualities, however, besides those of good fellowship, to make a worthy Freeman, and of these he was given an example before the evening was over. The whisky bottle had passed round many times, and the men were flushed and ripe for mischief, when their bodymaster rose once more to address them.

'Boys,' said he, 'there's one man in this town that wants trimming up, and it's for you to see that he gets it. I'm speaking of James Stanger, of the *Herald*. You've seen how he's been opening his mouth against us again?'

There was a murmur of assent, with many a muttered oath. McGinty took a slip of paper from his waistcoat pocket.

' "Law and Order!" That's how he heads it. "Reign of Terror in the Coal and Iron District. Twelve years have now elapsed since the first assassinations which proved the existence of a criminal organization in our midst. From that day these outrages have never ceased, until now they have reached a pitch which makes us the opprobrium of the civilized world. Is it for such results as this that our great country welcomes to its bosom the alien who flies from the despotisms of Europe? Is it that they shall themselves become tyrants over the very men who have given them shelter, and that a state of terrorism and lawlessness should be established under the very shadow of the sacred folds of the starry flag of freedom which would raise horror in our minds if we read of it as existing under the most effete monarchy of the East? The men are known. The organization is patent and public. How long are we to endure it? Can we for ever live –" Sure, I've read enough of the slush!' cried the chairman, tossing the paper down upon the table. 'That's what he says of us. The question I'm asking you is, What shall we say to him?'

'Kill him!' cried a dozen fierce voices.

'I protest against that,' said Brother Morris, the man of the good brow and shaven face. 'I tell you, brethren, that our hand is too heavy in this valley, and that there will come a point where, in self-defence, every man will unite to crush us out. James Stanger is an old man. He is respected in the township and the district. His paper stands for all that is solid in the valley. If that man is struck down, there will be a stir through this State that will only end with our destruction.'

'And how would they bring about our destruction, Mister Stand-back?' cried McGinty. 'Is it by the police? Sure, half of them are in our pay and half of them afraid of us. Or is it by the law courts and the judge? Haven't we tried that before now, and what ever came of it?'

'There is a Judge Lynch that might try the case,' said Brother Morris.

A general shout of anger greeted the suggestion.

'I have but to raise my finger,' cried McGinty, 'and I could put two hundred men into this town that would clear it out from end to end.' Then, suddenly raising his voice and bending his huge black brows into a terrible frown: 'See here, Brother Morris, I have my eye on you, and have had for some time. You've no heart yourself, and you try to take the heart out of others. It will be an ill day for you, Brother Morris, when your own name comes on our agenda paper, and I'm thinking that it's just there that I ought to place it.'

Morris had turned deadly pale and his knees seemed to give way under him as he fell back into his chair. He raised his glass in his trembling hand and drank before he could answer.

'I apologize, Worshipful Master, to you and to every brother in this Lodge if I have said more than I should. I am a faithful member – you all know that – and it is my fear lest evil come to the Lodge which makes me speak in anxious words. But I have greater trust in your judgement than in my own, Worshipful Master, and I promise you that I will not offend again.'

The bodymaster's scowl relaxed as he listened to the humble words.

'Very good, Brother Morris. It's myself that would be sorry if it were needful to give you a lesson. But so long as I am in this chair we shall be a united Lodge in word and in deed. And now, boys,' he continued, looking round at the company, 'I'll say this much – that if Stanger got his full deserts there would be more trouble than we need ask for. These editors hang together, and every journal in the State would be crying out for police and troops. But I guess you can give him a pretty severe warning. Will you fix it, Brother Baldwin?'

'Sure!' said the young man, eagerly.

'How many will you take?'

'Half-a-dozen, and two to guard the door. You'll come, Gower, and you, Mansel, and you, Scanlan, and the two Willabys.'

'I promised the new brother he should go,' said the chairman.

Ted Baldwin looked at McMurdo with eyes which showed that he had not forgotten nor forgiven.

'Well, he can come if he wants,' he said, in a surly voice. 'That's enough. The sooner we get to work the better.'

The company broke up with shouts and yells and snatches of drunken song. The bar was still crowded with revellers, and many of the brethren remained there. The little band who had been told off for duty passed out into the street, proceeding in twos and threes along the sidewalk so as not to provoke attention. It was a bitterly cold night, with a half-moon shining brilliantly in a frosty, star-spangled sky. The men stopped and gathered in a yard which faced a high building. The words 'Vermissa Herald' were printed in gold lettering between the brightly lit windows. From within came the clanking of the printing-press.

'Here, you,' said Baldwin to McMurdo; 'you can stand below at the door and see that the road is kept open for us. Arthur Willaby can stay with you. You others come with me. Have no fear, boys, for we have a dozen witnesses that we are in the Union bar at this very moment.'

It was nearly midnight, and the street was deserted save for one or two revellers upon their way home. The party crossed the road and, pushing open the door of the newspaper office, Baldwin and his men rushed in and up the stair which faced them. McMurdo and another remained below. From the room above came a shout, a cry for help, and then the sound of trampling feet and of falling chairs. An instant later a grey-haired man rushed out on to the landing. He was seized before he could get farther, and his spectacles came tinkling down to McMurdo's feet. There was a thud and a groan. He was on his face and half-a-dozen sticks were clattering together as they fell upon him. He writhed, and his long, thin limbs quivered under the blows. The others ceased at last, but Baldwin, his cruel face set in an infernal smile, was hacking at the man's head, which he vainly endeavoured to defend with his arms. His white hair was dabbled with patches of blood. Baldwin was still stooping over his victim, putting in a short, vicious blow whenever he could see a part exposed, when McMurdo dashed up the stair and pushed him back.

'You'll kill the man,' said he. 'Drop it!'

Baldwin looked at him in amazement.

'Curse you!' he cried. 'Who are you to interfere – you that are new to the Lodge? Stand back!' He raised his stick, but McMurdo had whipped his pistol out of his hip pocket.

'Stand back yourself!' he cried. 'I'll blow your face in if you lay a hand on me. As to the Lodge, wasn't it the order of the body-master that the man was not to be killed, and what are you doing but killing him?'

'It's truth he says,' remarked one of the men.

'By gosh, you'd best hurry yourselves!' cried the man below. 'The windows are all lighting up and you'll have the whole township on your back inside of five minutes.'

There was indeed the sound of shouting in the street, and a little group of compositors and typesetters was forming in the hall below and nerving itself to action. Leaving the limp and motionless body of the editor at the head of the stair, the criminals rushed down and made their way swiftly along the street. Having reached the Union House, some of them mixed with the crowd in McGinty's saloon, whispering across the bar to the Boss that the job had been well carried through. Others, and among them McMurdo, broke away into side-streets, and so by devious paths to their own homes.

Chapter Four
The Valley of Fear

When McMurdo awoke next morning he had good reason to remember his initiation into the Lodge. His head ached with the effect of the drink, and his arm, where he had been branded, was hot and swollen. Having his own peculiar source of income, he was irregular in his attendance at his work, so he had a late breakfast and remained at home for the morning, writing a long letter to a friend. Afterwards he read the *Daily Herald*. In a special column, put in at the last moment, he read, 'Outrage at the *Herald* Office. Editor seriously injured.' It was a short account of the facts with which he was himself more familiar than the writer could have been. It ended with the statement:

> The matter is now in the hands of the police, but it can hardly be hoped that their exertions will be attended by any better results than in the past. Some of the men were recognized, and there is hope that a conviction may be obtained. The source of the outrage was, it need hardly be said, that infamous society which has held this community in bondage for so long a period, and against which the *Herald* has taken so uncompromising a stand. Mr Stanger's many friends will rejoice to hear that, though he has been cruelly and brutally beaten and has sustained severe injuries about the head, there is no immediate danger to his life.

Below, it stated that a guard of Coal and Iron Police, armed with Winchester rifles, had been requisitioned for the defence of the office.

McMurdo had laid down the paper, and was lighting his pipe

with a hand which was shaky from the excesses of the previous evening, when there was a knock outside, and his landlady brought to him a note which had just been handed in by a lad. It was unsigned, and ran thus:

I should wish to speak to you, but had rather not do so in your house. You will find me beside the flagstaff upon Miller Hill. If you will come there now I have something which it is important for you to hear and for me to say.

McMurdo read the note twice with the utmost surprise, for he could not imagine what it meant or who was the author of it. Had it been in a feminine hand he might have imagined that it was the beginning of one of those adventures which had been familiar enough in his past life. But it was the writing of a man, and of a well-educated one, too. Finally, after some hesitation, he determined to see the matter through.

Miller Hill is an ill-kept public park in the very centre of the town. In summer it is a favourite resort of the people, but in winter it is desolate enough. From the top of it one has a view not only of the whole grimy, straggling town, but of the winding valley beneath, with its scattered mines and factories blackening the snow on either side of it, and of the wooded and white-capped ranges which flank it. McMurdo strolled up the winding path hedged in with evergreen until he reached the deserted restaurant which forms the centre of summer gaiety. Beside it was a bare flagstaff, and underneath it a man, his hat drawn down and the collar of his overcoat raised up. When he turned his face McMurdo saw that it was Brother Morris, he who had incurred the anger of the bodymaster the night before. The Lodge sign was given and exchanged as they met.

'I wanted to have a word with you, Mr McMurdo,' said the older man, speaking with a hesitation which showed that he was on delicate ground. 'It was kind of you to come.'

'Why did you not put your name to the note?'

'One has to be cautious, mister. One never knows in times like these how a thing may come back to one. One never knows either who to trust or who not to trust.'

'Surely one may trust brothers of the Lodge?'

'No, no; not always,' cried Morris, with vehemence. 'Whatever we say, even what we think, seems to go back to that man, McGinty.'

'Look here,' said McMurdo, sternly; 'it was only last night, as you know well, that I swore good faith to our bodymaster. Would you be asking me to break my oath?'

'If that is the view you take,' said Morris, sadly, 'I can only say that I am sorry I gave you the trouble to come to meet me. Things have come to a bad pass when two free citizens cannot speak their thoughts to each other.'

McMurdo, who had been watching his companion very narrowly, relaxed somewhat in his bearing.

'Sure, I spoke for myself only,' said he. 'I am a newcomer, as you know, and I am strange to it all. It is not for me to open my mouth, Mr Morris, and if you think well to say anything to me I am here to hear it.'

'And to take it back to Boss McGinty,' said Morris, bitterly.

'Indeed, then, you do me injustice there,' cried McMurdo. 'For myself I am loyal to the Lodge, and so I tell you straight, but I would be a poor creature if I were to repeat to any other what you might say to me in confidence. It will go no further than me, though I warn you that you may get neither help nor sympathy.'

'I have given up looking for either the one or the other,' said Morris. 'I may be putting my very life in your hands by what I say, but, bad as you are – and it seemed to me last night that you were shaping to be as bad as the worst – still you are new to it, and your conscience cannot yet be as hardened as theirs. That was why I thought to speak with you.'

'Well, what have you to say?'

'If you give me away, may a curse be on you!'

'Sure, I said I would not.'

'I would ask you, then, when you joined the Freemen's Society in Chicago, and swore vows of charity and fidelity, did ever it cross your mind that you might find it would lead you to crime?'

'If you call it crime,' McMurdo answered.

'Call it crime!' cried Morris, his voice vibrating with passion. 'You have seen little of it if you can call it anything else. Was it crime last night when a man, old enough to be your father, was beaten till the blood dripped from his white hairs? Was that crime – or what else would you call it?'

'There are some would say it was war,' said McMurdo. 'A war of two classes with all in, so that each struck as best it could.'

'Well, did you think of such a thing when you joined the Freemen's Society in Chicago?'

'No, I'm bound to say I did not.'

'Nor did I when I joined it at Philadelphia. It was just a benefit club and a meeting-place for one's fellows. Then I heard of this place – curse the hour that the name first fell upon my ears! – and I came to better myself. My God, to better myself! My wife and three children came with me. I started a dry-goods store in Market Square, and I prospered well. The word had gone round that I was a Freeman, and I was forced to join the local Lodge, same as you did last night. I've the badge of shame on my forearm, and something worse branded on my heart. I found that I was under the orders of a black villain, and caught in a meshwork of crime. What could I do? Every word I said to make things better was taken as treason, same as it was last night. I can't get away, for all I have in the world is in my store. If I leave the society, I know well that it means murder to me, and God knows what to my wife and children. Oh, man, it is awful – awful!' He put his hands to his face, and his body shook with convulsive sobs.

McMurdo shrugged his shoulders.

'You were too soft for the job,' said he. 'You are the wrong sort
for such work.'

'I had a conscience and a religion, but they made me a criminal
among them. I was chosen for a job. If I backed down I knew well
what would come to me. Maybe I'm a coward. Maybe it's the
thought of my poor little woman and the children that makes me
one. Anyhow, I went. I guess it will haunt me for ever. It was a
lonely house, twenty miles from here, over the range yonder. I
was told off for the door, same as you were last night. They could
not trust me with the job. The others went in. When they came
out their hands were crimson to the wrists. As we turned away a
child was screaming out of the house behind us. It was a boy of
five who had seen his father murdered. I nearly fainted with the
horror of it, and yet I had to keep a bold and smiling face, for well
I knew that if I did not it would be out of my house that they
would come next with their bloody hands, and it would be my
little Fred that would be screaming for his father. But I was a
criminal then – part sharer in a murder, lost for ever in this world,
and lost also in the next. I am a good Catholic, but the priest
would have no word with me when he heard I was a Scowrer, and
I am excommunicated from my faith. That's how it stands with
me. And I see you going down the same road, and I ask you what
the end is to be? Are you ready to be a cold-blooded murderer
also, or can we do anything to stop it?'

'What would you do?' asked McMurdo, abruptly. 'You would
not inform?'

'God forbid!' cried Morris. 'Sure, the very thought would cost
me my life.'

'That's well,' said McMurdo. 'I'm thinking that you are a weak
man, and that you make too much of the matter.'

'Too much! Wait till you have lived here longer. Look down
the valley. See the cloud of a hundred chimneys that over-shadows
it. I tell you that the cloud of murder hangs thicker and lower

than that over the heads of the people. It is the Valley of Fear – the Valley of Death. The terror is in the hearts of the people from the dusk to the dawn. Wait, young man, and you will learn for yourself.'

'Well, I'll let you know what I think when I have seen more,' said McMurdo, carelessly. 'What is very clear is that you are not the man for the place, and that the sooner you sell out – if you only get a dime a dollar for what the business is worth – the better it will be for you. What you have said is safe with me, but, by gosh! if I thought you were an informer –'

'No, no!' cried Morris, piteously.

'Well, let it rest at that. I'll bear what you have said in mind, and maybe some day I'll come back to it. I expect you meant kindly by speaking to me like this. Now I'll be getting home.'

'One word before you go,' said Morris. 'We may have been seen together. They may want to know what we have spoken about.'

'Ah, that's well thought of.'

'I offer you a clerkship in my store.'

'And I refuse it. That's our business. Well, so long, Brother Morris, and may you find things go better with you in the future.'

That same afternoon, as McMurdo sat smoking, lost in thought, beside the stove of his sitting-room, the door swung open, and its framework was filled with the huge figure of Boss McGinty. He passed the sign, and then, seating himself opposite to the young man, he looked at him steadily for some time, a look which was as steadily returned.

'I'm not much of a visitor, Brother McMurdo,' he said, at last. 'I guess I am too busy over the folk that visit me. But I thought I'd stretch a point and drop down to see you in your own house.'

'I'm proud to see you here, Councillor,' McMurdo answered, heartily, bringing his whisky-bottle out of the cupboard. 'It's an honour that I had not expected.'

'How's the arm?' asked the Boss.

McMurdo made a wry face.

'Well, I'm not forgetting it,' he said. 'But it's worth it.'

'Yes, it's worth it,' the other answered, 'to those that are loyal, and go through with it, and are a help to the Lodge. What were you speaking to Brother Morris about on Miller Hill this morning?'

The question came so suddenly that it was well that he had his answer prepared. He burst into a hearty laugh.

'Morris didn't know I could earn a living here at home. He sha'n't know either, for he has got too much conscience for the likes of me. But he's a good-hearted old chap. It was his idea that I was at a loose end, and that he would do me a good turn by offering me a clerkship in a dry-goods store.'

'Oh, that was it?'

'Yes, that was it.'

'And you refused it?'

'Sure. Couldn't I earn ten times as much in my own bedroom with four hours' work?'

'That's so. But I wouldn't get about too much with Morris.'

'Why not?'

'Well, I guess because I tell you not. That's enough for most folk in these parts.'

'It may be enough for most folks, but it ain't enough for me, Councillor,' said McMurdo, boldly. 'If you are a judge of men you'll know that.'

The swarthy giant glared at him, and his hairy paw closed for an instant round the glass as though he would hurl it at the head of his companion. Then he laughed in his loud, boisterous, insincere fashion.

'You're a queer card, for sure,' said he. 'Well, if you want reasons I'll give them. Did Morris say nothing to you against the Lodge?'

'No.'

'Nor against me?'

'No.'

'Well, that's because he daren't trust you. But in his heart he is not a loyal brother. We know that well, so we watch him, and we wait for the time to admonish him. I'm thinking that the time is drawing near. There's no room for scabby sheep in our pen. But if you keep company with a disloyal man, we might think that you were disloyal, too. See?'

'There's no chance of my keeping company with him, for I dislike the man,' McMurdo answered. 'As to being disloyal, if it was any man but you, he would not use the word to me twice.'

'Well, that's enough,' said McGinty, draining off his glass. 'I came down to give you a word in season, and you've had it.'

'I'd like to know,' said McMurdo, 'how you ever came to learn that I had spoken with Morris at all.'

McGinty laughed.

'It's my business to know what goes on in this township,' said he. 'I guess you'd best reckon on my hearing all that passes. Well, time's up, and I'll just say –'

But his leave-taking was cut short in a very unexpected fashion. With a sudden crash the door flew open, and three frowning, intent faces glared in at them from under the peaks of police caps. McMurdo sprang to his feet and half drew his revolver, but his arm stopped midway as he became conscious that two Winchester rifles were levelled at his head. A man in uniform advanced into the room, a six-shooter in his hand. It was Captain Marvin, once of Chicago, and now of the Coal and Iron Constabulary. He shook his head with a half smile at McMurdo.

'I thought you'd be getting into trouble, Mr Crooked McMurdo of Chicago,' said he. 'Can't keep out of it, can you? Take your hat and come along with us.'

'I guess you'll pay for this, Captain Marvin,' said McGinty. 'Who are you, I'd like to know, to break into a house in this fashion, and molest honest, law-abiding men?'

'You're standing out in this deal, Councillor McGinty,' said the police captain. 'We are not out after you, but after this man McMurdo. It is for you to help, not to hinder us in our duty.'

'He is a friend of mine, and I'll answer for his conduct,' said the Boss.

'By all accounts, Mr McGinty, you may have to answer for your own conduct some of these days,' the police captain answered. 'This man McMurdo was a crook before ever he came here, and he's a crook still. Cover him, patrolman, while I disarm him.'

'There's my pistol,' said McMurdo, coolly. 'Maybe, Captain Marvin, if you and I were alone and face to face, you would not take me so easily.'

'Where's your warrant?' asked McGinty. 'By gosh! a man might as well live in Russia as in Vermissa while folk like you are running the police. It's a capitalist outrage, and you'll hear more of it, I reckon.'

'You do what you think is your duty the best way you can, Councillor. We'll look after ours.'

'What am I accused of?' asked McMurdo.

'Of being concerned in the beating of old Editor Stanger at the *Herald* office. It wasn't your fault that it isn't a murder charge.'

'Well, if that's all you have against him,' cried McGinty, with a laugh, 'you can save yourself a deal of trouble by dropping it right now. This man was with me in my saloon playing poker up to midnight, and I can bring a dozen to prove it.'

'That's your affair, and I guess you can settle it in court tomorrow. Meanwhile, come on, McMurdo, and come quietly if you don't want a gun-butt across your head. You stand wide, Mr McGinty, for I warn you I will brook no resistance when I am on duty.'

So determined was the appearance of the captain that both McMurdo and his Boss were forced to accept the situation. The latter managed to have a few whispered words with the prisoner before they parted.

'What about –' He jerked his thumb upwards to signify the coining plant.

'All right,' whispered McMurdo, who had devised a safe hiding-place under the floor.

'I'll bid you good-bye,' said the Boss, shaking hands. 'I'll see Reilly, the lawyer, and take the defence upon myself. Take my word for it that they won't be able to hold you.'

'I wouldn't bet on that. Guard the prisoner, you two, and shoot him if he tries any games. I'll search the house before I leave.'

Marvin did so, but apparently found no trace of the concealed plant. When he had descended he and his men escorted McMurdo to the headquarters. Darkness had fallen and a keen blizzard was blowing, so that the streets were nearly deserted, but a few loiterers followed the group and, emboldened by invisibility, shouted imprecations at the prisoner.

'Lynch the cursed Scowrer!' they cried. 'Lynch him!' They laughed and jeered as he was pushed into the police depot. After a short formal examination from the inspector-in-charge, he was handed on to the common cell. Here he found Baldwin and three other criminals of the night before, all arrested that afternoon, and waiting their trial next morning.

But even within this inner fortress of the law the long arm of the Freemen was able to extend. Late at night there came a jailer with a straw bundle for their bedding, out of which he extracted two bottles of whisky, some glasses, and a pack of cards. They spent an hilarious night without an anxious thought as to the ordeal of the morning.

Nor had they cause, as the result was to show. The magistrate could not possibly, on the evidence, have brought in the sentence which would have carried the matter to a higher court. On the one hand, the compositors and pressmen were forced to admit that the light was uncertain, that they were themselves much perturbed, and that it was difficult for them to absolutely swear to the identity of the assailants, although they believed that the accused were among them. Cross-examined by the clever attorney who had been engaged by McGinty, they were even more nebulous in their evidence.

The injured man had already deposed that he was so taken by surprise by the suddenness of the attack that he could state nothing beyond the fact that the first man who struck him wore a moustache. He added that he knew them to be Scowrers, since no one else in the community could possibly have any enmity to him, and he had long been threatened on account of his outspoken editorials. On the other hand, it was clearly shown by the united and unfaltering evidence of six citizens, including that high municipal official Councillor McGinty, that the men had been at a card party at the Union House until an hour very much later than the commission of the outrage. Needless to say that they were discharged with something very near to an apology from the Bench for the inconvenience to which they had been put, together with an implied censure of Captain Marvin and the police for their officious zeal.

The verdict was greeted with loud applause by a Court in which McMurdo saw many familiar faces. Brothers of the Lodge smiled and waved. But there were others who sat with compressed lips and brooding eyes as the men filed out of the dock. One of them, a little dark-bearded, resolute fellow, put the thoughts of himself and comrades into words as the ex-prisoners passed him.

'You damned murderers!' he said. 'We'll fix you yet.'

Chapter Five

The Darkest Hour

If anything had been needed to give an impetus to Jack McMurdo's popularity among his fellows, it would have been his arrest and acquittal. That a man on the very night of joining the Lodge should have done something which brought him before the magistrate was a new record in the annals of the society. Already he had earned the reputation of a good boon companion, a cheery reveller, and withal a man of high temper, who would not take an insult even from the all-powerful Boss himself. But, in addition to this, he impressed his comrades with the idea that among them all there was not one whose brain was so ready to devise a bloodthirsty scheme, or whose hand would be more capable of carrying it out. 'He'll be the boy for the clean job,' said the oldsters to each other, and waited their time until they could set him to his work. McGinty had instruments enough already, but he recognized that this was a supremely able one. He felt like a man holding a fierce bloodhound in leash. There were curs to do the smaller work, but some day he would slip this creature upon its prey. A few members of the Lodge, Ted Baldwin among them, resented the rapid rise of the stranger, and hated him for it, but they kept clear of him, for he was as ready to fight as to laugh.

But if he gained favour with his fellows, there was another quarter, one which had become even more vital to him, in which he lost it. Ettie Shafter's father would have nothing more to do with him, nor would he allow him to enter the house. Ettie herself was too deeply in love to give him up altogether, and yet her own good sense warned her of what would come from a marriage with a man who was regarded as a criminal. One morning after a sleepless night she determined to see him, possibly for the last time, and make one strong endeavour to draw him from those evil influences which were sucking him down. She went to his house, as he had often begged her to do, and made her way into the room which he used as his sitting-room. He was seated at a table with his back turned and a letter in front of him. A sudden spirit of girlish mischief came over her – she was still only nineteen. He had not heard her when she pushed open the door. Now she tip-toed forward, and laid her hand lightly upon his bended shoulders.

If she had expected to startle him, she certainly succeeded, but only in turn to be startled herself. With a tiger spring he turned on her, and his right hand was feeling for her throat. At the same instant, with the other hand he crumpled up the paper that lay before him. For a moment he stood glaring. Then astonishment and joy took the place of the ferocity which had convulsed his features – a ferocity which had sent her shrinking back in horror as from something which had never before intruded into her gentle life.

'It's you!' said he, mopping his brow. 'And to think that you should come to me, heart of my hearts, and I should find nothing better to do than to want to strangle you! Come then, darling,' and he held out his arms. 'Let me make it up to you.'

But she had not recovered from that sudden glimpse of guilty fear which she had read in the man's face. All her woman's instinct told her that it was not the mere fright of a man who is startled. Guilt – that was it – guilt and fear.

'What's come over you, Jack?' she cried. 'Why were you so scared of me? Oh, Jack, if your conscience was at ease, you would not have looked at me like that.'

'Sure, I was thinking of other things, and when you came tripping so lightly on those fairy feet of yours –'

'No, no; it was more than that, Jack.' Then a sudden suspicion seized her. 'Let me see that letter you were writing.'

'Ah, Ettie, I couldn't do that.'

Her suspicions became certainties.

'It's to another woman!' she cried. 'I know it. Why else should you hold it from me? Was it to your wife that you were writing? How am I to know that you are not a married man – you, a stranger, that nobody knows?'

'I am not married, Ettie. See now, I swear it. You're the only one woman on earth to me. By the Cross of Christ, I swear it!'

He was so white with passionate earnestness that she could not but believe him.

'Well, then,' she cried, 'why will you not show me the letter?'

'I'll tell you, acushla,' said he. 'I'm under oath not to show it, and just as I wouldn't break my word to you, so I would keep it to those who hold my promise. It's the business of the Lodge, and even to you it's secret. And if I was scared when a hand fell on me, can't you understand it when it might have been the hand of a detective?'

She felt that he was telling the truth. He gathered her into his arms, and kissed away her fears and doubts.

'Sit here by me, then. It's a queer throne for such a queen, but it's the best your poor lover can find. He'll do better for you some of these days, I'm thinking. Now your mind is easy once again, is it not?'

'How can it ever be at ease, Jack, when I know that you are a criminal among criminals – when I never know the day that I may hear that you are in the dock for murder? McMurdo the Scowrer – that was what one of our boarders called you yesterday. It went through my heart like a knife.'

'Sure, hard words break no bones.'

'But they were true.'

'Well, dear, it's not as bad as you think. We are but poor men that are trying in our own way to get our rights.'

Ettie threw her arms round her lover's neck.

'Give it up, Jack! For my sake – for God's sake, give it up! It was to ask you that I came here today. Oh, Jack, see, I beg it of you on my bended knees. Kneeling here before you, I implore you to give it up.'

He raised her, and soothed her with her head against his breast.

'Sure, my darlin', you don't know what it is you are asking. How could I give it up when it would be to break my oath and to desert my comrades? If you could see how things stand with me, you could never ask it of me. Besides, if I wanted to, how could I do it? You don't suppose that the Lodge would let a man go free with all its secrets?'

'I've thought of that, Jack. I've planned it all. Father has saved some money. He is weary of this place, where the fear of these people darkens our lives. He is ready to go. We would fly together to Philadelphia or New York, where we should be safe from them.'

McMurdo laughed.

'The Lodge has a long arm. Do you think it could not stretch from here to Philadelphia or New York?'

'Well, then, to the West, or to England, or to Sweden, whence father came. Anywhere to get away from this Valley of Fear.'

McMurdo thought of old Brother Morris.

'Sure, it is the second time I have heard the valley so named,' said he. 'The shadow does indeed seem to lie heavy on some of you.'

'It darkens every moment of our lives. Do you suppose that Ted Baldwin has ever forgiven us? If it were not that he fears you, what do you suppose that our chances would be? If you saw the look in those dark, hungry eyes of his when they fall on me!'

'By gosh! I'd teach him better manners if I caught him at it. But see here, little girl. I can't leave here. I can't. Take that from me once and for all. But if you will leave me to find my own way, I will try to prepare a way of getting honourably out of it.'

'There is no honour in such a matter.'

'Well, well, it's just how you look at it. But if you'll give me six months I'll work it so as I can leave without being ashamed to look others in the face.'

The girl laughed with joy.

'Six months!' she cried. 'Is it a promise?'

'Well, it may be seven or eight. But within a year at the farthest we will leave the valley behind us.'

It was the most that Ettie could obtain, and yet it was something. There was this distant light to illuminate the gloom of the immediate future. She returned to her father's house more light-hearted than she had ever been since Jack McMurdo had come into her life.

It might be thought that as a member all the doings of the society would be told to him, but he was soon to discover that the organization was wider and more complex than the simple Lodge. Even Boss McGinty was ignorant as to many things, for there was an official named the county delegate, living at Hobson's Patch, farther down the line, who had power over several different Lodges, which he wielded in a sudden and arbitrary way. Only once did McMurdo see him, a sly little grey-haired rat of a man with a slinking gait and a sidelong glance which was charged with malice. Evans Pott was his name, and even the great Boss of Vermissa felt towards him something of the repulsion and fear which the huge Danton may have felt for the puny but dangerous Robespierre.

One day Scanlan, who was McMurdo's fellow-boarder, received a note from McGinty, enclosing one from Evans Pott, which informed him that he was sending over two good men, Lawler and Andrews, who had instructions to act in the neighbourhood, though it was best for the cause that no particulars as to their objects should be given. Would the bodymaster see to it that suitable arrangements be made for their lodgings and comfort until the time for action should arrive? McGinty added that it was impossible for any one to remain secret at the Union House, and that, therefore, he would be obliged if McMurdo and Scanlan would put the strangers up for a few days in their boarding-house.

The same evening the two men arrived, each carrying his grip-sack. Lawler was an elderly man, shrewd, silent, and self-contained, clad in an old black frock-coat, which, with his soft felt hat and ragged, grizzled beard, gave him a general resemblance to an itinerant preacher. His companion, Andrews, was little more than a boy, frank-faced and cheerful, with the breezy manner of one who is out for a holiday, and means to enjoy every minute of it. Both of the men were total abstainers, and behaved in all ways as exemplary members of society, with the one single exception that they were assassins who had often proved themselves to be most capable instruments for this Association of murder. Lawler had already carried out fourteen commissions of the kind, and Andrews three.

They were, as McMurdo found, quite ready to converse about their deeds in the past, which they recounted with the half-bashful pride of men who had done good and unselfish service for the community. They were reticent, however, as to the immediate job in hand.

'They chose us because neither I nor the boy here drink,' Lawler explained. 'They can count on us saying no more than we should. You must not take it amiss but it is the orders of the county delegate that we obey.'

'Sure, we are all in it together,' said Scanlan, McMurdo's mate, as the four sat together at supper.

'That's true enough, and we'll talk till the cows come home of the killing of Charlie Williams, or of Simon Bird, or any other job in the past. But till the work is done we say nothing.'

'There are half-a-dozen about here that I have a word to say to,' said McMurdo, with an oath. 'I suppose it isn't Jack Knox, of Ironhill, that you are after? I'd go some way to see him get his deserts.'

'No; it's not him yet.'

'Or Herman Strauss?'

'No, nor him either.'

'Well, if you won't tell us, we can't make you, but I'd be glad to know.'

Lawler smiled, and shook his head. He was not to be drawn.

In spite of the reticence of their guests, Scanlan and McMurdo were quite determined to be present at what they called the 'fun'. When, therefore, at an early hour one morning McMurdo heard them creeping down the stairs, he awakened Scanlan, and the two hurried on their clothes. When they were dressed they found that the others had stolen out, leaving the door open behind them. It was not yet dawn, and by the light of the lamps they could see the two men some distance down the street. They followed them warily, treading noiselessly in the deep snow.

The boarding-house was near the edge of the township, and soon they were at the cross-roads which are beyond its boundary. Here three men were waiting, with whom Lawler and Andrews held a short, eager conversation. Then they all moved on together. It was clearly some notable job which needed numbers. At this point there are several trails which lead to various mines. The strangers took that which led to the Crow Hill, a huge business which was in strong hands, who had been able, thanks to their energetic and fearless New England manager, Josiah H. Dunn, to keep some order and discipline during the long reign of terror.

Day was breaking now, and a line of workmen were slowly making their way, singly and in groups, along the blackened path.

McMurdo and Scanlan strolled on with the others, keeping in sight of the men whom they followed. A thick mist lay over them, and from the heart of it there came the sudden scream of a steam whistle. It was the ten-minute signal before the cages descended and the day's labour began.

When they reached the open space round the mineshaft there were a hundred miners waiting, stamping their feet and blowing on their fingers, for it was bitterly cold. The strangers stood in a little group under the shadow of the engine-house. Scanlan and McMurdo climbed a heap of slag, from which the whole scene lay before them. They saw the mine engineer, a great bearded Scotsman named Menzies, come out of the engine-house and blow his whistle for the cages to be lowered. At the same instant a tall, loose-framed young man, with a clean-shaven, earnest face, advanced eagerly towards the pit-head. As he came forward his eyes fell upon the group, silent and motionless, under the engine-house. The men had drawn down their hats and turned up their collars to screen their faces. For a moment the presentiment of death laid its cold hand upon the manager's heart. At the next he had shaken it off and saw only his duty towards intrusive strangers.

'Who are you?' he asked, as he advanced. 'What are you loitering there for?'

There was no answer, but the lad Andrews stepped forward and shot him in the stomach. The hundred waiting miners stood as motionless and helpless as if they were paralysed. The manager clapped his two hands to the wound and doubled himself up. Then he staggered away, but another of the assassins fired, and he went down sideways, kicking and clawing among a heap of clinkers. Menzies, the Scotsman, gave a roar of rage at the sight, and rushed with an iron spanner at the murderers, but was met by two balls in the face, which dropped him dead at their very feet. There was a surge forward of some of the miners, and an inarticulate cry of pity and of anger, but a couple of the strangers emptied their six-shooters over the heads of the crowd, and they broke and scattered, some of them rushing wildly back to their homes in Vermissa. When a few of the bravest had rallied, and there was a return to the mine, the murderous gang had vanished in the mists of the morning without a single witness being able to swear to the identity of these men who in front of a hundred spectators had wrought this double crime.

Scanlan and McMurdo made their way back, Scanlan some-what subdued, for it was the first murder job that he had seen with his own eyes, and it appeared less funny than he had been led to believe. The horrible screams of the dead manager's wife pursued them as they hurried to the town. McMurdo was absorbed and silent, but he showed no sympathy for the weaken-ing of his companion.

'Sure, it is like a war,' he repeated. 'What is it but a war between us and them, and we hit back where we best can?'

There was high revel in the Lodge room at the Union House that night, not only over the killing of the manager and engineer of the Crow Hill mine, which would bring this organization into line with the other blackmailed and terror-stricken companies of the district, but also over a distant triumph which had been wrought by the hands of the Lodge itself. It would appear that when the county delegate had sent over five good men to strike a blow in Vermissa, he had demanded that, in return, three Vermissa men should be secretly selected and sent across to kill William Hales, of Stake Royal, one of the best-known and most popular mine-owners in the Gilmerton district, a man who was believed not to have an enemy in the world, for he was in all ways a pattern employer. He had insisted, however, upon efficiency in the work, and had there-fore paid off certain drunken and idle *employés* who were members of the all-powerful society. Coffin notices hung outside his door had not weakened his resolution, and so in a free, civilized country he found himself condemned to death.

The execution had now been duly carried out. Ted Baldwin, who sprawled in the seat of honour beside the bodymaster, had been the chief of the party. His flushed face and glazed, blood-shot eyes told of sleeplessness and drink. He and his two comrades had spent the night before among the mountains. They were unkempt and weather-stained. But no heroes, returning from a forlorn hope, could have had a warmer welcome from their com-rades. The story was told and retold amid cries of delight and shouts of laughter. They had waited for their man as he drove home at nightfall, taking their station at the top of a steep hill, where his horse must be at a walk. He was so furred to keep out the cold that he could not lay his hand on his pistol. They had pulled him out and shot him again and again.

None of them knew the man, but there is eternal drama in a killing, and they had shown the Scowrers of Gilmerton that the Vermissa men were to be relied upon. There had been one *contre-temps*, for a man and his wife had driven up while they were still emptying their revolvers into the silent body. It had been suggested that they should shoot them both, but they were harmless folk who were not connected with the mines, so they were sternly bidden to drive on and keep silent, lest a worse thing befall them. And so the blood-mottled figure had been left as a warning to all such hard-hearted employers, and the three noble avengers had hurried off into the mountains where unbroken Nature comes down to the very edge of the furnaces and the slag-heaps.

It had been a great day for the Scowrers. The shadow had fallen even darker over the valley. But as the wise general chooses the moment of victory in which to redouble his efforts, so that his foes may have no time to steady themselves after disaster, so Boss McGinty, looking out upon the scene of his operations with brooding and malicious eyes, had devised a new attack upon those who opposed him. That very night, as the half-drunken company broke up, he touched McMurdo on the arm and led him aside into that inner room where they had their first interview.

'See here, my lad,' said he, 'I've got a job that's worthy of you at last. You'll have the doing of it in your own hands.'

'Proud I am to hear it,' McMurdo answered.

'You can take two men with you – Manders and Reilly. They have been warned for service. We'll never be right in this district until Chester Wilcox has been settled, and you'll have the thanks of every Lodge in the coalfields if you can down him.'

'I'll do my best, anyhow. Who is he, and where shall I find him?'

McGinty took his eternal half-chewed, half-smoked cigar from the corner of his mouth, and proceeded to draw a rough diagram on a page torn from his notebook.

'He's the chief foreman of the Iron Dyke Company. He's a hard citizen, an old colour-sergeant of the war, all scars and grizzle. We've had two tries at him, but had no luck, and Jim Carnaway lost his life over it. Now it's for you to take it over. That's the house, all alone at the Iron Dyke cross-road, same as you see here in the map, without another within earshot. It's no good by day. He's armed, and shoots quick and straight, with no questions asked. But at night – well, there he is, with his wife, three children, and a hired help. You can't pick or choose. It's all or none. If you could get a bag of blasting powder at the front door with a slow match to it –'

'What's the man done?'

'Didn't I tell you he shot Jim Carnaway?'

'Why did he shoot him?'

'What in thunder has that to do with you? Carnaway was about his house at night, and he shot him. That's enough for me and you. You've got to set the thing right.'

'There's these two women and the children. Do they go up, too?'

'They have to, else how can we get him?'

'It seems hard on them, for they've done nothing amiss.'

'What sort of talk is this? Do you stand back from it?'

'Easy, Councillor, easy. What have I ever said or done that you should think I would be after standing back from an order of the bodymaster of my own Lodge? If it's right or if it's wrong it's for you to decide.'

'You'll do it, then?'

'Of course I will do it.'

'When?'

'Well, you had best give me a night or two that I may see the house and make my plans. Then –'

'Very good,' said McGinty, shaking him by the hand. 'I leave it with you. It will be a great day when you bring us the news. It's just the last stroke that will bring them all to their knees.'

McMurdo thought long and deeply over the commission which had been so suddenly placed in his hands. The isolated house in which Chester Wilcox lived was about five miles off in an adjacent valley. That very night he started off all alone to prepare for the attempt. It was daylight before he returned from his reconnaissance. Next day he interviewed his two subordinates, Manders and Reilly, reckless youngsters, who were as elated as if it were a deer hunt. Two nights later they met outside the town, all three armed, and one of them carrying a sack stuffed with the powder which was used in the quarries. It was two in the morning before they came to the lonely house. The night was a windy one, with broken clouds drifting swiftly across the face of a three-quarter moon. They had been warned to be on their guard against bloodhounds, so they moved forward cautiously, with their pistols cocked in their hands. But there was no sound save the howling of the wind and no movement but the swaying branches above them. McMurdo listened at the door of the lonely house, but all was still within. Then he leaned the powder bag against it, ripped a hole in it with his knife, and attached the fuse. When it was well alight, he and his two companions took to their heels, and were some distance off, safe and snug in a sheltering ditch, before the shattering roar of the explosion, with the low, deep rumble of the collapsing building, told them that their work was done. No cleaner job had ever been carried out in the blood-stained annals of the society. But, alas, that work so well organized and boldly conceived should all have gone for nothing! Warned by the fate of the various victims, and knowing that he was marked down for destruction, Chester Wilcox had moved himself and his family only the day before to some safer and less known quarters, where a guard of police should watch over them. It was an empty house which had been torn down by the gunpowder, and the grim old colour-sergeant of the war was still teaching discipline to the miners of Iron Dyke.

'Leave him to me,' said McMurdo. 'He's my man, and I'll get him sure, if I have to wait a year for him.'

A vote of thanks and confidence was passed in full Lodge, and so for the time the matter ended. When a few weeks later it was reported in the papers that Wilcox had been shot at from an ambuscade, it was an open secret that McMurdo was still at work upon his unfinished job.

Such were the methods of the Society of Freemen, and such were the deeds of the Scowrers by which they spread their rule of fear over the great and rich district which was for so long a period haunted by their terrible presence. Why should these pages be stained by further crimes? Have I not said enough to show the men and their methods? These deeds are written in history, and there are records wherein one may read the details of them. There one may learn of the shooting of Policemen Hunt and Evans because they had ventured to arrest two members of the society – a double outrage planned at the Vermissa Lodge, and carried out in cold blood upon two helpless and disarmed men. There also one may read of the shooting of Mrs Larbey whilst she was nursing her husband, who had been beaten almost to death by orders of Boss McGinty. The killing of the elder Jenkins, shortly followed by that of his brother, the mutilation of James Murdoch, the blowing-up of the Staphouse family, and the murder of the Stendals all followed hard upon each other in the same terrible winter. Darkly the shadow lay upon the Valley of Fear. The spring had come with running brooks and blossoming trees. There was hope for all Nature, bound so long in an iron grip; but nowhere was there any hope for the men and women who lived under the yoke of the terror. Never had the cloud above them been so dark and hopeless as in the early summer of the year '75.

Chapter Six

Danger

It was the height of the reign of terror. McMurdo, who had already been appointed inner Deacon, with every prospect of some day succeeding McGinty as bodymaster, was now so necessary to the councils of his comrades that nothing was done without his help and advice. The more popular he became, however, with the Freemen, the blacker were the scowls which greeted him as he passed along the streets of Vermissa. In spite of their terror the citizens were taking heart to bind themselves together against their oppressors. Rumours had reached the Lodge of secret gatherings in the *Herald* office and of distribution of firearms among the law-abiding people. But McGinty and his men were undisturbed by such reports. They were numerous, resolute, and well armed. Their opponents were scattered and powerless. It would all end, as it had done in the past, in aimless talk, and possibly in impotent arrests. So said McGinty, McMurdo, and all the bolder spirits.

It was a Saturday evening in May. Saturday was always the Lodge night, and McMurdo was leaving his house to attend it, when Morris, the weaker brother of the Order, came to see him. His brow was creased with care and his kindly face was drawn and haggard.

'Can I speak with you freely, Mr McMurdo?'

'Sure.'

'I can't forget that I spoke my heart to you once, and that you kept it to yourself, even though the Boss himself came to ask you about it.'

'What else could I do if you trusted me? It wasn't that I agreed with what you said.'

'I know that well. But you are the one here I can speak to and be safe. I've a secret here' – he put his hand to his breast – 'and it is just burning the life out of me. I wish it had come to any one of you but me. If I tell it, it will mean murder, for sure. If I don't, it may bring the end of us all. God help me, but I am near out of my wits over it!'

McMurdo looked at the man earnestly. He was trembling in every limb. He poured some whisky into a glass and handed it to him.

'That's the physic for the likes of you,' said he. 'Now let me hear of it.'

Morris drank, and his white face took a tinge of colour.

'I can tell it you all in one sentence,' said he. 'There's a detective on our trail.'

McMurdo stared at him in astonishment.

'Why, man, you're crazy!' he said. 'Isn't the place full of police and detectives, and what harm did they ever do us?'

'No, no; it's no man of the district. As you say, we know them, and it is little that they can do. But you've heard of Pinkerton's?'

'I've read of some folk of that name.'

'Well, you can take it from me you've no show when they are on your trail. It's not a take-it-or-miss-it Government concern. It's a dead earnest business proposition that's out for results, and keeps out till, by hook or by crook, it gets them. If a Pinkerton man is deep in this business we are all destroyed.'

'We must kill him.'

'Ah, it's the first thought that came to you! So it will be up at the Lodge. Didn't I say to you that it would end in murder?'

'Sure, what is murder? Isn't it common enough in these parts?'

'It is indeed, but it's not for me to point out the man that is to be murdered. I'd never rest easy again. And yet it's our own necks that may be at stake. In God's name what shall I do?' He rocked to and fro in his agony of indecision.

But his words had moved McMurdo deeply. It was easy to see

that he shared the other's opinion as to the danger, and the need for meeting it. He gripped Morris's shoulder, and shook him in his earnestness.

'See here, man,' he cried, and he almost screeched the words in his excitement, 'you won't gain anything by sitting keening like an old wife at a wake. Let's have the facts. Who is the fellow? Where is he? How did you hear of him? Why did you come to me?'

'I came to you, for you are the one man that would advise me. I told you that I had a store in the East before I came here. I left good friends behind me, and one of them is in the telegraph service. Here's a letter that I had from him yesterday. It's this part from the top of the page. You can read it for yourself.'

This was what McMurdo read:

'How are the Scowrers getting on in your parts? We read plenty of them in the papers. Between you and me I expect to hear news from you before long. Five big corporations and the two railroads have taken the thing up in dead earnest. They mean it, and you can bet they'll get there. They are right deep down into it. Pinkerton has taken hold under their orders, and his best man, Birdy Edwards, is operating. The thing has got to be stopped right now.'

'Now read the postscript.'

'Of course, what I give you is what I learned in business, so it goes no further. It's a queer cipher that you handle by the yard every day and can get no meaning from.'

McMurdo sat in silence for some time with the letter in his restless hands. The mist had lifted for a moment, and there was the abyss before him.

'Does anyone else know of this?' he asked.

'I have told no one else.'

'But this man – your friend – has he any other person that he would be likely to write to?'

'Well, I dare say he knows one or two more.'

'Of the Lodge?'

'It's likely enough.'

'I was asking because it is likely that he may have given some description of this fellow, Birdy Edwards. Then we could get on his trail.'

'Well, it's possible. But I should not think he knew him. He is just telling me the news that came to him by way of business. How would he know this Pinkerton man?'

McMurdo gave a violent start.

'By gosh!' he cried, 'I've got him. What a fool I was not to know it! Lord, but we're in luck! We will fix him before he can do any harm. See here, Morris; will you leave this thing in my hands?'

'Sure, if you will only take it off mine!'

'I'll do that. You can stand right back and let me run it. Even your name need not be mentioned. I'll take it all on myself as if it were to me that this letter has come. Will that content you?'

'It's just what I would ask.'

'Then leave it at that and keep your head shut. Now I'll get down to the Lodge, and we'll soon make old man Pinkerton sorry for himself.'

'You wouldn't kill this man?'

'The less you know, friend Morris, the easier your conscience will be and the better you will sleep. Ask no questions, and let things settle themselves. I have hold of it now.'

Morris shook his head sadly as he left.

'I feel that his blood is on my hands,' he groaned.

'Self-protection is no murder, anyhow,' said McMurdo, smiling grimly. 'It's him or us. I guess this man would destroy us all if we left him long in the valley. Why, Brother Morris, we'll have to elect you bodymaster yet, for you've surely saved the Lodge.'

And yet it was clear from his actions that he thought more seriously of this new intrusion than his words would show. It may have been his guilty conscience; it may have been the reputation of the Pinkerton organization; it may have been the knowledge that great rich corporations had set themselves the task of clearing out the Scowrers; but, whatever his reason, his actions were those of a man who is preparing for the worst. Every paper which could incriminate him was destroyed before he left the house. After that he gave a long sigh of satisfaction, for it seemed to him that he was safe; and yet the danger must still have pressed somewhat upon him, for on his way to the Lodge he stopped at old Shafter's. The house was forbidden him, but when he tapped at the window Ettie came out to him. The dancing Irish devilry had gone from her lover's eyes. She read his danger in his earnest face.

'Something has happened!' she cried. 'Oh, Jack, you are in danger!'

'Sure, it is not very bad, my sweetheart. And yet it may be wise that we make a move before it is worse.'

'Make a move!'

'I promised you once that I would go some day. I think the time is coming. I had news tonight – bad news – and I see trouble coming.'

'The police?'

'Well, a Pinkerton. But, sure, you wouldn't know what that is, acushla, nor what it may mean to the likes of me. I'm too deep in this thing, and I may have to get out of it quick. You said you would come with me if I went.'

'Oh, Jack, it would be the saving of you.'

'I'm an honest man in some things, Ettie. I wouldn't hurt a hair of your bonnie head for all that the world can give, nor ever pull you down one inch from the golden throne above the clouds where I always see you. Would you trust me?'

She put her hand in his without a word.

'Well, then, listen to what I say and do as I order you, for indeed it's the only way for us. Things are going to happen in this valley. I feel it in my bones. There may be many of us that will have to look out for ourselves. I'm one, anyhow. If I go, by day or night, it's you that must come with me!'

'I'd come after you, Jack.'

'No, no; you shall come *with* me. If this valley is closed to me and I can never come back, how can I leave you behind, and me perhaps in hiding from the police with never a chance of a message? It's with me you must come. I know a good woman in the place I come from, and it's there I'd leave you till we can get married. Will you come?'

'Yes, Jack, I will come.'

'God bless you for your trust in me. It's a fiend out of hell that I should be if I abused it. Now, mark you, Ettie, it will be just a word to you, and when it reaches you you will drop everything and come right down to the waiting-hall at the depot and stay there till I come for you.'

'Day or night, I'll come at the word, Jack.'

Somewhat eased in mind now that his own preparations for escape had been begun, McMurdo went on to the Lodge. It had already assembled, and only by complicated signs and countersigns could he pass through the outer guard and inner guard who close-tiled it. A buzz of pleasure and welcome greeted him as he entered. The long room was crowded, and through the haze of tobacco-smoke he saw the tangled black mane of the bodymaster, the cruel, unfriendly features of Baldwin, the vulture face of Harraway, the secretary, and a dozen more who were among the leaders of the Lodge. He rejoiced that they should all be there to take counsel over his news.

'Indeed, it's glad we are to see you, brother!' cried the chairman. 'There's business here that wants a Solomon in judgement to set it right.'

'It's Lander and Egan,' explained his neighbour, as he took his seat. 'They both claim the head-money given by the Lodge for the shooting of old man Crabbe over at Stylestown, and who's to say which fired the bullet?'

McMurdo rose in his place and raised his hand. The expression of his face froze the attention of the audience. There was a dead hush of expectation.

'Worshipful Master,' he said, in a solemn voice, 'I claim urgency.'

'Brother McMurdo claims urgency,' said McGinty. 'It's a claim that by the rules of this Lodge takes precedence. Now, brother, we attend you.'

McMurdo took the letter from his pocket.

'Worshipful Master and brethren,' he said, 'I am the bearer of ill news this day, but it is better that it should be known and discussed than that a blow should fall upon us without warning which would destroy us all. I have information that the most powerful and richest organizations in this State have bound themselves together for our destruction, and that at this very moment there is a Pinkerton detective, one Birdy Edwards, at work in the valley collecting the evidence which may put a rope round the neck of many of us, and send every man in this room into a felon's cell. That is the situation for the discussion of which I have made a claim of urgency.'

There was a dead silence in the room. It was broken by the chairman.

'What is your evidence for this, Brother McMurdo?' he asked.

'It is in this letter which has come into my hands,' said McMurdo. He read the passage aloud. 'It is a matter of honour with me that I can give no further particulars about the letter, nor put it into your hands, but I assure you that there is nothing else in it which can affect the interests of the Lodge. I put the case before you as it has reached me.'

'Let me say, Mr Chairman,' said one of the older brethren, 'that I have heard of Birdy Edwards, and that he has the name of being the best man in the Pinkerton service.'

'Does any one know him by sight?' asked McGinty.

'Yes,' said McMurdo, 'I do.'

There was a murmur of astonishment through the hall.

'I believe we hold him in the hollow of our hands,' he continued, with an exulting smile upon his face. 'If we act quickly and wisely we can cut this thing short. If I have your confidence and your help it is little that we have to fear.'

'What have we to fear anyhow? What can he know of our affairs?'

'You might say so if all were as staunch as you, Councillor. But this man has all the millions of the capitalists at his back. Do you think there is no weaker brother among all our Lodges that could not be bought? He will get at our secrets – maybe has got them already. There's only one sure cure.'

'That he never leaves the valley,' said Baldwin.

McMurdo nodded.

'Good for you, Brother Baldwin,' he said. 'You and I have had our differences, but you have said the true word tonight.'

'Where is he, then? How shall we know him?'

'Worshipful Master,' said McMurdo, earnestly, 'I would put it to you that this is too vital a thing for us to discuss in open Lodge. God forbid that I should throw a doubt on anyone here, but if so much as a word of gossip got to the ears of this man there would be an end of any chance of our getting him. I would ask the Lodge to choose a trusty committee, Mr Chairman – yourself, if I might suggest it, and Brother Baldwin here, and five more. Then I can talk freely of what I know and of what I would advise should be done.'

The proposition was at once adopted and the committee chosen. Besides the chairman and Baldwin, there were the vulture-faced secretary, Harraway; Tiger Cormac, the brutal young assassin; Carter, the treasurer; and the brothers Willaby, who were fearless and desperate men who would stick at nothing.

The usual revelry of the Lodge was short and subdued, for there was a cloud upon the men's spirits, and many there for the first time began to see the cloud of avenging Law drifting up in that serene sky under which they had dwelled so long. The horrors which they had dealt out to others had been so much a part of their settled lives that the thought of retribution had become a remote one, and so seemed the more startling now that it came so closely upon them. They broke up early and left their leaders to their council.

'Now, McMurdo,' said McGinty, when they were alone. The seven men sat frozen in their seats.

'I said just now that I knew Birdy Edwards,' McMurdo explained. 'I need not tell you that he is not here under that name. He's a brave man, I dare bet, but not a crazy one. He passes under the name of Steve Wilson, and he is lodging at Hobson's Patch.'

'How do you know this?'

'Because I fell into talk with him. I thought little of it at the time, nor would have given it a second thought but for this letter, but now I'm sure it's the man. I met him on the cars when I went down the line on Wednesday – a hard case if ever there was one. He said he was a pressman. I believed it for the moment. Wanted to know all he could get about the Scowrers and what he called "the outrages" for the *New York Press*. Asked me every kind of question so as to get something for his paper. You bet I was giving nothing away. "I'd pay for it, and pay well," said he, "if I could get some stuff that would suit my editor." I said what I thought would please him best, and he handed me a twenty-dollar bill for my information. "There's ten times that for you," said he, "if you can find me all that I want."'

'What did you tell him, then?'

'Any stuff I could make up.'

'How do you know he wasn't a newspaper man?'

'I'll tell you. He got out at Hobson's Patch, and so did I. I chanced into the telegraph bureau, and he was leaving it.

' "See here," said the operator, after he'd gone out, "I guess we should charge double rates for this," "I guess you should," said I. He had filled the form with stuff that might have been Chinese for all we could make of it. "He fires a sheet of this off every day," said the clerk. "Yes," said I; "it's special news for his paper, and he's scared that the others should tap it." That was what the operator thought and what I thought at the time, but I think different now.'

'By gosh, I believe you are right!' said McGinty. 'But what do you allow that we should do about it?'

'Why not go right down now and fix him?' someone suggested.

'Aye, the sooner the better.'

'I'd start this next minute if I knew where we could find him,' said McMurdo. 'He's in Hobson's Patch, but I don't know the house. I've got a plan, though, if you'll only take my advice.'

'Well, what is it?'

'I'll go to the Patch tomorrow morning. I'll find him through the operator. He can locate him, I guess. Well, then, I'll tell him that I'm a Freeman myself. I'll offer him all the secrets of the Lodge for a price. You bet he'll tumble to it. I'll tell him the papers are at my house, and that it's as much as my life would be worth to let him come while folk were about. He'll see that that's horse sense. Let him come at ten o'clock at night, and he shall see everything. That will fetch him, sure.'

'Well?'

'You can plan the rest for yourselves. Widow MacNamara's is a lonely house. She's as true as steel and as deaf as a post. There's only Scanlan and me in the house. If I get his promise – and I'll let you know if I do – I'd have the whole seven of you come to me by nine o'clock. We'll get him in. If ever he gets out alive – well, he can talk of Birdy Edwards's luck for the rest of his days.'

'There's going to be a vacancy at Pinkerton's or I'm mistaken,' said McGinty. 'Leave it at that, McMurdo. At nine tomorrow we shall be with you. You once get the door shut behind him, and you can leave the rest with us.'

Chapter Seven

The Trapping of Birdy Edwards

As McMurdo had said, the house in which he lived was a lonely one and very well suited for such a crime as they had planned. It was on the extreme fringe of the town, and stood well back from the road. In any other case the conspirators would have simply called out their man, as they had many a time before, and emptied their pistols into his body; but in this instance it was very necessary to find out how much he knew, how he knew it, and what had been passed on to his employers. It was possible that they were already too late and that the work had been done. If that were indeed so, they could at least have their revenge upon the man who had done it. But they were hopeful that nothing of great importance had yet come to the detective's knowledge, as otherwise, they argued, he would not have troubled to write down and forward such trivial information as McMurdo claimed to have given him. However, all this they would learn from his own lips. Once in their power they would find a way to make him speak. It was not the first time they had handled an unwilling witness.

McMurdo went to Hobson's Patch as agreed. The police seemed to take a particular interest in him that morning, and Captain Marvin – he who had claimed the old acquaintance with him at Chicago – actually addressed him as he waited at the depot. McMurdo turned away and refused to speak with him. He was back from his mission in the afternoon, and saw McGinty at the Union House.

'He is coming,' he said.

'Good!' said McGinty. The giant was in his shirtsleeves, with chains and seals gleaming athwart his ample waistcoat and a diamond twinkling through the fringe of his bristling beard. Drink and politics had made the Boss a very rich as well as powerful man. The more terrible, therefore, seemed that glimpse of the prison or the gallows which had risen before him the night before.

'Do you reckon he knows much?' he asked, anxiously.

McMurdo shook his head gloomily.

'He's been here some time – six weeks at the least. I guess he didn't come into these parts to look at the prospect. If he has been working among us all that time with the railroad money at his back, I should expect that he has got results, and that he has passed them on.'

'There's not a weak man in the Lodge,' cried McGinty. 'True as steel, every man of them. And yet, by the Lord, there is that skunk Morris. What about him? If any man gives us away it would be he. I've a mind to send a couple of the boys round before evening to give him a beating up and see what they can get from him.'

'Well, there would be no harm in that,' McMurdo answered. 'I won't deny that I have a liking for Morris and would be sorry to see him come to harm. He has spoken to me once or twice over Lodge matters, and though he may not see them the same as you or I, he never seemed the sort that squeals. But still, it is not for me to stand between him and you.'

'I'll fix the old devil,' said McGinty, with an oath. 'I've had my eye on him this year past.'

'Well, you know best about that,' McMurdo answered. 'But whatever you do must be tomorrow, for we must lie low until the Pinkerton affair is settled up. We can't afford to set the police buzzing today of all days.'

'True for you,' said McGinty. 'And we'll learn from Birdy Edwards himself where he got his news, if we have to cut his heart out first. Did he seem to scent a trap?'

McMurdo laughed.

'I guess I took him on his weak point,' he said. 'If he could get on a good trail of the Scowrers he's ready to follow it home. I took his money' – McMurdo grinned as he produced a wad of dollar notes – 'and as much more when he has seen all my papers.'

'What papers?'

'Well, there are no papers. But I filled him up about constitutions and books of rules and forms of membership. He expects to get right down to the end of everything before he leaves.'

'Faith, he's right there,' said McGinty, grimly. 'Didn't he ask you why you didn't bring him the papers?'

'As if I would carry such things, and me a suspected man, and Captain Marvin after speaking to me this very day at the depot!'

'Aye, I heard of that,' said McGinty. 'I guess the heavy end of this business is coming on to you. We could put him down an old shaft when we've done with him, but however we work it we can't get past the man living at Hobson's Patch and you being there today.'

McMurdo shrugged his shoulders.

'If we handle it right they can never prove the killing,' said he. 'No one can see him come to the house after dark, and I'll lay to it that no one will see him go. Now, see here, Councillor. I'll show you my plan, and I'll ask you to fit the others into it. You will all come in good time. Very well. He comes at ten. He is to tap three times, and me to open the door for him. Then I'll get behind him and shut it. He's our man then.'

'That's all easy and plain.'

'Yes, but the next step wants considering. He's a hard proposition. He's heavily armed. I've fooled him proper, and yet he is likely to be on his guard. Suppose I show him right into a room with seven men in it where he expected to find me alone. There is going to be shooting and somebody is going to be hurt.'

'That's so.'

'And the noise is going to bring every blamed copper in the township on to the top of us.'

'I guess you are right.'

'This is how I should work it. You will all be in the big

room – same as you saw when you had a chat with me. I'll open the door for him, show him into the parlour beside the door, and leave him there while I get the papers. That will give me the chance of telling you how things are shaping. Then I will go back to him with some faked papers. As he is reading them I will jump for him and get my grip on his pistol arm. You'll hear me call, and in you will rush. The quicker the better, for he is as strong a man as I, and I may have more than I can manage. But I allow that I can hold him till you come.'

'It's a good plan,' said McGinty. 'The Lodge will owe you a debt for this. I guess when I move out of the chair I can put a name to the man that's coming after me.'

'Sure, Councillor, I am little more than a recruit,' said McMurdo, but his face showed what he thought of the great man's compliment.

When he had returned home he made his own preparations for the grim evening in front of him. First he cleaned, oiled, and loaded his Smith and Wesson revolver. Then he surveyed the room in which the detective was to be trapped. It was a large apartment, with a long deal table in the centre and the big stove at one end. At each of the other sides were windows. There were no shutters to these – only light curtains which drew across. McMurdo examined these attentively. No doubt it must have struck him that the apartment was very exposed for so secret a matter. Yet its distance from the road made it of less consequence. Finally he discussed the matter with his fellow-lodger. Scanlan, though a Scowrer, was an inoffensive little man who was too weak to stand against the opinion of his comrades, but was secretly horrified by the deeds of blood at which he had sometimes been forced to assist. McMurdo told him shortly what was intended.

'And if I were you, Mike Scanlan, I would take a night off and keep clear of it. There will be bloody work here before morning.'

'Well, indeed, then, Mac,' Scanlan answered, 'it's not the will but the nerve that is wanting in me. When I saw Manager Dunn go down at the colliery yonder it was just more than I could stand. I'm not made for it, same as you or McGinty. If the Lodge will think none the worse of me, I'll just do as you advise, and leave you to yourselves for the evening.'

The men came in good time as arranged. They were outwardly respectable citizens, well-clad and cleanly, but a judge of faces would have read little hope for Birdy Edwards in those hard mouths and remorseless eyes. There was not a man in the room whose hands had not been reddened a dozen times before. They were as hardened to human murder as a butcher to sheep. Foremost, of course, both in appearance and in guilt, was the formidable Boss. Harraway, the secretary, was a lean, bitter man, with a long, scraggy neck and nervous, jerky limbs – a man of incorruptible fidelity where the finances of the Order were concerned, and with no notion of justice or honesty to anyone beyond. The treasurer, Carter, was a middle-aged man with an impassive, rather sulky expression and a yellow parchment skin. He was a capable organizer, and the actual details of nearly every outrage had sprung from his plotting brain. The two Willabys were men of action, tall, lithe young fellows with determined faces, while their companion, Tiger Cormac, a heavy, dark youth, was feared even by his own comrades for the ferocity of his disposition. These were the men who assembled that night under the roof of McMurdo for the killing of the Pinkerton detective.

Their host had placed whisky upon the table, and they had hastened to prime themselves for the work before them. Baldwin and Cormac were already half drunk, and the liquor had brought out all their ferocity. Cormac placed his hands on the stove for an instant – it had been lighted, for the spring nights were still cold.

'That will do,' said he, with an oath.

'Aye,' said Baldwin, catching his meaning. 'If he is strapped to that we will have the truth out of him.'

'We'll have the truth out of him, never fear,' said McMurdo.

He had nerves of steel, this man, for, though the whole weight of the affair was on him, his manner was as cool and unconcerned as ever. The others marked it and applauded.

'You are the one to handle him,' said the Boss, approvingly. 'Not a warning will he get till your hand is on his throat. It's a pity there are no shutters to your windows.'

McMurdo went from one to the other and drew the curtain tighter.

'Sure, no one can spy upon us now. It's close upon the hour.'

'Maybe he won't come. Maybe he'll get a sniff of danger,' said the secretary.

'He'll come, never fear,' McMurdo answered. 'He is as eager to come as you can be to see him. Hark to that!'

They all sat like wax figures, some with their glasses arrested halfway to their lips. Three loud knocks had sounded at the door.

'Hush!'

McMurdo raised his hand in caution. An exulting glance went round the circle and hands were laid upon hidden weapons.

'Not a sound for your lives!' McMurdo whispered, as he went from the room, closing the door carefully behind him.

With strained ears the murderers waited. They counted the steps of their comrade down the passage. Then they heard him open the outer door. There were a few words as of greeting. Then they were aware of a strange step inside and of an unfamiliar voice. An instant later came the slam of the door and the turning of the key in the lock. Their prey was safe within the trap. Tiger Cormac laughed horribly, and Boss McGinty clapped his great hand across his mouth.

'Be quiet, you fool!' he whispered. 'You'll be the undoing of us yet.'

There was a mutter of conversation from the next room. It seemed interminable. Then the door opened and McMurdo appeared, his finger upon his lip.

He came to the end of the table and looked round at them. A

subtle change had come over him. His manner was as of one who has great work to do. His face had set into granite firmness. His eyes shone with a fierce excitement behind his spectacles. He had become a visible leader of men. They stared at him with eager interest, but he said nothing. Still with the same singular gaze, he looked from man to man.

'Well,' cried Boss McGinty at last, 'is he here? Is Birdy Edwards here?'

'Yes,' McMurdo answered slowly. 'Birdy Edwards is here. I am Birdy Edwards!'

There were ten seconds after that brief speech during which the room might have been empty, so profound was the silence. The hissing of a kettle upon the stove rose sharp and strident to the ear. Seven white faces, all turned upwards to this man who dominated them, were set motionless with utter terror. Then, with a sudden shivering of glass, a bristle of glistening rifle-barrels broke through each window, while the curtains were torn from their hangings. At the sight Boss McGinty gave the roar of a wounded bear and plunged for the half-opened door. A levelled revolver met him there, with the stern blue eyes of Captain Marvin of the Coal and Iron Police gleaming behind the sights. The Boss recoiled and fell back into his chair.

'You're safer there, Councillor,' said the man whom they had known as McMurdo. 'And you, Baldwin, if you don't take your hand off your gun you'll cheat the hangman yet. Pull it out, or, by the Lord that made me – There, that will do. There are forty armed men round this house, and you can figure it out for yourselves what chance you have. Take their guns, Marvin!'

There was no possible resistance under the menace of those rifles. The men were disarmed. Sulky, sheepish, and very amazed, they still sat round the table.

'I'd like to say a word to you before we separate,' said the man who had trapped them. 'I guess we may not meet again until you see me on the stand in the courthouse. I'll give you something to think over betwixt now and then. You know me now for what I am. At last I can put my cards on the table. I am Birdy Edwards, of Pinkerton's. I was chosen to break up your gang. I had a hard and a dangerous game to play. Not a soul, not one soul, not my nearest and dearest knew that I was playing it, except Captain Marvin here and my employers. But it's over tonight, thank God, and I am the winner!'

The seven pale, rigid faces looked up at him. There was an unappeasable hatred in their eyes. He read the relentless threat.

'Maybe you think that the game is not over yet. Well, I take my chance on that. Anyhow, some of you will take no further hand, and there are sixty more besides yourselves that will see a jail this night. I'll tell you this, that when I was put upon this job I never believed there was such a society as yours. I thought it was paper talk, and that I would prove it so. They told me it was to do with the Freemen, so I went to Chicago and was made one. Then I was surer than ever that it was just paper talk, for I found no harm in the society, but a deal of good. Still, I had to carry out my job, and I came for the coal valleys. When I reached this place I learned that I was wrong and that it wasn't a dime novel after all. So I stayed to look after it. I never killed a man in Chicago. I never minted a dollar in my life. Those I gave you were as good as any others, but I never spent money better. I knew the way into your good wishes, and so I pretended to you that the law was after me. It all worked just as I thought.

'So I joined your infernal Lodge and I took my share in your councils. Maybe they will say that I was as bad as you. They can say what they like, so long as I get you. But what is the truth? The night I joined you beat up old man Stanger. I could not warn him, for there was no time, but I held your hand, Baldwin, when you would have killed him. If ever I have suggested things, so as to keep my place among you, they were things which I knew that I could prevent. I could not save Dunn and Menzies, for I did not know enough, but I will see that their murderers are hanged. I gave Chester Wilcox warning, so that when I blew his house in he and his folk were in hiding. There was many a crime that I could not stop, but if you look back and think how often your man came home the other road, or was down in town when you went for him, or stayed indoors when you thought that he would come out, you'll see my work.'

'You blasted traitor!' hissed McGinty, through his closed teeth.

'Aye, John McGinty, you may call me that if it eases your smart. You and your like have been the enemy of God and man in these parts. It took a man to get between you and the poor devils of men and women that you held under your grip. There was just one way of doing it, and I did it. You call me a "traitor", but I guess there's many a thousand will call me a "deliverer" that went down into hell to save them. I've had three months of it. I wouldn't have three such months again if they let me loose in the Treasury at Washington for it. I had to stay till I had it all, every man and every secret, right here in this hand. I'd have waited a little longer if it hadn't come to my knowledge that my secret was coming out. A letter had come into the town that would have set you wise to it all. Then I had to act, and act quickly. I've nothing more to say to you, except that when my time comes I'll die the easier when I think of the work I have done in this valley. Now, Marvin, I'll keep you no more. Have them in and get it over.'

There is little more to tell. Scanlan had been given a sealed note to be left at the address of Miss Ettie Shafter – a mission which he had accepted with a wink and a knowing smile. In the early hours of the morning a beautiful woman and a much-muffled man boarded a special train which had been sent by the railroad company, and made a swift, unbroken journey out of the land of danger. It was the last time that ever either Ettie or her lover set foot in the Valley of Fear. Ten days later they were married in Chicago, with old Jacob Shafter as witness of the wedding.

The trial of the Scowrers was held far from the place where

their adherents might have terrified the guardians of the law. In vain they struggled. In vain the money of the Lodge – money squeezed by blackmail out of the whole countryside – was spent like water in the attempt to save them. That cold, clear, unimpassioned statement from one who knew every detail of their lives, their organization, and their crimes was unshaken by all the wiles of their defenders. At last, after so many years, they were broken and scattered. The cloud was lifted for ever from the valley. McGinty met his fate upon the scaffold, cringing and whining when the last hour came. Eight of his chief followers shared his fate. Fifty odd had various degrees of imprisonment. The work of Birdy Edwards was complete.

And yet, as he had guessed, the game was not over yet. There was another hand to be played, and yet another and another. Ted Baldwin, for one, had escaped the scaffold; so had the Willabys; so had several other of the fiercest spirits of the gang. For ten years they were out of the world, and then came a day when they were free once more – a day which Edwards, who knew his men, was very sure would be an end of his life of peace. They had sworn an oath on all that they thought holy to have his blood as a vengeance for their comrades. And well they strove to keep their vow. From Chicago he was chased, after two attempts so near to success that it was sure that the third would get him. From Chicago he went, under a changed name, to California, and it was there that the light went for a time out of his life when Ettie Edwards died. Once again he was nearly killed, and once again, under the name of Douglas, he worked in a lonely canyon, where, with an English partner named Barker, he amassed a fortune. At last there came a warning to him that the bloodhounds were on his track once more, and he cleared – only just in time – for England. And here came the John Douglas who for a second time married a worthy mate and lived for five years as a Sussex country gentleman – a life which ended with the strange happenings of which we have heard.

Epilogue

The police-court proceedings had passed, in which the case of John Douglas was referred to a higher court. So had the Assizes, at which he was acquitted as having acted in self-defence. 'Get him out of England at any cost,' wrote Holmes to the wife. 'There are forces here which may be more dangerous than those he has escaped. There is no safety for your husband in England.'

Two months had gone by, and the case had to some extent passed from our minds. Then one morning there came an enigmatic note slipped into our letter-box. 'Dear me, Mr Holmes! Dear me!' said this singular epistle. There was neither superscription nor signature. I laughed at the quaint message, but Holmes showed an unwonted seriousness.

'Devilry, Watson!' he remarked, and sat long with a clouded brow.

Late that night Mrs Hudson, our landlady, brought up a message that a gentleman wished to see Holmes, and that the matter was of the utmost importance. Close at the heels of his messenger came Mr Cecil Barker, our friend of the moated Manor House. His face was drawn and haggard.

'I've had bad news – terrible news, Mr Holmes,' said he.

'I feared as much,' said Holmes.

'You have not had a cable, have you?'

'I have had a note from someone who has.'

'It's poor Douglas. They tell me his name is Edwards, but he will always be Jack Douglas of Benito Canyon to me. I told you that they started together for South Africa in the *Palmyra* three weeks ago.'

'Exactly.'

'The ship reached Cape Town last night. I received this cable from Mrs Douglas this morning:

' "Jack has been lost overboard in gale off St Helena. No one knows how accident occurred – Ivy Douglas." '

'Ha! It came like that, did it?' said Holmes, thoughtfully. 'Well, I've no doubt it was well stage-managed.'

'You mean that you think there was no accident?'

'None in the world.'

'He was murdered?'

'Surely!'

'So I think also. These infernal Scowrers, this cursed vindictive nest of criminals –'

'No, no, my good sir,' said Holmes. 'There is a master hand here. It is no case of sawed-off shot-guns and clumsy six-shooters. You can tell an old master by the sweep of his brush. I can tell a Moriarty when I see one. This crime is from London, not from America.'

'But for what motive?'

'Because it is done by a man who cannot afford to fail – one whose whole unique position depends upon the fact that all he does must succeed. A great brain and a huge organization have been turned to the extinction of one man. It is crushing the nut with the hammer – an absurd extravagance of energy – but the nut is very effectually crushed all the same.'

'How came this man to have anything to do with it?'

'I can only say that the first word that ever came to us of the business was from one of his lieutenants. These Americans were well advised. Having an English job to do, they took into partnership, as any foreign criminal could do, this great consultant in crime. From that moment their man was doomed. At first he would content himself by using his machinery in order to find their victim. Then he would indicate how the matter might be treated. Finally, when he read in the reports of the failure of his agent, he would step in himself with a master touch. You heard me warn this man at Birlstone Manor House that the coming danger was greater than the past. Was I right?'

Barker beat his head with his clenched fist in his impotent anger.

'Do you tell me that we have to sit down under this? Do you say that no one can ever get level with this king-devil?'

'No, I don't say that,' said Holmes, and his eyes seemed to be looking far into the future. 'I don't say that he can't be beat. But you must give me time – you must give me time!'

We all sat in silence for some minutes, while those fateful eyes still strained to pierce the veil.

'A Case of [Mistaken?] Identity': Conan Doyle, Sherlock Holmes and *fin de siècle* London[1]

by David Cannadine

The late 1880s were a remarkable and transformative era in the history of London, which suddenly attained an unprecedented prominence (but also an unrivalled notoriety) as the national capital, as the imperial metropolis, and as the one place on the globe that was uniquely and incomparably (yet also worryingly and troublingly) *the* 'world city'; and that pre-eminence would last until the outbreak of war in 1914.[2] There was a new awareness of its imperial, royal and historic associations, as exemplified by the popularity of the Colonial and Indian Exhibition held at South Kensington in 1886, by the successful staging of Queen Victoria's Golden Jubilee in the following year, and by the starring part given to the venerable fabric of the Tower of London in Gilbert and Sullivan's *The Yeoman of the Guard* (1888). There were major changes in the government of the metropolis, most of which would henceforward be administered by the newly established and democratically elected London County Council (hereafter LCC), which was created in 1888, even as the ancient City preserved its traditional autonomy and successfully fended off reform, in part by scaling up the glitter and the pageantry associated with its Lord Mayor.[3] But there was also a growing concern about what seemed to be the widening gap between the affluent and aristocratic 'West End', and the impoverished and indigent 'East End'; and these anxieties were intensified and reinforced by the Trafalgar Square riots of the unemployed in 1886 and 1887, by the notorious 'Jack the Ripper' murders of 1888, and by the great

London dock strike of 1889.[4] There were two revealing and con-
trasted responses to these varied events and developments: the
construction of New Scotland Yard was undertaken as the headquarters of the rapidly expanding London Metropolitan Police
force; and in the same year as the London dock strike, Charles
Booth published the first volume of what would become his
monumental investigation into *Life and Labour in London*, which
concluded that one third of the inhabitants of the world's greatest city were, in fact, living in poverty.[5]

Booth was merely one of many writers and thinkers, pundits
and critics, journalists and commentators from Britain and far
beyond who, beginning in the mid-1880s, described the metropolis as the place where both the challenges and the possibilities of
contemporary urban living were displayed in their most extreme
and exaggerated forms.[6] From one perspective, London debased
and degraded humankind in new, troubling and horrifying ways;
from another it offered redemptive scope for personal fulfilment
and individual achievement; and the young Arthur Conan Doyle
embraced both these developing conventional wisdoms in two
early writings which date from this time. In *A Study in Scarlet*, published in 1887, Dr Watson returned home, invalided from the
army, with limited funds and knowing scarcely anyone, and he
naturally – but reluctantly – gravitated to the nation's capital,
which he described and deplored as that 'great cesspool into which
all the loungers and idlers of the Empire are irresistibly drawn'.
But a year later, Conan Doyle produced a very different piece,
entitled 'On the Geographical Distribution of British Intellect',
where he argued that in recent decades, London had 'clearly produced very much more than its numerical share of the intellect of
the nation.' This was, he went on, 'as might be expected when one
takes into account the centralization of wealth in London, and the
way in which for centuries back the brightest intellects in every
walk of life have been drawn towards the metropolis.'[7] Here were
two contrasting images of London that would significantly inform

Conan Doyle's Sherlock Holmes stories: the city as a great wen or 'Modern Babylon', which harboured and attracted dangerous undesirables, who had to be sought out and apprehended; and the city as a great wonder or the 'New Jerusalem', which offered unprecedented possibilities and limitless opportunities, and which nurtured and drew in people of spirit and distinction, such as Sherlock Holmes himself, who would spend the whole of his professional life based in *fin de siècle* London.[8]

I

It has been often claimed that there are three principal characters in the Holmes and Watson stories: the great detective, the good doctor, and the ever-present metropolis, and up to a point (although only up to a point) this is true. Like the Tower of London in *The Yeoman of the Guard*, so this argument goes, the city was more than just the passive backdrop or the inert setting for Conan Doyle's fiction: it was for him, 'as it was for Dickens, a condition of possibility for the form and content of the tales'.[9] Yet London was not where Holmes started out: for his background was rural and gentrified, he was descended from a long line of country squires, he had attended a 'college' in a small university town, and his first two cases, 'The Gloria Scott' (set in 1874) and 'The Musgrave Ritual' (set in 1879) took him respectively to Norfolk and Sussex.[10] But sometime in between, he decided to make a career as the world's first 'consulting detective', establishing himself in London: initially in Montague Street, near the British Museum, and subsequently at 221B Baker Street. There he settled, in 1881, with Dr Watson, as recounted in *A Study in Scarlet*, and there he practised for ten years until he disappeared, presumed dead, after his encounter with Professor Moriarty at the Reichenbach Falls in 'The Final Problem' (set in 1891).[11] Holmes later returned to Baker Street as described in

'The Empty House' (set in 1894), and he detected for almost another decade, until late in 1903, as explained in 'The Creeping Man' (set in that year). At that point, he left London for good, and retired to 'that little farm of my dreams' on the South Downs near Eastbourne, to keep bees and study philosophy, and his last two recorded cases took place, like his first two, in out of town locations: 'The Lion's Mane' (set in 1907) on the coast near his home in Sussex; and 'His Last Bow' (set in 1914) near Harwich.[12] But during the 1880s, the mid and late 1890s, and on into the early 1900s, Sherlock Holmes was permanently residing in Baker Street, and it is with the London of those years that he has always been subsequently regarded as synonymous.[13]

Yet this close connection between the sleuth and the city was in several ways a misleading literary sleight of hand. Unlike his fictional detective, whose 'knowledge of the byways of London was extraordinary', Conan Doyle's personal acquaintance with the great metropolis was relatively limited, for the time he lived there was of brief duration, and he never became a 'London' novelist in the close, intimate and well-observed way that Dickens had been before him, or that Gissing or H. G. Wells were during his own era.[14] His forbears were Irish (hence both 'Conan' and 'Doyle'), but he was born in 1859 in Edinburgh, and he was educated as a Catholic at Stonyhurst College in Lancashire and subsequently at Feldkirch in Austria, before returning to his home town to study medicine. While a student, he worked as a medical assistant in Birmingham; he went on two extended (and Joseph Conrad-like) voyages as a ship's surgeon to the north Atlantic and to west Africa; he was briefly a partner in an ill-fated Plymouth practice; and he transferred to Southsea, near Portsmouth, where he was more successful (and married in 1885). It was while he was living on the south coast that Conan Doyle wrote his first Sherlock Holmes stories, and it was only in 1891 that he and his family moved to London, where he hoped to make a career as an eye specialist: initially living at Montague Place (with his consulting rooms at 2 Devonshire Place at the top of Wimpole Street) and subsequently in the suburb of South Norwood (by which time he had abandoned his medical ambitions for full-time writing).[15] But the metropolitan sojourn was brief, for in 1893 Conan Doyle's wife contracted tuberculosis, and after two years' travelling in warmer climes, the family left London for the country, settling at Hindhead, in Surrey, in 1896. The departure was permanent, and on the death of his wife ten years later, Conan Doyle remarried, and moved to Windlesham in Sussex where he lived for the rest of his life. Although by then he had become a prominent member of the London literary, social and political establishments, and kept a small flat in town for overnight stays, he was never again a full-time city resident.[16]

This helps explain why Conan Doyle's familiarity with the *fin de siècle* metropolis was nothing like as detailed or as commanding as that which he claimed for his greatest fictional creation, or as that which Dickens or Gissing or Wells displayed. When he wrote *A Study in Scarlet* and *The Sign of Four*, he had only visited London briefly and infrequently; his knowledge of the city during the late 1880s was largely derived from the perusal of contemporary street atlases; and his subsequent four years' residence in the 'world city' did not deepen his close acquaintance all that much. Conan Doyle never became a committed, let alone a life-long Londoner, the Holmes and Watson stories were littered with descriptive and topographical errors, and he had little feel for what Henry James called the city's 'inconceivable immensity', or for particular neighbourhoods or buildings, which he often enumerated but rarely described. Indeed, on one occasion, late in his life, Conan Doyle claimed that he had never even set foot in Baker Street. This cannot have been literally true, since in 1874 he had visited Madame Tussaud's when it was located there; but although that famous thoroughfare loomed so large and so central in the Holmes and Watson stories, Conan Doyle never embellished or evoked it with any residential specificity or architectural details.[17]

Such limitations and lacunae lend support to Owen Dudley Edwards's contention that Sherlock Holmes's London of the 1880s and 1890s was not in fact the great metropolis at all, but was instead a thinly disguised version of Conan Doyle's Edinburgh of the 1860s and 1870s, with its narrow alleys, its close juxtaposition of the grand and the squalid, and a strong sense of cohesive community that did not exist in the larger and more dispersed 'world city'. In the same way, the Baker Street Irregulars were not so much a late-nineteenth-century-London gang: rather, they were modelled on a bunch of mid-Victorian Edinburgh youths with whom Conan Doyle had for a time gone about.[18]

Conan Doyle's brief and superficial acquaintance with the metropolis also helps explain why Holmes undertook so much of his work outside London: often in Sussex and Surrey, and sometimes in the West Country and Birmingham, which were the parts of England that he knew better than he did the capital city. Of the four novellas, *A Study in Scarlet*, although set in London, had a substantial American back story; *The Sign of Four* was also located in the metropolis, but was much concerned with prior events in India; *The Hound of the Baskervilles* took place predominantly in the West Country, albeit with London interludes; and *The Valley of Fear* unfolded in Sussex with another lengthy American sub plot. Among the fifty-six short stories, more than one third were primarily located outside London: in addition to the four already mentioned, set at the beginning and end of his career, they included such renowned episodes as 'Silver Blaze' (the West Country), 'The Speckled Band' (Surrey), 'The Crooked Man' (Aldershot), and 'The Priory School' (the 'north of England'). Many of Holmes's clients journeyed from the provinces up to the city, seeking his help in solving a rural problem, often centring on a remote country house, such as Baskerville Hall, and he went back with them to investigate, which was why he and Watson were so often heading to or from the great metropolitan railway stations. It was on just such a train journey, in 'The Copper

Beeches', that Holmes observed, drawing on his own experience, that 'the lowest and vilest alleys of London do not present a more dreadful record of sin than does the smiling and beautiful countryside.' There were also frequent allusions in the stories to Holmes's many continental cases, undertaken on behalf of such high-end clients as the ruling houses of Holland and Scandinavia, and the Pope and the Sultan of Turkey; his brilliant exposure of Baron Maupertius as 'the most accomplished swindler in Europe' left him triumphant but prostrated in a Lyon hotel; it was in Switzerland, not London, that Holmes allegedly fell to his death at the Reichenbach Falls; and in the three-year 'hiatus' that followed, he travelled extensively in Europe, Asia and North Africa.[19]

To be sure, many of the stories, wherever they eventually led and ended, did begin in the heart of central London, with Holmes and Watson comfortably ensconced at 221B Baker Street, and with the gas-lamps and hansom cabs – and often the next, anxious, footpath-pacing client – indistinctly glimpsed through the windows. Here is one such opening, from 'The Copper Beeches':

> It was a cold morning of the early spring, and we sat after breakfast on either side of a cheery fire in the old room at Baker Street. A thick fog rolled down between the lines of dun-coloured houses, and the opposing windows loomed like dark, shapeless blurs through the heavy yellow wreaths.[20]

In thus describing London's dense, yellow, pea-soup fog, and the feelings of mystery and menace which it conjured up, Conan Doyle rightly recognized a metropolitan phenomenon, which had become increasingly oppressive during the 1880s and 1890s, and which preoccupied contemporary meteorologists and environmentalists, and also such writers as Henry James and Oscar Wilde, and such artists as Whistler and Monet.[21] James loved the capital's 'atmosphere, with its magnificent mystifications, which flatters and superfuses, makes everything brown, rich, dim vague.' 'Without the fog', Monet once remarked, 'London would not be a beautiful city. It's the fog that gives it its magnificent breadth.'[22] Yet Conan Doyle never wrote about London fog so rhapsodically or so evocatively: in fact he rarely wrote about it at all, for a cursory search of the Holmes and Watson texts throws up only thirty-five references to fog, of which the majority come from one single story ('The Bruce-Partington Plans'), set in London, and from one novella (*The Hound of the Baskervilles*), set in Devon. Indeed, the Holmes and Watson stories paid scant attention to London's atmospherics: not only the fog, but also the stench of the smoke and the horse droppings, the squalor of the pavements and the streets, the unrelenting noise of horses' hooves on the cobble stones, and the almost intolerable traffic congestion, were rarely mentioned.[23]

But his treatment of fog was not the only limitation to Conan Doyle's urban vision. As G. M. Young once observed, the metropolis of the 1880s and 1890s, which was quintessentially Holmes's London, was gradually being transformed from 'the vast and shapeless city which Dickens knew – fog bound and fever haunted, brooding over its dark, mysterious river' into 'the imperial capital, of Whitehall, the Thames Embankment and South Kensington.'[24] Yet the fevers, like the fogs, received little notice from Conan Doyle: their only significant mention was in 'The Dying Detective', when Holmes claimed to have contracted 'a coolie disease from Sumatra,' which was 'infallibly deadly and horribly contagious', as a result of working on 'a case down at Rotherhithe, in an alley near the river.' And the evocation of the 'mysterious' Thames in *The Sign of Four* was little more than another catalogue of names and places, as Holmes and Watson went on a 'wild chase . . . through the pool, past the West India Docks, down the long Deptford Reach, and up again after rounding the Isle of Dogs', in pursuit of the villains and their misbegotten 'Agra treasure'. Nor was 'imperial' London much in

evidence in the stories, since most of that metropolitan transformation took place after Holmes had retired early in the first
decade of the twentieth century (of which more later).[25] Apart
from one reference to the Royal Albert Hall, the museum complex of South Kensington barely rated a mention; and although
Holmes and Watson regularly crossed the Thames, they never
did so by Tower Bridge, which had been completed in 1895,
shortly after Holmes's 'return'. As for Whitehall: Holmes's
brother Mycroft was employed there, and the Foreign Office was
mentioned in 'The Naval Treaty'; but Owen Dudley Edwards has
argued that the description of the interior was not based on Sir
George Gilbert Scott's recent, expansive neo-classical creation,
but was modelled on the cramped and dingy chambers of Edinburgh lawyers.[26]

Not surprisingly, the parts of the great metropolis that
appeared most frequently were the two areas of the city where
Conan Doyle lived during his brief period of residence in the
early 1890s. The first was in central London, extending from
Bloomsbury to Marylebone, which was bounded (for Holmes)
by Montague Street and Baker Street, and (for Conan Doyle) by
Montague Place and Wimpole Street, bisected by the two major
thoroughfares of Tottenham Court Road and Oxford Street:
here was their shared urban heartland. The second, reflecting
Conan Doyle's subsequent move to Norwood, was the sprawling
suburbia south of the Thames, 'the monster tentacles which the
giant city was throwing out into the country': not just Norwood
itself, and such neighbouring communities as Sydenham and
Streatham, but also Lambeth and Kennington, Lewisham and
Woolwich, Blackheath and Greenwich, Brixton and Croydon,
Wimbledon and Wandsworth.[27] Other parts of London were
also frequently alluded to: the City, the docks and the east end;
Clerkenwell and Covent Garden; Mayfair, St James's and Pall
Mall; Regent Street and Piccadilly; Trafalgar Square, Fleet Street
and the Strand; Kensington, Hyde Park and Notting Hill;

Chiswick, Hammersmith and Fulham; and (but rarely) Hampstead and Harrow. Railway stations were the most significant buildings, especially Paddington, Charing Cross, Waterloo, London Bridge and Victoria (most of Holmes's out of town adventures took place to the south or west of London). Also mentioned were the British Museum, the Royal Albert Hall, the Foreign Office, the Houses of Parliament and Westminster Abbey, St Paul's Cathedral and the Crystal Palace; an assortment of theatres, hotels and restaurants, some of which were real (the Haymarket, the Langham and Simpsons), some not; St Bartholomew's, Charing Cross and King's College Hospitals (in part in homage to Dr Watson); and Waterloo, Hammersmith and Vauxhall Bridges (though London Bridge, like Tower Bridge, was ignored).[28]

This wearying list of names (and, indeed, addresses) accurately reflects the limitations of Conan Doyle's mode of metropolitan evocation, and also it raises a further point often overlooked: for while some of Holmes's London was genuinely old, such as Westminster Abbey and the British Museum, the great aristocratic estates in Covent Garden, Bloomsbury and Mayfair, and John Nash's Regent Street, much of his city had been only recently constructed, immediately before or during his own lifetime (Holmes, like Conan Doyle, had been born in the 1850s). Waterloo Station had opened in 1848, Paddington was completed in 1854, and Victoria and Charing Cross followed in 1860 and 1864. The underground Metropolitan Railway was inaugurated in 1863, linking King's Cross, St Pancras, Euston and Paddington Stations; and it was outside Aldgate Station, its eastern terminus, that the body of Arthur Cadogan West was discovered in 'The Bruce-Partington Plans'.[29] Among other buildings mentioned in the stories, the Crystal Palace at Sydenham had been put up in Hyde Park for the Great Exhibition of 1851, the Palace of Westminster and the Foreign Office were completed during the 1860s, and the Royal Albert Hall was opened in 1871.

Charing Cross Road, Shaftesbury Avenue, Clerkenwell Road, Victoria Street and the Thames Embankment were mid-Victorian developments, while Northumberland Avenue and Rosebery Avenue were both laid out during Holmes's time in London. Most of the sprawling suburbia extending some eight or nine miles from Charing Cross was built during the second half of the nineteenth century, and was serviced by horse-drawn omnibuses and new commuter railway lines; while hotels, restaurants and theatres only became a pronounced feature of the central London scene from the 1870s. As one contemporary observed in 1888: 'this monster London is really a new city.' That may have been an exaggeration, yet the most striking feature of the great metropolis of Holmes and Watson was not (as it has since become) its nostalgic antiquity but its pervasive *modernity*.[30]

To be sure, for much of its history London had been the home of the royal court, the government, the judiciary and the legislature; it was also the hub of commerce and culture, politics and society, and literary and scientific endeavour; and it was a great port, a thriving manufacturing locale, and a major financial centre. But during the late nineteenth century, all these activities (with the exception of manufacturing) expanded and up-scaled, as London reasserted its dominance over the rest of the United Kingdom, and also became the financial and imperial capital of the world in ways that had never been quite true before.[31] Hence the dramatic increase in its population during the years Sherlock Holmes resided there: in the area governed by the LCC from 3.8 million in 1881 to 4.5 million twenty years later; and across greater London as a whole, from 4.7 million to 6.6 million. Hence the arrival of immigrants and workers from all over Britain, from Europe, North America and the rest of the world. Hence the massive proliferation of clerks and office workers, who were employed in the City, but lived in the new lower-middle-class suburbs (*vide* Mr Pooter).[32] Hence the unprecedented expansion in the numbers of middle class businessmen and professionals, and the influx of visitors and residents from the empire and the United States. Thus enlarged and extended, the great metropolis became more varied and diverse than ever, as Conan Doyle acknowledged when he described how Holmes and Watson once passed, in rapid succession, 'through the fringe of fashionable London, hotel London, theatrical London, literary London, commercial London and, finally, maritime London.'[33] Yet as a depiction of the great, multi-functional world city, this was a characteristic combination of precision, vagueness and selectivity, for while fashionable, commercial and maritime London might be exactly located, the same could hardly be said of the others. If Conan Doyle, or Holmes and Watson, had ordered the driver of a hansom cab to take them to 'hotel London' or 'literary London', he would not have had the faintest (or even the foggiest) idea where they could be found.

II

Such was Conan Doyle's idiosyncratic image of *fin de siècle* London, which was every bit as selective and impressionistic as Monet's contemporary canvases. But what, more substantively, lay behind this highly personal metropolitan vision, which Conan Doyle had created, and Sherlock Holmes inhabited? As many contemporaries recognized, the answer was less than straightforward. Late nineteenth-century London may have been the one authentic and undisputed 'world city', but it was far from clear that its global supremacy would last: for the United States and Germany were industrializing at prodigiously rapid rates, they would soon overtake Britain in manufacturing, and they seemed set to do so in finance as well; and New York, with its multi-ethnic energy, its massive territorial consolidation of the five boroughs, and (following Chicago) its pioneering skyscrapers, seemed to offer a very different and more challenging version of the urban future, as Conan Doyle recognized on his first visit there in 1894.[34] Moreover, London's position as the pre-eminent imperial metropolis was not quite what it seemed. The 'Scramble for Africa', the creation of the Australian Commonwealth and the conquest of the Boer Republics meant imperial euphoria was at its zenith, especially in the beating heart of empire; but the murder of General Gordon at Khartoum, the agitation for Home Rule in Ireland, the creation of the Congress Party demanding independence for India, and the humiliating defeats Britain suffered in South Africa, told a very different story; and by 1900, there were many young Africans and Asians, who would later become nationalist leaders, who were gaining a legal education in London. As a royal capital, London was certainly en fête and on parade during these years: Victoria's Golden Jubilee was followed by her Diamond Jubilee of 1897 and her funeral, and then by the Coronation of King Edward VII – an innovative sequence of royal pageants celebrating a newly apotheosized monarchy.[35] But among those in the know, there was an underlying concern about royal scandal, resulting from the gambling and extra-marital liaisons of the Prince of Wales (later Edward VII), and from the delinquencies of his eldest son, Prince Eddy.

Here were cross-currents and complexities a-plenty in fin de siècle London, and there were others that were equally significant. The ethos of British government, as exemplified by those two late Victorian titans, Lord Salisbury and Mr Gladstone, remained masculine, high minded, public spirited, incorruptible – and heterosexual. But the 1880s and 1890s were also an era of moral panic, of growing concerns about decadence, decay, disintegration and degeneracy, of anxiety about the 'new women' and the threat they presented to conventional gender relations, and of fears that London high society was mired in scandal, as instanced by the trial of Oscar Wilde for 'gross indecency', and the revelations concerning a homosexual brothel in Cleveland Street which, it was alleged (probably mistakenly), was frequented by

Prince Eddy.[36] Nor were the next generation of political leaders men of unimpeachable reputation or standing. It was rumoured in well-informed social and political circles that Gladstone's successor, Lord Rosebery, was homosexual; while his Eton contemporary, Arthur Balfour, who was Lord Salisbury's nephew and political heir, was known in the same quarters as 'Fanny', or 'the hermaphrodite'.[37] In terms of party politics, it was the Conservatives and the Unionists, led by Salisbury, and then by Balfour, who were the dominant force in government and national politics for most of Holmes's period of residence in London, and they were pledged to uphold the British monarchy, to safeguard the British Empire, and to preserve the Union with Ireland. But the local politics of the great metropolis ran along very different lines: for while the Conservatives had set up the LCC in the hope it would effectively be controlled, until 1907, by a left of centre 'Progressive' alliance of Liberals, Fabians and Socialists, with a more radical agenda. This was not the outcome Salisbury's government had wanted, and in an effort to rein in their non-compliant creature, they established a new tier of twenty-eight metropolitan boroughs in 1899, as a deliberate counterweight.[38]

There were many other contrasts and contradictions in late-nineteenth-century London, of which the greatest seemed to remain that between those whom Disraeli had earlier termed 'the rich' and 'the poor'. The Prince of Wales presided over a glittering and gaudy alternative court at Marlborough House, frequented by fast aristocrats, rich Jewish bankers and serial adulterers. Landowners lucky enough to enjoy extensive income from shares, mineral royalties and urban estates still kept up spectacular state in London during the season, whereas peers and gentry who depended solely on their farm rents were less lucky, as agricultural prices tumbled during the 'great depression'. Elsewhere in Park Lane and Mayfair, South African 'Randlords' and American millionaires mingled with home-grown plutocrats such as Edward Guinness (Lord Iveagh), Alfred Harmsworth

(Lord Northcliffe), and Weetman Pearson (Lord Cowdray), and their opulent presence reinforced the conventional view that late Victorian London was the richest city in the world. Yet what struck many observers during the 1880s and 1890s was the continued co-existence, amidst so much plenty, of so much poverty. The particular sense of social crisis and division, associated with the riots and strikes of the late 1880s, was soon averted, but the awareness that London was *the* pre-eminent social problem nevertheless remained. Charles Booth produced a second edition of *Life and Labour* in nine volumes between 1892 and 1897, and a third version in seventeen volumes between 1902 and 1903. His namesake, General William Booth, the founder of the Salvation Army, published *In Darkest England and the Way Out* in 1890, depicting London as an urban jungle, parts of which were inhabited by 'savages' who were physically deformed and spiritually decayed. The General's co-author, W. T. Stead, had earlier drawn attention to the scandal of child prostitution in London; and during and after the Ripper murders, the increasingly sensationalist – and increasingly national – press repeatedly described Holmes's London as the global capital of crime and vice.[39]

Yet while the facts of poverty and prostitution were undeniable, the London of Sherlock Holmes was actually becoming *much safer*, as all the reliable indices of crime began to fall from the 1850s, and they continued to do so until the outbreak of the First World War. The *Report of the Commissioner of Police of the Metropolis* for 1882 declared London to be 'the safest capital for life and property in the world', and fifteen years later the criminal registrar at the Home Office, surveying trends during the Queen's reign, flatly announced that 'crime has immensely decreased since 1836.'[40] There were many causes and consequences of these developments. By the 1880s, the uniformed police stood higher in public esteem than at any earlier time; they were widely thought to be decent, fair, brave and incorruptible, if not over bright; and they were affectionately parodied in Gilbert and Sullivan's *The*

Pirates of Penzance.[41] The men in blue were joined by plain-clothes detectives working for the new Criminal Investigation Department, who shared their colleagues' positive if plodding characteristics; and the scientific study of crime was also being initiated by a new breed of international experts known as criminologists (who created a growing body of literature to which Holmes himself contributed 'several monographs'). As policing and detection changed, so did the nature of crime. In the London of Charles Dickens, it had been public, brutal and violent; robbery and murder had been its visible and often horrific manifestations; and criminals were deemed to belong to the 'dangerous classes', who presented a systemic threat to social order. But in the London of Sherlock Holmes, crime was more likely to occur in private and in ostensibly 'respectable' dwellings; to be less violent because it was often concerned with fraud or embezzlement or blackmail; to require brain power rather than physical strength to uncover its perpetrators; and to represent less of a threat to the social order because wrong-doers were increasingly regarded as flawed individuals and criminal 'professionals' rather than as belonging to some generic, ill-defined and lawless underclass.[42]

Such was the *fin de siècle* metropolitan environment in which Conan Doyle briefly established himself, and although he was no Londoner, he was very much a product of those times, reflecting in his own life and attitudes many of their contradictions and ambiguities. From one perspective, he appeared to be a quintessential late-Victorian conservative – conscious and proud of his race's innate superiority, unswervingly loyal to the British throne, devoted to the British Empire, and deeply patriotic. He rejected his Irish heritage and Irish nationalism, and for most of his life was a fervent opponent of Home Rule, which he saw as portending the break-up of the British Empire; he idolized Queen Victoria ('the very heart of our lives . . . the dear mother of us all'), and was a staunch admirer of King Edward VII (he was overwhelmed by the 'majesty . . . colour . . . and variety' of his funeral); he volunteered for medical service in South Africa and wrote books justifying Britain's conduct during the Boer War, for which he received a knighthood; he stood (unsuccessfully) as a Unionist candidate at the general election in 1900 and again six years later; he opposed giving votes to women; and he was a fervid supporter and chronicler of Britain's war effort between 1914 and 1918.[43] Indeed, with his love of sport, his adherence to a chivalric code of gentlemanly conduct, his military bearing and his handlebar moustache, Conan Doyle might well have been Colonel Blimp before his time. It was a non-Blimpish version of this image which his family later sought to cultivate and embellish, via their commissioned biography from John Dickinson Carr, which (somewhat implausibly) insisted that Conan Doyle was in many ways his own Sherlock Holmes, as embodied in the phrase 'steel true, blade straight', which was engraved on his tombstone. Some recent commentators have also accepted this interpretation, although with the very different aim of denouncing Conan Doyle as an unreconstructed racist and diehard imperialist.[44]

Yet Conan Doyle was far from sympathetic to many of the conventional conservative pieties of late Victorian Britain and its Empire. He was a European cosmopolitan, at ease in the cultures and languages of Germany and France, he set many of his historical romances on the continent rather than in Britain, and he admiringly intruded thinly disguised versions of Gladstone ('austere, high-nosed, eagle-eyed and dominant') and Lord Rosebery ('endowed with every beauty of body and mind') as Sherlock Holmes's clients in 'The Second Stain'. He was 'gladdened' that the Progressives won control of the newly established LCC, he disapproved of the hereditary House of Lords as a second chamber and of the 'bad monopoly' of the 'unearned increment' of the great ground landlords of London, he favoured the reform and liberalization of the 'deplorable' divorce laws, and he eventually came round to supporting Irish Home Rule. He rejected the Roman Catholicism in which he had been brought up and educated, and with it all other forms of Christianity, and from early adulthood he was drawn to Spiritualism.[45] His father was an alcoholic, he wrote about syphilis in his Edinburgh MD dissertation, he explored such issues as homosexuality in some of his (non-Sherlockian) stories, and he admired and knew Oscar Wilde and thought his imprisonment unjust. He maintained a long-term liaison with another woman, Jean Leckie, while his first wife was ill with tuberculosis, he gave a thinly disguised account of their relationship in his novel, *A Duet* (1899), and he married Jean as soon as he decently could once he was widowed.[46] He was also an admirer of the American anti-slavery campaigner Henry Highland Garnet; he feared that on occasions Britain was too intrusive and interfering in its imperial mission; he opposed (as did Joseph Conrad) the selfish and exploitative conduct of the Belgian monarch in the Congo (where his allies included Roger Casement and E. D. Morrel); and in campaigning against miscarriages of justice in the British legal system, he intervened on behalf of a South Asian and a German-born Jew.[47]

Like his creator, albeit in different ways, Sherlock Holmes was also, in the complexities and contradictions of his character, very much a creature of the 1880s and 1890s. In one guise, Conan Doyle made him almost superhuman: a 'wizard' invested with 'special knowledge and special powers' that seemed to verge on the miraculous, and which meant he could 'outwit any adversary, however cunning, and solve any puzzle, however bizarre.' His mind constituted the most perfect reasoning machine ever created, his clients marvelled at his capacity for observation and deduction, and his handling of his greatest cases, such as 'The Bruce-Partington Plans', was astonishingly skilful. 'A masterpiece', Watson told him. 'You have never risen to greater heights.' Holmes was also exceptionally brave, strong, bold, fearless, resourceful, masterful, commanding and audacious; he was a chivalrous and patriotic 'knight-errant', adhering to a strict gentlemanly code of honour and conduct; he rebuked aristocrats and plutocrats when he believed they had behaved improperly or inappropriately; and as 'a benefactor of the race' he repeatedly restored order in a world constantly threatened by subversion.[48] To this end, he saw himself as being above the law: he burgled private residences without a qualm (and could clearly have been a first-class criminal had he chosen); he acquitted murderers he had detected if he thought their cause was morally just; he could count, whenever needed, on the influence and support of people in the very highest of places; he never appeared in dock, either as a witness or defendant; and he was the self-appointed and self-constituted 'last and highest court of appeal' who 'represented justice'. As such, Sherlock Holmes was an early version of Superman, the character introduced by Nietzsche as Ubermensch in *Thus Spoke Zarathustra*, initially published in 1883 in German (a language Conan Doyle read widely and well), and translated into English in 1896.[49]

But in an alternative guise, which was so utterly contradictory as to be almost completely inconsistent, Sherlock Holmes was not so much a reassuring Superman but his very antithesis – a self-indulgent, drug-addicted Bohemian, a *fin de siècle* aesthete and decadent, and an isolated and alienated intellectual, who might have stepped straight from the pages, not of Nietzsche, but rather of Oscar Wilde.[50] For much of the time, he suffered from boredom and ennui; his sexuality was unclear, he had few if any friends apart from Watson, and he had an 'aversion to women'; he took heroin and cocaine (albeit only a 'seven per cent solution'); he enjoyed pipes, cigars and cigarettes, and 221B Baker Street was often wreathed in foul and impenetrable smoke; he played the violin, tunelessly, at all hours of the day and night; he was neurotic, lethargic and frequently depressed; and in such moods he was not a man of action and affairs, but 'an introspective and pallid dreamer'.[51] And for all his claims to be a cold and calculating reasoning machine, Holmes also possessed a strong artistic and theatrical streak, and he could have been a great actor (as well as a great criminal). He loved producing dramatic dénouements to his cases, he relished the applause of his admirers, and it was both a professional necessity and a personal pleasure for him to dress up, put on make-up, and disguise himself as another man – or as a woman. 'With Vaseline upon one's forehead', he told Watson in 'The Dying Detective', as if proclaiming a decadent manifesto, 'belladonna in one's eyes, rouge over the cheek bones, and crusts of beeswax around one's lips, a very satisfying effect can be produced.' What, then, was it about late nineteenth-century London which Sherlock Holmes found alternatively, and contradictorily, so stultifying yet also so stimulating, and what were the circumstances under which, as Dr Watson so frequently observed, Holmes changed 'in an instant . . . from the languid dreamer to the man of action'?[52]

III

At first glance, the answer to those questions is obvious, for during the 1880s and 1890s 'the dark jungle of criminal London' was widely regarded as a place of squalor, danger, evil and wrongdoing on a uniquely massive and unrivalled scale, which meant it offered greater investigative opportunities and criminological possibilities than Holmes could ever have found in the 'stagnant' provinces, in Glasgow or Cardiff or Birmingham or Bristol, or in any other European town or continental capital. Hence his wholly understandable decision to set up, as the world's first consulting detective, in the first city of the world. 'He loved to lie', Dr Watson observed at the beginning of 'The Resident Patient', 'in the very centre of five millions of people, with his filaments stretching out and running through them, responsive to every little rumour or suspicion of unsolved crime.' 'Amid the action and reaction of so dense a swarm of humanity', Holmes told the good doctor on another occasion, 'every possible combination of events may be expected to take place.'[53] But in practice, and all too often, such high Holmesian expectations went unmet, for in an era of falling crime rates and enhanced policing, and despite the contrary claims of the sensationalist press, London was becoming a much safer city, violent crime had diminished, most wrongdoing was on a small and petty scale and, like prostitution, it was generally confined to the working classes.[54] Hence Holmes's constant lament that, despite his best hopes and intentions, *there was nothing for him to do*. 'There are,' he repeatedly complained, 'no crimes and no criminals in these days'; 'man, or at least criminal man, has lost all enterprise and originality'; 'audacity and romance seems to have passed for ever from the criminal world.' Crime was 'commonplace' (a key word), which meant existence was commonplace: and instead of interesting and challenging cases, there was merely 'some bungling villainy with a motive so transparent that even a Scotland Yard official can see through it.'[55]

This meant that for Holmes, the default mode of London living was languid depression and Wildean ennui: for all too often, he was a detective with nothing worthwhile to detect. Only on those relatively rare occasions when he was confronted by an 'interesting little problem' was his attention engaged, as the lethargic Bohemian was suddenly aroused into the (super) man of action. But a relatively small proportion of these cases involved murder or grievous bodily harm, some were 'entirely free' from any form of 'legal crime', and they tended to be domestic and conspiratorial, and professional and white-collar, rather than public, violent and working class. As a result, much of Holmes's work was involved with the complications and consequences of *secrecy*: with exposing individual duplicity and concealment, or fraud and embezzlement; or, alternatively, with the 'hushing up' of 'scandal' (another key word) that would result in shame and disgrace among the high-born, and with the recovery of sensitive government documents that had gone missing.[56] In 'A Case of Identity' and 'The Man with the Twisted Lip', the two wrong-doers, though they broke no laws, were perpetrators of cruel deceptions. In 'The Norwood Builder', Holmes foiled an attempt by the eponymous contractor to 'swindle his creditors', and in 'Black Peter', the plot hinged on the theft of securities from a disgraced banker. In 'A Scandal in Bohemia', Holmes (vainly) tried to recover compromising love letters from the eponymous King to his former lover Irene Adler; 'The Priory School' revolved around the existence and concealment of the illegitimate son of a duke; and in 'Charles Augustus Milverton', Holmes took on 'the king of all blackmailers'. His services to the British government were similar: in 'The Naval Treaty', he successfully recovered a confidential agreement between Britain and Italy; in 'The Second Stain', an intemperate and indiscreet 'letter from a foreign poten-tate' had gone missing, which, if published, would involve 'this country in a great war'; and in 'The Bruce-Partington Plans', the designs of a new submarine, 'the most jealously guarded of all government secrets', had 'gone – stolen, vanished.'[57]

Many of Holmes's London cases were concerned with unmasking wrongdoings which individuals sought to keep secret, or with recovering documents that governments sought to keep confidential. This in turn meant that despite his oft-repeated claim that it was the interest of the problem rather than the stat-ure of the client that appealed to him, in practice few of those who sought his assistance came from the lower echelons of soci-ety; and as the example of 'The Priory School' makes plain, his clients were often of similar status when Holmes investigated out-side the capital. There, too, the cases were frequently concerned with fraud, deception, blackmail or secrecy, most famously in *The Hound of the Baskervilles*, but also in 'The Boscombe Valley Mys-tery', 'Silver Blaze' and 'Shoscombe Old Place'. And even when Holmes investigated outside the great metropolis, the parts of the United Kingdom to which he ventured were generally extensions of the city, for the centre of gravity of the out-of-town stories was emphatically the Home Counties of Sussex, Surrey, Berkshire and Kent. Wales did not feature at all: the closest Holmes ever got to it was Herefordshire. Nor, despite Conan Doyle's own upbringing, did his hero ever visit Scotland on a case, and Scottish figures rarely appeared in the stories. As for Ireland: it was the land of Conan Doyle's forbears, but he rejected its Catholicism and (for most of his life) he also deplored Irish nationalism. So it is no surprise that Holmes never crossed the Irish Sea, and that the few Irish figures in the stories tended to be villains: the murderous American gang called the 'Scowrers', based on the 'Molly Maguires', that feature in *The Valley of Fear*; Professor Moriarty, whose name was taken from an Irish school contemporary of Conan Doyle's, in 'The Final Problem'; and Holmes himself, when impersonating an Irish-American with strong anti-British and pro-German feelings in 'His Last Bow'.[58]

In a domestic context, then, the Holmes and Watson stories were preoccupied with the great metropolis, or with the London-dominated south-east, while the rest of England and the remainder of the United Kingdom scarcely counted. As this compact and connected geography suggests, they often focused on the interlinked worlds of monarchy and government, aristocracy and plutocracy, financiers and rentiers, diplomats and military men, that were spreading across much of the city itself and out into the moneyed and mansioned Home Counties – worlds that were also being vividly depicted (and deplored) by J. A. Hobson in his book, *Imperialism: A Study*, which he first published in 1902, the same year that Conan Doyle produced *The Hound of the Baskervilles*, and also resolved to bring his discarded hero more permanently back to life.[59] This, in turn, suggests a more convincing justification for Holmes's need to live and work in London than that which he habitually – but somewhat implausibly – advanced: for what really attracted the great detective to the great metropolis was that it was the epicentre of that large and growing nexus of national and imperial 'gentlemanly capitalists' that Hobson so perceptively identified in his powerful anti-imperial polemic. Thus understood, Holmes was not so much concerned with 'interesting problems', whatever they might be, and regardless of the social standing of the client: instead, he acted as the resident troubleshooter for those generally privileged but sometimes unfortunate people, living in the south east of England, who were the agents and the beneficiaries – or the victims – of Britain's late-nineteenth-century imperial pre-eminence and financial supremacy. And the kings and the princes, the popes and the presidents, the monarchs and the bankers, who constituted Holmes's more extended continental clientele, belonged to a similar world, and they turned to him with similar problems.[60]

Sherlock Holmes's London was not only the financial capital of the United Kingdom and the European continent, but also of trans-Atlantic Anglo-America, a concept and a construct that were becoming closer yet also more competitive during the 1880s and 1890s. On the one hand, this was a growing era of international rapprochement and cultural interconnectedness, as the two Anglo-Saxon nations increasingly began to appreciate the things they had in common; but it was also a time when the United States was beginning to challenge the United Kingdom as the world's industrial and financial hegemon, and to acquire its own imperial and maritime ambitions. 'We've got to go into partnership with them, or be overshadowed by them', Conan Doyle perceptively concluded after his first visit, when he sensed American hostility to Britain even as he relished American friendship, and he had earlier dedicated *The White Company* 'To the hope of the future, the reunion of the English-speaking races'. These Anglo-American ambivalences were well caught in the Holmes-and-Watson stories. The great detective derived his surname from Oliver Wendell Holmes, the American writer and doctor who was one of Conan Doyle's lifelong heroes; and in 'The Noble Bachelor', he expressed his creator's views when he declared: 'It is always a joy to meet an American . . . for I am one of those who believe that the folly of a monarch and the blundering of a minister in far-gone years will not prevent our children from being someday citizens of the same world-wide country under a flag which shall be a quartering of the Union Jack with the Stars and Stripes.'[61] But elsewhere, the view of America conveyed in the stories was less appreciative and optimistic: the Mormons were roundly criticized in *A Study in Scarlet*; the Ku Klux Klan was denounced in 'The Five Orange Pips'; the 'Scowrers' received similar treatment in *The Valley of Fear*; in 'The Dancing Men' and 'The Three Garridebs', the villains were both Americans 'of sinister and murderous reputation'; and the central character in 'The Problem of Thor Bridge' was the American 'Gold King', Neil Gibson, who was also singularly unattractive.[62]

The British Empire, of which London was even more the capital than it was of Anglo-America, was also treated by Conan Doyle with a certain degree of equivocation. In one guise, London was the place to which Britons returned after imperial service overseas, most famously in the case of Dr Watson himself, recovering from the wound received while on military duty in Afghanistan. Some Britons, having made their fortune in the Empire by honourable means, went home hoping to live in peace and prosperity in the mother country. In *The Hound of the Baskervilles*, Sir Charles Baskerville came back to Britain, 'having made large sums of money in South African speculation', with the aim of improving his house and estate in the West Country. In 'The Boscombe Valley Mystery', John Turner 'made his money in Australia and returned some years ago to the old country.' And in 'A Case of Identity', Miss Mary Sutherland enjoyed an income left to her by her Uncle Ned which was derived from 'New Zealand stock, paying 4.5 per cent.'[63] In another guise, the British Empire was the destination where those who had erred in Britain might venture forth to seek redemption on the frontier. In 'The Devil's

Foot', the 'great lion-hunter and explorer', Dr Leon Sterndale, was urged by Holmes to 'bury himself' in central Africa, having poisoned his enemies in a terrible (if justified) act of revenge. In 'The Priory School', the illegitimate son of the Duke of Holdernesse, who resorted to kidnapping and condoned murder, was banished 'to seek his fortune in Australia'. The undergraduate caught cheating in 'The Three Students' set out for a new life in the colonies. 'I trust', Holmes tells him, 'that a bright future awaits you in Rhodesia. For once you have fallen low. Let us see, in the future, how high you can rise.' And there was Empire as a place, not of atonement and redemption, but of freedom and opportunity: as in 'The Copper Beeches', where Mr Fowler and Miss Ruscastle escaped a wicked family by Fowler accepting 'a government appointment on the Island of Mauritius.'[64]

But there was also a 'persistent querying of Empire in the Sherlock Holmes canon', for Conan Doyle often depicted it as a sinister place, where desperate men did terrible things, which subsequently became a source of embarrassment or (more likely) revenge when they returned home. *The Sign of Four*, which owed much to Robert Louis Stevenson and Wilkie Collins, featured two villains who had stolen the 'Agra treasure' in India, but had later been imprisoned there; they eventually escaped and were determined to get the treasure back; they sought both restitution and retribution in London; and they were accompanied by an evil and 'savage' pygmy. In 'The Disappearance of Lady Frances Carfax', the wrongdoer was 'Holy' Peters, who preyed on lonely, credulous, upper-class women: Holmes described him as 'one of the most unscrupulous rascals that Australia has ever evolved' and he added, for good measure, 'for a young country it has turned out some very finished types.'[65] Similar vengeful returnees from the Antipodes and South Africa were to be found in such stories as 'The Gloria Scott', 'The Solitary Cyclist', 'The Creeping Man' and 'The Boscombe Valley Mystery'; but they were all surpassed, in 'The Speckled Band', by the violent-tempered and 'dissolute and wasteful' Dr Grimesby Roylott. As the scion of a fading gentry family, he trained as a doctor and went out to India where he 'beat his native butler to death . . . narrowly escaped a capital sentence', and went to prison for a long time. He also acquired 'a passion for Indian animals', and returned to Britain, 'morose and disappointed', accompanied by a cheetah and a baboon which roamed the grounds of his country house; and he murdered one stepdaughter, and nearly eliminated the second, by setting on them both 'a swamp adder . . . the deadliest snake in India.'[66] From this perspective, Conan Doyle's version of the Empire came close to aligning with Hobson's: it was a place inhabited by 'damaged characters' who had gone out from Britain; but when they returned, the 'frontier narrative came home to roost'.[67]

IV

It was into this fluid and fertile late-nineteenth-century world, by turns local and metropolitan, rural and national, European and North American, imperial and global, but always seemingly focused and centred on London, that Conan Doyle introduced his detective and his doctor. That elaborate and extended context helps explain many of the contradictions and paradoxes to be found in their creator, in the stories, in their central characters, and in the treatment of London; but the picture is further complicated because the time period over which Conan Doyle wrote about Holmes and Watson – and London – was considerably longer than that in which the two friends were actively working. It bears repeating that the majority of the cases were set in the period from 1881 to 1891, and from 1894 to 1903. But *A Study in Scarlet* and *The Sign of Four*, and *The Adventures* and *The Memoirs of Sherlock Holmes*, which culminated in the great detective's 'death', were written between 1887 and 1893; *The Hound of the Baskervilles*,

The Return of Sherlock Holmes and *The Valley of Fear* were published between 1902 and 1914; and the two final collections, *His Last Bow* and *The Case-Book of Sherlock Holmes*, came out in 1917 and 1927, the second only three years before Conan Doyle died. By the time the author bade his final farewell to his most famous creation, it was almost a quarter of a century since Holmes had retired, and getting on for half a century since he had made his debut in *A Study in Scarlet*.[68] As Conan Doyle remarked in 1927, 'he began his adventures in the very heart of the Victorian era, carried it through the all-too-short reign of Edward, and has managed to hold his own little niche even in these feverish days.' This meant the perspective Conan Doyle offered on the 1880s and 1890s soon ceased to be contemporary, and became increasingly distant and anachronistic; and by the 1920s, the London of the 'bright young things' was a very different place from the 'world city' of the 1880s.[69]

The first two novellas and the first two collections of short stories that Conan Doyle wrote between 1887 and 1893 were the closest to the period in which they were fictionally set, and this gave them an immediacy and a vitality which subsequent instalments never quite recaptured. Moreover, because Conan Doyle later repeated what was essentially the same formula fifty-six times across nearly forty years, it is almost impossible to appreciate the audacious originality and powerful contemporaneity of those pioneering short stories.[70] In his identity and his methods, their central character owed something to the earlier sleuths who had appeared in the works of Charles Dickens, Edgar Allan Poe and Wilkie Collins, but Conan Doyle also drew on the personality and the techniques of Dr Joseph Bell, under whom he had studied at Edinburgh. In terms of their structure and construction, the short stories benefited from Conan Doyle's earlier experience in writing logical and ordered scientific papers, and they were also indebted to the example of Poe and much more to Maupassant (so it was not altogether surprising that Holmes was given one

French forbear). But he was the first author to establish *the detective story* as a recognizable genre, creating a format that was initially highly inventive, yet which soon became reassuringly familiar. To borrow and adapt one of Holmes's Shakespearian quotations: age could not wither them, nor custom stale their infinite monotony.[71] As such, they were also perfectly judged for the new, mass, popular readership that had come into being in the aftermath of W. E. Forster's Education Act of 1870, for it was an audience that was increasingly informed and entertained by new, high-circulation, late-Victorian newspapers and periodicals, among them *The Strand Magazine*, in which the Holmes and Watson short stories initially appeared.[72] And similar transatlantic developments in publishing (and the simultaneous tightening up of the copyright law in the United States) meant Conan Doyle was among the first generation of British authors who was also able to exploit the growing outlets provided by American periodicals, in particular *Lippincott's Monthly Magazine*.[73]

There were other ways in which the early novels and short stories were both innovative and contemporary that have long since become difficult to recover. London was a – indeed, the – *modern* city: the great stations, the Houses of Parliament and the Royal Albert Hall were scarcely a generation old. The technological infrastructure provided by railways, telegrams and hansom cabs (but rarely horse-drawn buses or the underground, or telephones or typewriters), on which Holmes relied, was also a recent creation: it was not until the mid-1870s that the hansom had reached its final form, and the number of cabs on the streets had grown ten-fold between the 1830s and the 1880s.[74] In the same way, Holmes was working with (and, often, against) state of the art policing: the uniformed force had only recently become widely recognized and esteemed by the general public; the London CID, which employed such well-meaning but plodding figures as Inspectors Gregson and Lestrade, had only been re-established on a serious footing in 1878, less than a decade before *A Study in*

Scarlet appeared; and Norman Shaw's New Scotland Yard was built between 1887 and 1890, the very years in which the first two Holmes novellas were published. Indeed, the collaboration (and, often, confusion) of the constabulary was both a novel but an essential ingredient for, as Reginald Hill has observed, 'without a police force there can be no detective fiction.'[75] Three of the early stories, 'A Case of Identity', 'The Speckled Band', and 'The Copper Beeches', described the attempts by hostile (step) fathers to prevent their (step) daughters from keeping their rightful inheritances if they took a husband, in vain defiance of the Married Women's Property Act, which had only been passed in 1882. These early writings also resonated with the intensifying conservative political culture of these years, with their support of the established order of monarchy and empire: on the walls of 221B Baker Street were the letters VR, the royal cypher of Queen Victoria, which Holmes had 'patriotically' shot in bullets, and there was a picture of General Gordon, who had been killed at Khartoum in 1885.[76]

Yet these first fictions were also liberal, indeed radical, for they were often as much concerned with the promotion of social justice as with the detection of criminal acts. Hence Holmes's praise, in 'The Naval Treaty', of the board schools that had been brought into being by the Education Act, one of the major reforms of Gladstone's first ministry which had been in power from 1868 to 1874. They were, he assured Watson, 'Light-houses. Beacons of the future!', which would help create a 'wiser, better England.' This ringing support for improved opportunities for those low down the social scale was accompanied by sympathy for mixed-race marriages (in 'The Yellow Face'), and by a sustained criticism of the misdoings of those at the top.[77] Both 'A Scandal in Bohemia', centring on sexual licence, and 'The Beryl Coronet', dealing with serious private indebtedness, were concerned with the misdemeanours and delinquencies of royalty; and as such they were a thinly veiled criticism of the wayward behaviour of the Prince of Wales and his eldest son, Prince Eddy (the Tranby

Croft affair took place in 1890 and the Cleveland Street Scandal erupted two years later). In 'The Red-Headed League', the villain, John Clay, described as a 'murderer, thief, smasher and forger', was descended from a royal duke. Although Conan Doyle later wrote of aristocrats and landowners in hushed and obsequious tones, as possessing the greatest names and most venerable lineages in the land, he did not treat them so well in these opening stories: Sir George Burnwell was a wicked baronet straight out of melodrama, and the snobbish Lord Robert St Simon, son of the impoverished Duke of Balmoral (another hit at royalty?), sought to repair the family fortunes by unscrupulously marrying an American heiress for her money.[78] Equally in Conan Doyle's sights in these early adventures was official incompetence: as he initially depicted them, Inspectors Gregson and Lestrade were both arrogant and incapable, and on several occasions, their reputations were saved by Holmes's superior brilliance and self-effacing magnanimity.

For almost a decade after 1893, Conan Doyle wrote no Sherlock Holmes stories; but in 1902, he brought his detective back in *The Hound of the Baskervilles*, which was supposedly an overlooked adventure set more than a decade earlier before his 'death'; and he then resurrected him for real in 'The Empty House', where it was revealed that Holmes had survived his encounter with Moriarty. That story was first published towards the end of 1903, and inaugurated a second phase of authorial activity which would last up to 1914 (*The Valley of Fear*, and all but the eponymous finale in *His Last Bow*, were completed just before the First World War began). But 'The Empty House' was set in 1894, which meant the gap was gradually widening between the time when the stories took place and the date of their actual composition; and it would grow wider in the future, because Conan Doyle decided to retire Holmes late in 1903, the very year he had brought him back (and soon after Holmes refused a knighthood in fiction, whereas Conan Doyle accepted one in fact).[79] Yet while Holmes remained a late-Victorian figure, living in late-Victorian London, Conan

Doyle was increasingly writing about him from an Edwardian perspective, and with Edwardian preoccupations. In 'The Abbey Grange' and 'The Devil's Foot', he intruded his own contemporary concerns about the need to reform the divorce law. Although set in the 1890s, both 'The Second Stain' and 'The Bruce-Partington Plans' reflected the heightened international tensions of the 1900s, when 'the whole of Europe' was 'an armed camp'. In the same way, 'The Six Napoleons', 'The Golden Pince-Nez', 'Wisteria Lodge' and 'The Red Circle' explored fears about foreign nihilists, anarchists and revolutionaries that were Edwardian, rather than late-Victorian, concerns (and were being simultaneously treated by Joseph Conrad, who published *The Secret Agent* in 1907). And in 'The Devil's Foot', which was set in 1897, Holmes was on the brink of a total nervous collapse, necessitating convalescence in the west country; but his broken-down condition may also have been a reflection of the growing sense of crisis which engulfed the ruling classes in Britain between 1910 and 1914.[80]

At the same time, the Edwardian metropolis suddenly became a very different place from the London of the 1880s and 1890s, as it underwent an unprecedented phase of expansion and transformation. Most of the roads and buildings associated with 'imperial London' were constructed during the decade between Holmes's retirement to the Sussex Downs and the outbreak of the First World War. Among the new thoroughfares driven through the very centre of the city were Millbank, which extended the Thames embankment east from the Palace of Westminster; Kingsway and the Aldwych, which were pushed through areas of slums and squalid housing south of Bloomsbury; and the Mall, which linked together the recently constructed ceremonial ensemble of Admiralty Arch, the Victoria Monument and the refashioned frontage to Buckingham Palace. This grand processional route meant London could now compete with Vienna, Paris, Berlin and St Petersburg as a setting for royal and state spectaculars; and elsewhere across the central area of the city, many new buildings were constructed in the style of 'high Edwardian Baroque', including the War Office and Treasury in Whitehall; the Old Bailey and the headquarters of the Port of London Authority; luxurious department stores such as Harrods, Selfridges and Burberry; opulent hotels including the Ritz, the Piccadilly and the Waldorf; the London Coliseum and the theatres of Shaftesbury Avenue; and the Methodist Central Hall and the Royal Automobile Club; while a start was made on County Hall, to accommodate the LCC, south of the Thames.[81] As G. M. Young rightly noted, these changes fundamentally transformed the public face of the metropolis in the years immediately after Queen Victoria died and Holmes retired: indeed, they were so great that when Holmes and Watson set out, after their final encounter at the end of 'His Last Bow', to journey from Harwich to London, they would have found much of the place unrecognizable after their ten years away.

Even as they approached the outskirts of London, Holmes and Watson would have noticed many bewildering changes. They would have journeyed through a section of the whole new ring of suburbs that had sprung up, among them Acton, Barnes, Chingford, Golders Green, Merton and Morden. If they had paid a sentimental visit to their old haunts in Baker Street, they would have seen the vast modern blocks of mansion flats spreading across Marylebone and the area surrounding Marble Arch, offering a wholly different style of metropolitan living from that which Mrs Hudson had earlier provided at 221B. If they had gone to Scotland Yard, they would have discovered major innovations in methods of detection, among them the use of fingerprints and photography.[82] They would also have noticed that London transport had been revolutionized, in part because of the advent of electric trams and the extension of the underground to the new outlying suburbs. Even more significant was the virtual disappearance of the horse from the streets of London: in 1903 there were 3,623 horse buses and a mere 13 motor buses, but by 1913 only 142 horse buses remained to face 3,522 motor buses; and in the cab business, there had been over 11,000 hansoms and hackneys in 1903 and only one motor taxi cab, while in 1913 there were more than 8,000 motor taxi cabs and less than 2,000 horse vehicles left.[83] All this made Edwardian London a very different city from the late-Victorian metropolis: it was grander, bigger, and more technologically advanced. Indeed, it has been suggestively argued that it would have been impossible for Holmes to have operated in such a different urban environment, where gas lamps and hansoms had been superseded by electricity and motors, which was why Conan Doyle retired him in 1903, and continued setting his stories in the 1880s and 1890s and at the turn of the century. And Holmes's creator increasingly found Edwardian London too much changed for his own liking: in *The Poison Belt*, a science fiction story published in 1913, he came close to killing off the entire population of the 'dreadful, silent city', as the earth passed through clouds of apparently lethal gas.[84]

For Conan Doyle and his generation, the First World War destroyed much of late-nineteenth-century Britain. He lost a son and a brother as a result of the conflict, and he publicly embraced Spiritualism to which he had long been privately attracted; the promotion of that cause took up most of his time and energy thereafter, and it also exposed him to considerable public ridicule. Most of his writing was devoted to justifying his paranormal views, and he produced just a trickle of Holmes and Watson stories, which were collected – and concluded – in *The Case-Book of Sherlock Holmes*.[85] Yet despite Conan Doyle's own faith and credulity, the great detective remained convinced that this was the only world there was, and that reason and scepticism were the only sure guides to human behaviour, and in these valedictory pieces he denounced human cravings for the artificial prolongation of life, as well as rejecting suicide. These later stories were also characterized by explicit references to bodily mutilation, and they addressed sexual issues more candidly than he had done before, ranging from the 'lust diary' of Baron Gruner in 'The Illustrious Client' to Holmes's declaration of 'loyalty and love' for Watson in 'The Three Garridebs.'[86] These final fictions were also shorter than the earlier narratives, often offering 'flashing glimpses of human distress and deformity', and they were further diminished by the recognition that Holmes was no longer the superman he had once been, and that it had become impossible to sustain world order and safeguard national security by the heroic efforts of a single individual, however brilliant. Hence, in these last tales, an all-pervasive sense of resignation and melancholy: 'Is not all life', Holmes asked Watson at the beginning of 'The Retired Colourman', 'pathetic and futile?'[87] This was a very different sort of disenchantment from the languid, Wildean ennui of the 1880s and 1890s: a dazed bewilderment in the face of a post-war world more bleak than brave. And when Holmes feared that 'our poor world' was in danger of becoming 'a cesspool', he may have echoed Watson's original description of London in *A Study in Scarlet*, but this time offered no redemptive alternative to it.[88]

This resigned sense of disorientation may have been further intensified by the realization that much of Sherlock Holmes's 'world city' of the 1880s and 1890s had been transformed beyond recognition, as large parts of central London were redeveloped, and as the population of Greater London rose by another million between 1911 and 1931. On Piccadilly and Park Lane, many of the old aristocratic palaces were demolished to make way for flats, offices and shops. John Nash's Regent Street was pulled down, and rebuilt to the designs of Sir Reginald Bloomfield. New London headquarters were established for the dominions of Canada, Australia, New Zealand and South Africa, and also for India; and the protracted construction of County Hall was finally completed. Work on Bush House was begun in 1925, and on Broadcasting House three years later: new buildings for the new medium of the wireless and, eventually, television, which would also transform both the practice and the depiction of detection.[89] Horse-drawn cabs completely disappeared from the streets of London, and were replaced by motorized taxis, while the continuing extension of the Underground led to the creation of a further, expanded suburban 'Metroland', encompassing Ealing, Wembley, Hendon, Finchley, Purley, Coulsdon and Dagenham. And the making of the new Great West Road not only resulted in the similar expansion of Heston and Hounslow, but also in the building of the 'Golden Mile' at Brentford where, from 1925, a succession of iconic art deco factories were constructed.[90] Surveying these changes, in a work that appeared in the same year as *The Case-Book of Sherlock Holmes*, Harold Clunn concluded that London remained 'the largest city and the capital of the greatest Empire the world has ever seen'; but he was obliged to recognize that, in terms of numbers, it might soon be overtaken by New York. Yet by then, it had in fact already been surpassed, which meant the London of the 1920s was no longer the undisputed 'world city' it had been in its late-Victorian heyday, and it had ceased to be the place where the future – both bad and good – was already happening in the present.[91]

As early as 1914, when Conan Doyle had revisited America, he had been amazed at the changes that had taken place on Manhattan since he had first set foot there twenty years before. 'It seems', he observed, having made it to the top of the fifty-nine-storey Woolworth Building, 'as though someone had gone over the city with a watering pot, and these stupendous buildings had grown up overnight as a result . . . New York', he concluded, 'is a wonderful city, as America is a wonderful country, with a big future.'[92] In 1927, Erich Pommer and Fritz Lang made the same point even more emphatically in their epic science-fiction film, *Metropolis*, which was allegedly set one hundred years hence in a vast, high-rise city, but was in fact based on contemporary Manhattan, which was roaring and soaring upwards during the booming 'twenties, and offering a wholly original version of a 'jazz-age' new world city. Even following the Wall Street Crash, just a year before Conan Doyle died, New York continued to rise and reach for the stars, with the completion of the Chrysler Building and the Empire State Building, the world's tallest skyscrapers, and the construction of the Rockefeller Center, that great monument to philanthropic endeavour and art deco design. In 1938, Jerry Siegel and Joe Schuster created their own, comic book version of Nietzsche's Superman, who operated in a city called Metropolis, which owed much to the Lang and Pommer film; and in the following year, Bob Kane and Bill Finger responded with Batman, who was based in the fictional Gotham City, which was another scarcely disguised version of New York, albeit more at night than in the daytime.[93] Superman and Batman would become the iconic crusaders and knight errants of the twentieth century, they preferred tights and modern gadgets to deerstalkers and hansom cabs, they were much more credible in Manhattan than they would ever have been in Marylebone, and Batman even appropriated the accolade first bestowed on Conan Doyle's creation: for just as New York had surpassed London as the greatest 'world city', so Batman had superseded Sherlock Holmes as 'the World's Greatest Detective.'

V

Or had he? The considered answer to that question must surely be no: Batman had not, and has not, done any such thing, and nor has Superman. For while comic books and blockbuster movies, bringing Gotham City and Metropolis vividly to life, have endowed these high-tech crusaders with a certain amount of glitzy global glamour, they have scarcely begun to compete with Sherlock Holmes's extraordinary and enduring appeal and his still-expanding multi-media longevity. During the last hundred years, the novels and short stories have been translated into virtually every major language, and they have never been out of print in English. In Conan Doyle's lifetime, some stories were transferred from the page to the stage, beginning in 1899 with the American actor William Gillette, who recreated Holmes as a theatrical figure, and played the part for many years on both sides of the Atlantic. The first silent film, entitled *Sherlock Holmes Baffled*, appeared as early as 1900, and forty-five shorts and two feature length movies were produced by Stoll Pictures between 1921 and 1923. The first sound film to feature Sherlock Holmes was made in 1929, and Basil Rathbone and Nigel Bruce made fourteen American Holmes-and-Watson talkies between 1939 and 1946.[94] Since then, Holmes has gone on to the wireless, including a complete adaptation of every novel and story on BBC Radio 4 broadcast between 1989 and 1998, and there have been many television versions, among them those starring Douglas Wilmer, then Peter Cushing between 1964 and 1968, and Jeremy Brett from 1984 to 1994. Many 'new' Sherlock Holmes stories have been written, broadcast and filmed, and statues have been unveiled to him in London, Edinburgh and Moscow.[95] In 1934, the Sherlock Holmes Society was founded in London, and the Baker Street Irregulars in New York, the first of many world-wide groups extending as far as Australia, India and Japan, and they in turn have spawned a strange, obsessive-compulsive world of 'Sherlockian' pseudo-scholarship.[96] The result is that Conan Doyle's creation has remained, in P. D. James's words, 'the unchallenged Great Detective', and he has become the most famous fictional character in the English language and the most portrayed movie character, with more than seventy actors playing the part in over two hundred films.[97]

All this means that Sherlock Holmes has long since left behind the time and the place in which he was originally created, and has taken on a life (indeed, many lives) of his own, far beyond the particular confines of late-nineteenth-century London in which he first appeared. Indeed, that process had already begun while

Conan Doyle was still alive and writing new stories in the 1920s, as Holmes and Watson, and the late Victorian city they inhabited, were already being looked back on with a kind of wistful longing for what seemed to have been a happier place in an earlier time. At the end of that decade, T. S. Eliot noted that 'in the Sherlock Holmes stories, the late nineteenth century is always romantic, always nostalgic', and that 'the pleasant externals' of the city were an essential part of that nostalgia and romance. For Eliot, as for a growing number of his inter-war generation, Conan Doyle's stories had become a welcome fantasy escape from the 'waste land' of modernity embodied in the damp-pavement (and still fog-bound) dinginess of contemporary London. Indeed, Eliot went further, and predicted that the nostalgia and romance would only increase and intensify among those future Holmes and Watson devotees who would have had no first-hand recollection of the nineteenth century.[98] And posterity has abundantly vindicated that prediction, as countless readers, listeners and viewers the world over remain beguiled by what they *imagine* to have been London in 1895, with its sinister and omnipresent fogs, and with Holmes sporting his deerstalker hat, his curved Calabash pipe and his Inverness cape. But it bears repeating that London fog in the 1880s and 1890s was more widespread in the city than it was in the pages of Conan Doyle's stories, and that only after the passing of the Clean Air Act in 1953 could such life-threatening environmental pollutants become an object of nostalgia; while Holmes's hat, pipe and cape owed more to the illustrations of Sydney Paget and the films starring Basil Rathbone than they did to Conan Doyle's original texts (and they were less in evidence in the television series starring Jeremy Brett, which sought to be more true to the original stories).[99]

Yet such fuzzy, romantic, gas-lit nostalgia conveniently disregards the many 'unpleasant externals' of late-nineteenth-century London: the filth and the stench, the noise and the congestion, the squalor and the poverty.[100] It shows no awareness of the limitations, the inadequacies, the idiosyncracies of Conan Doyle's vision of the 'world city', or of the alternative inspirations for it, which owed at least as much to Edinburgh as to the great metropolis itself. It fails to appreciate the time-bound specificity and uniqueness of Sherlock Holmes, and also of his creator, who in their contradictory personalities resonated so powerfully with the 1880s and 1890s, two decades in which anxiety and hope, poverty and progress, were so challengingly co-mingled. It also ignores the way in which works that were initially innovative and contemporary became, even during the author's later lifetime, increasingly formulaic and anachronistic, and since then have become ever more disconnected from their historic time and place of origin. Thus understood, Holmes's posthumous career, in the decades since Conan Doyle's death, is itself a subject worthy of serious attention: as a classic instance, like Gilbert and Sullivan's operettas, and P. G. Wodehouse's Jeeves and Wooster stories, of an original literary genre long and successfully outliving the circumstances in which it was first created.[101] But Holmes's own life in his own time in his own city is more fascinating still, for he was a fictional character who both embodied, yet also bridged, the gap between the two very different identities of late-nineteenth-century London – as the place where the squalid reality of urban despair co-existed with the romantic possibilities of metropolitan redemption.

Notes

1 Throughout these notes, I have used the following abbreviations:

ACD   Sir Arthur Conan Doyle

CASH   ACD, *The Penguin Complete Adventures of Sherlock Holmes* (Harmondsworth, 1984 edn)

CD   A. Lycett, *Conan Doyle: The Man Who Created Sherlock Holmes* (London, 2008)

LiL   J. Lellenberg, D. Stashower and C. Foley (eds), *Arthur Conan Doyle: A Life in Letters* (London, 2008)

SACD   J. Dickson Carr, *The Life of Sir Arthur Conan Doyle* (New York, 2003 edn)

2 A. Briggs, *Victorian Cities* (London, 1963), pp. 320–31. For the same description applied at an earlier time, see C. Fox (ed.), *London – World City, 1800–1840* (London, 1992).

3 J. Martin, 'Reinventing the Tower Beefeater in the Nineteenth Century', *History*, xcviii (2013), pp. 730–49; T. B. Smith, 'In Defence of Privilege': The City of London and the Challenge of Municipal Reform, 1875–1890', *Journal of Social History*, xxvii (1993), pp. 59–83.

4 G. Stedman Jones, *Outcast London: A Study in the Relationship between the Classes in Victorian Society* (Harmondsworth, 1976); W. J. Fishman, *East End 1888* (London, 1988); J. R. Walkowitz, *City of Dreadful Delight: Narratives of Sexual Danger in Late-Victorian London* (London, 1992); P. L. Garside, 'West End, East End: London, 1890–1940', in A. Sutcliffe (ed.), *Metropolis, 1890–1940* (London, 1984), pp. 221–35.

5 A. Service, *Edwardian Architecture: A Handbook to Building Design in Britain, 1890–1914* (London, 1977), pp. 43–44; C. Booth, *Life and Labour of the People of London* (2 vols., London, 1889–91).

6 D. Rodgers, *Atlantic Crossings: Social Politics in a Progressive Age* (Cambridge, Mass., 1998), pp. 132–42; A. Lees, 'The Metropolis and the Intellectual', in Sutcliffe (ed.), *Metropolis*, pp. 75–77, 79–81.

7 *CASH: A Study in Scarlet*, p. 15; ACD, 'On the Geographical Distribution of British Intellect', *The Nineteenth Century* (August 1888), p. 185; *CD*, p. 146.

8 M. Girouard, *Cities and People, A Social and Architectural History* (London, 1985), pp. 343–9; T. Hunt, *Building Jerusalem: The Rise and Fall of the Victorian City* (London, 2004). For contemporary views of the city as both the betrayer and redeemer of mankind, see G. Gilloch, *Myth and Metropolis: Walter Benjamin and the City* (Cambridge, 1996), pp. 1–5.

9 J. McLaughlin, *Writing the Urban Jungle: Reading Empire in London from Doyle to Eliot* (Charlottesville, 2000), p. 51.

10 There is a great deal of 'Sherlockian' pseudo-scholarship outlining the career and dating the cases of the great detective, as if he had been a 'real' person, among which are: W. S. Baring-Gould, *Sherlock Holmes: A Biography of the World's First Consulting Detective* (London, 1963); M. Harrison, *The World of Sherlock Holmes* (London, 1973); H. F. R. Keating, *Sherlock Holmes: The Man and His World* (New York, 1979); D. A. Redmond, *Sherlock Holmes: A Study in Sources* (Montreal, 1982).

11 *CASH*: 'The Greek Interpreter', p. 435; 'The Musgrave Ritual', p. 387; ACD, *Memories & Adventures* (London, 1988 edn), p. 99.

12 *CASH: His Last Bow*, preface, p. 869; 'The Creeping Man', p. 1080; 'The Lion's Mane', p. 1083.

13 J. G. Cawelti, *Adventure, Mystery and Romance: Formula Stories as Art and Popular Culture* (Chicago, 1976), p. 140; J. Conlin, *Tales of Two Cities: Paris, London and the Birth of the Modern City* (London, 2013), p. 175.

14 *CASH*: 'The Empty House', p. 489; A. Welsh, *The City of Dickens* (Oxford, 1971); F. S. Schwartzbach, *Dickens and the City* (London, 1979); Briggs, *Victorian Cities*, pp. 355–67.

15 ACD, *Memories & Adventures*, pp. 95–97; *LiL*, p. 291.

16 *SACD*, pp. 276, 280.

17 Girouard, *Cities and People*, p. v; J. *LiL*, pp. 63–71, 101–07; *CD*, pp. 42–43, 122; O. Dudley Edwards, *The Quest for Sherlock Holmes: A Biographical Study of Arthur Conan Doyle* (Edinburgh, 1983), pp. 39–40, 150–51.

18 *CASH: The Sign of Four*, p. 126; Dudley Edwards, *The Quest for Sherlock Holmes*, pp. 202–3, 249–50.

19 *CASH*: 'The Priory School', p. 540; 'The Copper Beeches', p. 323; 'The Reigate Puzzle', p. 398.

20 P. D. James, *Talking about Detective Fiction* (Oxford, 2009), p. 40; *CASH*: 'The Copper Beeches', p. 317.

21 F. J. Brodie, 'On the Prevalence of Fog in London During the 20 Years 1871 to 1890', *Quarterly Journal of the Royal Meteorological Society*, xviii (1892), pp. 40–45; idem, 'Decrease of Fog in London During Recent Years', *Quarterly Journal of the Royal Meteorological Society*, xxxi (1905), pp. 15–28; H. T. Bernstein, 'The Mysterious Disappearance of Edwardian London Fog', *The London Journal*, i (1975), pp. 189–206; P. Brimblecombe, *The Big Smoke: A History of Air Pollution in London Since Medieval Times* (London, 2011 edn), pp. 108–35.

22 H. James, *Essays on London and Elsewhere* (London, 1893), pp. 1, 9; G. Seiberling, *Monet in London* (Seattle, 1988), p. 55. See also S. F. Khan, 'Monet at the Savoy Hotel and the London Fogs, 1899–1901' (unpublished PhD dissertation, University of Birmingham, 2011).

23 F. M. L. Thompson, 'Nineteenth-Century Horse Sense', *Economic History Review*, new ser., xxix (1976), pp. 62–63, 77.

24 Briggs, *Victorian Cities*, p. 331; G. M. Young, *Victorian England: Portrait of an Age* (Oxford, 1977 edn.), p. 92.

25 *CASH*: 'The Dying Detective', p. 933; *The Sign of Four*, p. 138; A. Service, *London 1900* (London, 1979), pp. 1–7.

26 *CASH*: 'The Naval Treaty', p. 451; M. H. Port, *Imperial London: Civil Government Building in London, 1850–1915* (London,

1995), pp. 198–210; Dudley Edwards, *The Quest for Sherlock Holmes*, pp. 249–50.

27 *CASH*: 'The Blue Carbuncle', p. 251; *The Sign of Four*, p. 99.

28 There is also much 'Sherlockian' pseudo-scholarship on Holmes's London, which contains a great deal of valuable information, but is wholly lacking in historical awareness or perspective, for which see, among others: M. Harrison, *The London of Sherlock Holmes* (Newton Abbot, 1972); T. Kobayashi, A. Higashiyama and M. Uemura, *Sherlock Holmes's London: Following in the Footsteps of London's Master Detective* (San Francisco, 1983); D. Sinclair, *Sherlock Holmes's London* (London, 2009); D. Sinclair, *Close to Holmes: A look at the connections between historical London, Sherlock Holmes and Sir Arthur Conan Doyle* (London, 2009); T. Bruce Wheeler, *The London of Sherlock Holmes* (London, 2011); J. Christopher, *The London of Sherlock Holmes* (Stroud, 2012).

29 J. Summerson, *Georgian London* (London, 2003 edn), pp. 179–224; J. Mordaunt Crook, *London's Arcadia: John Nash & the Planning of Regent's Park* (London, 2001); R. Porter, *London: A Social History* (London, 1994), pp. 313–14; *CASH*: 'The Bruce-Partington Plans', p. 915.

30 D. J. Olsen, *The Growth of Victorian London* (London, 1976), p. 81; J. White, *London in the Nineteenth Century: 'A Human Awful Wonder of God'* (London, 2007), p. 477.

31 Briggs, *Victorian Cities*, p. 335; H. Pelling, *Social Geography of British Elections, 1885–1910* (London, 1967), p. 27.

32 G. Grossmith and W. Grossmith, *The Diary of a Nobody* (Bristol, 1892).

33 *CASH*: 'The Six Napoleons', p. 588.

34 *SACD*, pp. 84, 236; *LiL*, p. 343; N. Pevsner, *An Outline of European Architecture* (Harmondsworth, 7th edn., 1963), pp. 397–98, 444–46; K. T. Jackson, 'The Capital of Capitalism: the New York Metropolitan Region, 1890–1940', in Sutcliffe (ed.), *Metropolis*, pp. 321–24; Girouard, *Cities and People*, pp. 319–24.

35 J. Schneer, *London 1900: The Imperial Metropolis* (London, 1999), pp. 184–226; D. Cannadine, 'The Context, Performance and Meaning of Ritual: The British Monarchy and the "Invention of Tradition", c. 1820–1977', in E. J. Hobsbawm and T. Tanger (eds), *The Invention of Tradition* (Cambridge, 1983), pp. 108–38.

36 S. Ledger and R. Luckhurst, 'Introduction: Reading the "Fin de Siècle"', in idem (eds.), *The Fin de Siècle: A Reader in Cultural History, c1880–1900* (Oxford, 2000), pp. xvi–xviii; R. A. Kaye, 'Sexual Identity at the Fin de Siècle', in G. Marshall (ed.), *The Cambridge Companion to the Fin de Siècle* (Cambridge, 2007), pp. 53–72.

37 L. McKinstry, *Rosebery: Statesman in Turmoil* (London, 2005), pp. 348–68; R. F. Mackay, *Balfour: Intellectual Statesman* (Oxford, 1985), p. 8.

38 Briggs, *Victorian Cities*, pp. 342–55; P. Thompson, *Socialists, Liberals and Labour: The Struggle for London, 1885–1914* (London, 1967), pp. 80–82, 90–111; K. Young and P. Garside, *Metropolitan London. Politics and Urban Change, 1837–1981* (London, 1982), pp. 64–101; S. Pennybacker, *A Vision for London: Labour, Everyday Life and the LCC Experiment* (London, 1995), pp. 1–32.

39 J. Walkowitz, *City of Dreadful Delight: Narratives of Sexual Danger in Late-Victorian London* (Chicago, 1992), pp. 81–120, 191–228; D. Gray, 'Gang Crime and the Media in Late Nineteenth-Century London: The Regent's Park Murder of 1888', *Cultural and Social History*, x (2013), pp. 559–75.

40 V. A. C. Gatrell, 'The Decline of Theft and Violence in Victorian and Edwardian England', in V. A. C. Gatrell, B. Lenman and G. Parker (eds), *Crime and the Law: The Social History of Crime in Western Europe since 1500* (London, 1980), pp. 240–41, 280–86, 290–93; M. J. Wiener, *Reconstructing the Criminal: Culture, Law and Policy in England, 1830–1914* (Cambridge, 1990), pp. 216–17.

41 D. Cannadine, 'Gilbert and Sullivan: The Making and Un-Making of a British "Tradition"', and C. Emsley, 'The English

Bobby: An Indulgent Tradition', both in R. Porter (ed.), *Myths of the English* (Cambridge, 1993 edn), respectively p. 22, p. 120; James, *Detective Fiction*, pp. 18–19.

42 C. Emsley, *Crime, Police and Penal Policy: European Experiences, 1750–1940* (Oxford, 2007), pp. 142–59, 181–214; V. A. C. Gatrell, 'Crime, Authority and the Policeman State', in F. M. L. Thompson (ed.), *The Cambridge Social History of Britain*, vol. iii, *Social Agencies and Institutions* (Cambridge, 1990), pp. 306–10; Wiener, *Reconstructing the Criminal*, pp. 224–56.

43 *SACD*, pp. 48–49; *LiL*, pp. 267–68, 407–507, 566; ACD, *Memories & Adventures*, pp. 200–09; ACD, *The Great Boer War* (London, 1900); ACD, *The War in South Africa – Its Cause and Conduct* (London, 1902).

44 *SACD*, pp. xiv, 56–60, 163, 263–64, 276, 283; Schneer, *London 1900*, pp. 106–13; McLaughlin, *Writing the Urban Jungle*, pp. 27–78.

45 *CD*, p. 44; Dudley Edwards, *The Quest for Sherlock Holmes*, pp. 185–86, 189–90; *LiL*, pp. 313, 357–58, 532–33, 579–60, 623, 637; *CASH*: 'The Second Stain', p. 650.

46 *CASH*: 'The Devil's Foot', p. 968; ACD, *Memories & Adventures*, pp. 78–79; Dudley Edwards, *The Quest for Sherlock Holmes*, pp. 15–17; *SACD*, pp. 101–12; *CD*, pp. 242–46, 253–55, 259, 264–65, 277, 308–13, 320–21; *LiL*, pp. 412–18, 522.

47 *LiL*, pp. 365–66, 562–63; ACD, *Memories & Adventures*, pp. 55–56; ACD, *The Story of Mr George Edalji* (London, 1907); ACD, *The Case of Oscar Slater* (London, 1912); ACD, *The Crime of the Congo* (London, 1909); C. Wynne, *The Colonial Conan Doyle: British Imperialism, Irish Nationalism and the Gothic* (London, 2002), pp. 101–8.

48 James, *Detective Fiction*, p. 31; *CASH*: *The Sign of Four*, pp. 89, 96, 129; 'The Red-Headed League', p. 190; 'The Abbey Grange', pp. 642, 646; *The Hound of the Baskervilles*, p. 754; 'The Bruce-Partington Plans', p. 927.

49 CASH: 'The Bruce-Partington Plans', p. 913; 'The Illustrious Client', p. 999; 'The Three Gables', p. 1032; 'The Retired Colourman', p. 1120; Wiener, Reconstructing the Criminal, p. 222; Dudley Edwards, The Quest for Sherlock Holmes, pp. 127–28, 132–33; LiL, pp. 78–79; W. O. Aydelotte, 'The Detective Story as a Historical Source', in F. M. Nevins (ed.), The Mystery Writer's Art (Bowling Green, Ohio, 1970), p. 323–24.

50 CD, p. 120; R. Hill, 'Holmes: The Hamlet of Crime Fiction,' in H. F. R. Keating (ed.), Crime Writers (London, 1978), pp. 22–24.

51 CASH: 'The Greek Interpreter', p. 435; The Sign of Four, pp. 89–90; 'The Priory School', p. 547.

52 CD, p. 358; CASH: The Sign of Four, p. 13; 'A Scandal in Bohemia', p. 170; The Valley of Fear, pp. 776, 809; 'The Dying Detective', p. 941; The Hound of the Baskervilles, p. 689; 'The Bruce-Partington Plans', p. 920; 'The Mazarin Stone', pp. 1012–13, 1022.

53 CASH: 'The Empty House', p. 488; 'Wisteria Lodge', p. 879; 'The Norwood Builder', p. 496; 'The Resident Patient', p. 423; 'The Cardboard Box', p. 888; 'The Blue Carbuncle', p. 245.

54 Gatrell, 'Crime, Authority and the Policeman State', pp. 264–65, 270; J. Walkowitz, Prostitution and Victorian Society: Women, Class and the State (Cambridge, 1980), pp. 13–14, 29–31.

55 CASH: A Study in Scarlet, p. 25; The Sign of Four, pp. 89–90, 93; 'The Red-Headed League', p. 190; 'A Case of Identity', p. 197; 'The Copper Beeches', p. 317; 'Wisteria Lodge', p. 870.

56 CASH: 'The Empty House', p. 496; 'The Blue Carbuncle', p. 245; 'The Priory School', pp. 543, 545, 555–56; 'Charles Augustus Milverton', p. 582; 'The Three Students', p. 596; 'The Missing Three-Quarter', pp. 629–30, 635; 'The Abbey Grange', p. 640; 'The Second Stain', pp. 663, 666; The Hound of the Baskervilles, p. 695; 'The Problem of Thor Bridge', p. 1055; Wiener, Reconstructing the Criminal, pp. 219–20, 244–50; S. Knight, Form and Ideology in Crime Fiction (Bloomington, 1980), p. 88; Cawelti, Adventure, Mystery and Romance, pp. 95–96.

57 *CASH*: 'The Norwood Buiilder', p. 510; 'Charles Augustus Milverton', p. 572; 'The Second Stain', pp. 651–53; 'The Bruce-Partington Plans', p. 916.

58 Dudley Edwards, *The Quest for Sherlock Holmes*, pp. 117–18; *LiL*, p. 595; *CD*, pp. 24, 35, 364–65, 383; *CASH*: 'His Last Bow', p. 973.

59 J. A. Hobson, *Imperialism: A Study* (1965 edn), pp. 48, 51, 59; idem, 'The General Election: A Sociological Interpretation', *Sociological Review*, iii (1910), pp. 112–13; P. J. Cain, 'J. A. Hobson, Financial Capitalism and Imperialism in Late Victorian and Edwardian England', *Journal of Imperial and Commonwealth History*, xiii (1985), pp. 8–9; P. J. Cain and A. G. Hopkins, *British Imperialism*, vol. i, *Innovation and Expansion, 1688–1914* (Harlow, 1993), pp. 16–17, 199–200.

60 Hobson, *Imperialism*, p. 54.

61 H. Orel, *Sir Arthur Conan Doyle: Interviews and Recollections* (New York, 1991), p. 126; *LiL*, pp. 336–44; *CD*, pp. 21, 60, 82, 218–19; *CASH*: 'The Noble Bachelor', pp. 299–300.

62 *CASH*: 'The Five Orange Pips', pp. 226–27; *The Valley of Fear*, pp. 832–33; 'The Dancing Men', p. 523; 'The Three Garridebs', p. 1051; 'The Problem of Thor Bridge', pp. 1055–61.

63 *CASH*: *The Hound of the Baskervilles*, p. 676; 'The Boscombe Valley Mystery', pp. 203, 208; 'A Case of Identity', p. 193.

64 *CASH*: 'The Devil's Foot', pp. 961, 970; 'The Priory School', p. 558; 'The Three Students', pp. 606–07; 'The Copper Beeches', p. 332.

65 J. A. Kestner, *Sherlock's Men: Masculinity, Conan Doyle, and Cultural History* (Aldershot, 1997), p. 7; *CD*, p. 325; *CASH*: *The Sign of Four*, pp. 138–39; 'The Disappearance of Lady Frances Carfax', p. 947.

66 *CASH*: 'The Speckled Band', pp. 260, 268, 272.

67 McLaughlin, *Writing the Urban Jungle*, p. 51; Hobson, *Imperialism*, p. 51. Hobson and ACD (and, indeed, Joseph Conrad in *Heart of Darkness*) also shared views about Belgian involvement in the Congo: Hobson, *Imperialism*, p. 198.

68 Dudley Edwards, *The Quest for Sherlock Holmes*, p. 128.

69 *CASH: Case-Book*, preface, p. 983; Hill, 'Holmes: The Hamlet of Crime Fiction', p. 22.

70 *LiL*, p. 514.

71 *CASH*: 'The Empty House', p. 489; Dudley Edwards, *The Quest for Sherlock Holmes*, p. 143; Conlin, *Tales of Two Cities*, pp. 194–209.

72 Hill, 'Holmes: the Hamlet of Crime Fiction', pp. 28–31; A. Hennegan, 'Personalities and Principles: Aspects of Literature and Life in Fin de Siècle England', in M. Teich and R. Porter (eds), *Fin de Siècle and its Legacy* (Cambridge, 1990), pp. 173, 184; M. D. Stetz, 'Publishing Industries and Practices', in Marshall, *Cambridge Companion to the Fin de Siècle*, pp. 113–30.

73 *CD*, pp. 155–56, 173.

74 Thompson, 'Nineteenth-Century Horse Sense', p. 65.

75 Gatrell, 'Crime, Authority and the Policeman State', p. 261; Service, *Edwardian Architecture*, pp. 43–44; Hill, 'Holmes: the Hamlet of Crime Fiction', p. 33.

76 Kestner, *Sherlock's Men*, pp. 6, 88; *CASH*: 'The Musgrave Ritual', p. 386.

77 *CASH*: 'The Naval Treaty', pp. 456–57; 'The Yellow Face', pp. 361–62; Dudley Edwards, *The Quest for Sherlock Holmes*, pp. 273–76, 286–87.

78 *CASH*: 'The Red-Headed League', pp. 186, 189; 'The Beryl Coronet', pp. 304, 313; 'The Noble Bachelor', pp. 288–89; Dudley Edwards, *The Quest for Sherlock Holmes*, pp. 65–66.

79 *SACD*, pp. 159–61; *LiL*, pp. 494–507; *CASH*: 'The Three Garridebs', p. 1044.

80 *CASH*: 'The Abbey Grange', p. 148; 'The Devil's Foot', p. 968; 'The Second Stain', p. 653; 'The Six Napoleons', p. 588; 'The Golden Pince-Nez', p. 619; 'Wisteria Lodge', pp. 884–85; 'The Red Circle', pp. 908–09; 'The Devil's Foot', p. 955; Kestner, *Sherlock's Men*, pp. 165–76.

81 Service, *Edwardian Architecture*, pp. 140–69; idem, *London 1900*, pp. 109–29, 141–53, 217–45; Port, *Imperial London*, pp. 18–19.

82 Service, *London 1900*, pp. 60–71; Emsley, *Crime, Police and Penal Policy*, p. 187.

83 N. Barratt, *Greater London: The Story of the Suburbs* (London, 2012), pp. 343–56; Thompson, 'Nineteenth-Century Horse Sense', p. 61.

84 D. S. Davies, 'Introduction' to ACD, *The Best of Sherlock Holmes* (Ware, 1998), p. xi; ACD, *The Lost World & The Poison Belt* (San Francisco, 1989 edn), p. 242; *LiL*, pp. 586–87.

85 ACD, *The New Revelation* (London, 1918); ACD, *The Vital Message* (London, 1919); ACD, *The Wanderings of a Spiritualist* (London, 1921); ACD, *The Coming of the Fairies* (London, 1922); ACD, *The Case for Spirit Photography* (London, 1922); ACD, *The History of Spiritualism* (London, 1926); ACD, *The Edge of the Unknown* (London, 1930).

86 *CD*, pp. 424–25, 439–40; *CASH*: 'The Sussex Vampire', p. 1034; 'The Creeping Man', pp. 1082–83; 'The Veiled Lodger', pp. 1101–02; 'The Illustrious Client', p. 998; 'The Three Garridebs', p. 1053.

87 C. Clausen, 'Sherlock Holmes, Order and the Late-Victorian Mind', *The Georgia Review*, xxxviii (1984), p. 122; Dudley Edwards, *The Quest for Sherlock Holmes*, pp. 17–19, 113–14; Kestner, *Sherlock's Men*, pp. 176–200.

88 *CASH*, 'The Retired Colourman', p. 1113; 'The Creeping Man', p. 1083.

89 Service, *London 1900*, pp. 228–29, 250–51; Port, *Imperial London*, p. 19.

90 Barratt, *Greater London*, pp. 357–76; Porter, *London*, pp. 316–18; Thompson, 'Nineteenth-Century Horse Sense', p. 76.

91 H. Clunn, *London Rebuilt, 1897–1927* (London, 1927), pp. 9–1; A. Sutcliffe, 'Introduction: Urbanization, Planning and the Giant City', in Sutcliffe (ed), *Metropolis*, pp. 7, 11.

92 *LiL*, p. 596; *CD*, p. 368.

93 A. Sutcliffe, 'The Metropolis in the Cinema', in Sutcliffe (ed.), *Metropolis*, pp. 168–69.

94 ACD, *Memories & Adventures*, p. 106; *CD*, pp. 336, 406–07; R. W. Pohle and D. C. Hart, *Sherlock Holmes on the Screen: The Motion Picture Adventures of the World's Most Popular Detective* (South Brunswick, NJ, 1977); C. Steinbrunner and N. Michaels, *The Films of Sherlock Holmes* (Secaucus, NJ, 1978).

95 Adrian Conan Doyle and J. Dickson Carr, *The Exploits of Sherlock Holmes* (New York, 1954).

96 C. James, 'The Sherlockologists', *New York Review of Books*, 20 February 1975, pp. 15–18.

97 James, *Detective Fiction*, p. 31; ACD, *Sherlock Holmes: The Major Stories with Contemporary Critical Essays* (ed. J. A. Hodgson, Boston, 1994), pp. 437–41.

98 T. S. Eliot, 'Books of the Quarter', *Criterion*, viii (1929), p. 553.

99 *CD*, p. 455; Cawelti, *Adventure, Mystery and Romance*, p. 19; Brimblecombe, *Big Smoke*, pp. 161–78.

100 McLaughlin, *Writing the Urban Jungle*, p. 29.

101 Cannadine, 'Gilbert and Sullivan', pp. 12–32; idem, 'Another "Last Victorian"?: P. G. Wodehouse and His World', *South Atlantic Quarterly*, lxxvii (1978), pp. 470–91.

PENGUIN ENGLISH
LIBRARY

OTHER TITLES IN THIS SERIES

The Five Orange Pips and Other Cases
ARTHUR CONAN DOYLE

> "He is the Napoleon of crime, Watson ... He sits motion-less, like a spider in the centre of its web, but that web has a thousand radiations, and he knows well every quiver of each of them"

Witty and fiendishly clever, these tales of Sherlock Holmes and Doctor Watson see the duo solving the mysteries in London's foggy backstreets and behind the walls of country houses. In some of Conan Doyle's most famous and devilishly difficult problems, they face locked rooms, strange letters, separated twins, and beautiful, brilliant Irene Adler.

Hugely popular since publication, Arthur Conan Doyle's tales have been adapted countless times on stage and screen, and continue to influence crime writers today.

PENGUIN ENGLISH
LIBRARY

OTHER TITLES IN THIS SERIES

The Hound of the Baskervilles
ARTHUR CONAN DOYLE

"Mr Holmes, they were the footprints of a gigantic hound!"

The terrible spectacle of the beast, the fog of the moor, the discovery of a body: this classic horror story pits detective against dog, rationalism against the supernatural, good against evil. When Sir Charles Baskerville is found dead on the wild Devon moorland with the footprints of a giant hound nearby, the blame is placed on a family curse. It is left to Sherlock Holmes and Doctor Watson to solve the mystery of the legend of the phantom hound before Sir Charles's heir comes to an equally gruesome end. *The Hound of the Baskervilles* gripped readers when it was first serialized and has continued to hold its place in the popular imagination.

PENGUIN ENGLISH
LIBRARY

OTHER TITLES IN THIS SERIES

The Secret Agent
JOSEPH CONRAD

'Madness and despair! Give me that for a lever, and I'll move the world'

Prescient and shocking, *The Secret Agent* features terrorism, espionage and revolutionary groups in nineteenth-century London. Quiet shop-owner Verloc is a member of an anarchist group, and a secret agent for a foreign country, who becomes involved in a plot to blow up the Greenwich Observatory, with tragic consequences.

Inspired by the real-life Greenwich bomb of 1894, *The Secret Agent* is a masterpiece of failed lives and complex moral dilemmas.